BLACKOUT

This Large Print Book carries the
Seal of Approval of N.A.V.H.

BLACKOUT

Annie Solomon

Thorndike Press • Waterville, Maine

Published in 2006 by arrangement with Warner Books, Inc.

Thorndike Press® Large Print Basic.

The tree indicium is a trademark of Thorndike Press.

The text of this Large Print edition is unabridged.
Other aspects of the book may vary from the original edition.

Set in 16 pt. Plantin.

Printed in the United States on permanent paper.

Library of Congress Cataloging-in-Publication Data

Solomon, Annie.
    Blackout / by Annie Solomon.
       p. cm.
    "Thorndike Press large print basic" — T.p. verso.
    ISBN 0-7862-8863-9 (lg. print : hc : alk. paper)
    1. Amnesiacs — Fiction. 2. Murder — Investigation —
Fiction. 3. Washington (D.C.) — Fiction. 4. Large type
books. I. Title.
    PS3619.O433B63 2006
    813′.6—dc22   2006013703

Acknowledgments

Thanks to Marcia Epelbaum for help
with Spanish, and to Steven Akey for help
with neighborhoods in the DC area.

Much appreciation, too, to Pam Ahearn,
who came up with a brilliant idea
for the end.

And to Larry, for letting me drag his butt
all over DC and its environs,
I owe you one, pal.

1

Last night I killed a man.

Sliced into his tight white throat until the blood bloomed scarlet.

He gasped and struggled, breath gurgling. His knees, once strong enough to hold his weight, shuddered. They buckled, and he fell.

His eyes, whites wide and full of terrible knowledge, stared up at me from the floor where he lay.

I watched him die.

2

Moonlight washed the path with a low glow. The man checked his watch and peered out from behind the clump of trees. He tightened his hold on a branch, gaze riveted on the dirt trail.

She would come. He'd been assured of it.

And when she did, he'd be right behind her.

Automatically, he felt for the Night Raider on his thigh. The knife was just under the rim of his running shorts. Handy. Easy to reach.

Soon. She would be coming soon.

3

A scream ripped her awake. Her eyes snapped open. Saw shadows in the corner of the ceiling. Dark room. No light.

Sweat. She was sweating. Something had woken her.

Noise? Blood thudded in her ears. Was that it? She remembered dream images. Darkness blurred. Faces smeared. People? Person. Was someone screaming?

She listened hard. All was quiet.

Street light filtered in through a window. One by one she ticked off furnishings in the gloom-filled surroundings: dresser, mirror, rocking chair in corner. Clothes over the chair arm.

Hers. Of course, hers.

She was home. In her bedroom.

Yet . . . was it her bedroom?

It was dark. Why was it dark?

She snapped on the light, and it stabbed through her eyes into her brain. She turned it off, collapsed back down, stared up at the ceiling again.

A hammer pounded her skull.

Headaches were unusual. At least . . . she thought they were.

Why wasn't she sure?

She sat up, groaning. What time was it? The clock on the nightstand blared 12:00 a.m. in digital green.

She ran two fingers over her brow, pressed in the sides. Aspirin. She should take some aspirin.

She put her feet on the floor and stood. A wave of dizziness gripped her, and she stumbled to the chair for her robe. A pair of running shorts and a tank top were draped over the arm, sneakers stuffed with athletic socks sat on the floor.

Running. Fresh air, outdoors. The call was fierce and compelling. She could no more resist it than she could resist breathing. Aspirin forgotten, she slipped the clothes on. Immediate relief poured through her.

Pulling her tangled hair into a rough ponytail, she staggered down the stairs and let herself out the front door.

The night washed her with cool, gentle air. She gulped it in, feeling better, much better.

Setting off down the street, she started off slow, gradually increasing the pace until her legs pumped strength into the rest of her. At the end of the block she turned the corner. It was automatic, unthinking. Down the block and around the corner. What she had to do. Was meant to do.

Another three blocks and the park loomed to the left, the entrance a black mouth waiting to gobble her up. She headed for it unerringly, breathing easy, legs sure. Dumbarton Oaks Park. It closed at dark, the sign said, but she plunged past it, unable to stop even if she wanted to.

Here and there the city had put up a light, but for the most part the trail was dim, lit only by the moon. But her feet were steady, the path as familiar as the way home. She'd been here before.

At the second bend she headed right, and the first prickle ran over her. She listened hard. Heard nothing but her own steps.

She slowed, then picked up the pace. Branches brushed by, naked and bony against the moonlight. An owl screeched.

Was someone following her?

But when she turned, there was no one. Only the dim shade of the path behind her.

She plowed on, turning into the track that bordered the creek. The name drifted into her head. Rock Creek.

Water gurgled, swooshed and fell like

dark music. Shaking off the jitters, she pounded over the wood bridge. Her feet had just hit the trail again when she sensed him.

She checked behind, saw no one, turned back around. Ahead of her, a man had appeared on the trail, bent over one knee and blocking the way. Too late, her foot slammed into him and she went up and over, landing with a thud.

She grunted with the impact, but in the next instant, she'd sprung back up, crouched, ready. A distant part of her mind wondered how she'd done that. The rest focused on the man as he stood and backed away, limping.

"Whoa. It's okay. I'm harmless." He held his hands up. They were empty, unthreatening. "Sorry. New shoes." He pointed to his runners with one of his hands, keeping the other still raised. "Twisted my damn ankle."

She watched him warily, not moving.

"I . . . uh . . . didn't see you coming." He smiled tentatively. "Didn't know anyone else was crazy enough to run this time of night. You all right?"

Slowly, she straightened, unclenched her fists. "Fine."

"Good." He ran a hand over his head

with a sheepish expression. "Look, I, uh
. . . don't suppose you'd give me a hand?
My car is at the bottom of the trail, but my
ankle's pretty messed up."

He was tall and wiry, with long athletic
legs under loose, knee-length basketball
shorts. His shirt was tied around his waist,
so she could see his upper body. No
weapons. Why did she even notice that?
Better to notice that he was trim, muscled,
a fine specimen who obviously worked out
or was used to physical labor. His hair,
clipped tight to his skull, didn't hide much.

Military, came the word in her head, and
instantly she felt less threatened.

Why was that?

"Sure," she said, and a voice inside her
head said, *You could take him if you had
to.*

Take him where? How?

He untied his shirt, slipped it on, winced
as he limped toward her. Gingerly, he
wrapped an arm over her shoulder.
"Thanks." They started off, him using her
body to offset the pressure on his bad foot.
"I'm Jake, by the way. Jake Wise."

"Margo Scott." The name came to her
easily. Why shouldn't it?

"You looked pretty scary back there,
Margo. For a minute I thought you were

going to take my eyes out. You some kind of karate expert?"

The question echoed in her head, and for half a second she didn't know how to answer it. Then, as though it had been there all along, the response came.

She shook her head. "A bookseller. I own a store in Old Town. You?"

"Lawyer." He grunted the word, stumbling over a branch. "Here. Georgetown."

Neither construction worker nor soldier. She was vaguely surprised. "You should stick to a track."

"Don't I know it. Friend told me about this place. Was working late. Thought I'd try out my shoes." He smiled grimly. "I've had better ideas."

His car was parked on the street just outside the park entrance. She helped him to the driver's side, and he fished out a set of keys from a pocket inside his shorts. He opened the door, propped himself against it, and hopped around to face her. "Can I give you a lift? I owe you."

"That's okay. I only live a couple of blocks away. I'll run back."

He shrugged. "Suit yourself." He slipped into the seat. "Appreciate the help."

"No problem. Take it slow going home. Ice down that ankle."

14

"Will do." He closed the door, rolled down the window. "Thanks again."

She nodded and watched him drive away. Her headache was gone.

4

Margo Scott shrank in Jake's rearview mirror. A left turn, and she disappeared altogether. He hooked right, pulled into T Street, and stopped.

Didn't look like he'd need the knife sheathed on his thigh. The homes loomed close here, row houses tightly scrunched together, but dark. Everyone cozy. Everyone asleep.

Snapping open the glove compartment, he removed a cell phone and a palm-sized device that looked like a GameBoy. He punched a number into the phone and flipped open the device. A map of the area dissolved into view. In the middle, a flashing green dot progressed steadily over the streets heading away from the park.

The phone on the other end picked up. The voice of the man who answered was deep and smooth and very familiar. Jake didn't introduce himself.

"Done," he said.

"You're sure it was her?"

He pictured the woman. Tall and solid,

16

she'd shown muscular legs underneath her running shorts. Her toned arms and lithe body had little trouble holding his weight. She had a remarkable face, more arresting than lovely. Wide, mobile mouth, slashing cheekbones, strong nose, large dark eyes. Not a conventional face, but interesting. "I didn't ask to see her ID, but she bore a striking resemblance to her pictures. And she introduced herself as Margo Scott."

"Good. Condition?"

Idly, Jake watched the flashing green dot. It turned a corner and headed up a street two blocks away. "Normal as far as I could tell."

"No disorientation, slurred speech, dizziness?"

He recalled her voice. Nothing frail about it. Deep and smoky as the night. "Why? Should there be?"

"You know better than to ask that."

He did, but that wasn't going to stop him until he got the whole story. "Her instincts are sharp, I'll give you that. She wanted to take off my head."

"I gather you're still in one piece," the man said dryly.

"Oh, yeah. Though if anyone asks, I've twisted my ankle."

"Clumsy of you."

"I'll make a miraculous recovery."

"And then?"

"As planned."

"Good. Don't lose her."

Jake lifted his gaze from the monitor and stared at the blackness outside his windows. It seemed as thick and impenetrable as whatever truth the other man was keeping from him. "When are you going to tell me what this is all about?"

"When it's no longer necessary."

"Well, that's fair."

The man laughed. "No one ever said it would be."

Jake pursed his lips. Useless to pursue this further. He'd have to wait a day or two and try again. "You're the boss."

"And don't you forget it." There was mock severity behind the admonition and a hint of affection.

Jake returned it. "Not likely to."

"Tomorrow then."

"Tomorrow." He disconnected, twisted the ignition. The sense of the woman lingered as the car came to life. Like a scent dimly remembered.

Danika.

The name sprang out of the backlog in his head, a distant ache he rarely let himself think about anymore. It came at him

18

out of the blue, a sucker punch. Sharp, pungent.

When he could think again, when he could breathe without the slap of remembered pain, he wondered, *Why now?* It had been seven years since Dani's death. A good five since he'd buried his grief.

Well, he was working for Frank again. Maybe that's why.

He took one last look at the palm-sized monitor with its flashing dot.

Or maybe it was the woman and her taut, dark, *interesting* face. Nothing like Dani's towheaded mischievousness, but with the same . . . what? Self-possession? That isolationist, I-can-take-care-of-myself constraint?

Christ, he hoped not.

In the monitor, the dot stopped, then continued. He pressed a button, and a location appeared on the small screen. He smiled.

Welcome home, Margo.

5

The sun blared through the bedroom window. Margo groaned. How could she sleep so late? Eleven-forty-five and still in bed. Not like her.

Or was it?

Something knocked at the back of her mind.

What?

A quick mental inventory: no grogginess like the night before. No headache. Her mouth was dry.

She went into the bathroom, swished water around her mouth, then swallowed a palmful. Then another. And another. God, she was thirsty.

She showered, dressed, dried her hair. All the usual routine. But sluggish. Like she was underwater. She stared at a tube of toothpaste. Colgate. Her brand, right? It wavered, came back into focus.

Whoa.

She grabbed it, her fingers latching on to the solid shape. There. No problem. She was fine. Safe. Home. The home her great-aunt Frances had built.

The name conjured up an image, though it was distorted and hazy over ten years' time. It had been that long since her aunt had died and left Margo the house and bookstore. Tall and beak-nosed was what came through. How much longer until Margo couldn't remember her at all?

She squeezed toothpaste out, brushed, and spit. She should call St. Louis and have her sister, Barbara, fish around their parents' attic for pictures.

Downstairs, the house had the dusty charm of old wood and hulking furniture. Aunt Frances had been an antique seller's dream. Every surface was covered in old quilts or afghans or fussy lace Margo hadn't had the heart to throw away, though the clutter drove her crazy.

Bypassing the kitchen, she grabbed her purse and left. Outside, the sun banished all shadows. It was a gloriously bright day, warm and sunny and blue-sky perfect, and it made her stop short at her front door. The deep pink of a Japanese magnolia greeted her in the yard. Across the street, cherry trees fluffed white and baby pink.

Overnight the world had bloomed into color.

How was that possible? Yesterday the

21

branches had been bare, naked sticks. Today . . .

Uneasiness settled over her, like a crack in the earth. Yet the day was bright. The view calm. Nothing but front porches, latticed foundations. Rockers. Shrubs.

And blossoms. Lots of pink and white blossoms. Flowers that hadn't been there yesterday.

She headed for the shuttle, unwilling to fight traffic in her car. Under her feet, she tramped over dead blooms.

Her skin grew icy, nerves jangling.

The jumpy feeling chased her from the shuttle into the metro station at Foggy Bottom and onto the train. Was someone watching her? She shoved on a pair of sunglasses and examined the faces of her fellow passengers.

A man in a suit reading *USA Today*. A student with a backpack and iPod headphones. A woman holding a baby. No one paid her any attention.

And yet the shaky feeling stayed with her all the way in to Alexandria and her stop in Old Town.

Ordinarily she liked the long walk past the boutiques and bistros down King Street to the river. Today, she felt exposed and wished she'd opted for the car, traffic or no.

She stopped at Starbucks and bought a cup of coffee. On the way out, she saw a copy of the *Post*. For some reason, her heart quickened, and she picked it up. Headlines loomed. She stared at them without really seeing the words, then got distracted by the other papers nearby. Impulsively, she stacked a copy of the *City Paper*, the *Business Journal*, the *New York Times*, the *Wall Street Journal*, and the *Times-Daily* on top of the *Post*, paid for them all, and hurried out.

Anxiety gnawed at her. Something in the paper. Something she needed to find.

She searched her memory, couldn't recall what it was. But the nagging feeling kept her company through the cut over to Prince Street. Tourists flooded the way. They strutted out of Silverfoil with their jewelry boxes and into Ben & Jerry's. The smell of cheese and oregano wafted by from Marghetti's Pizza. She tramped down another block to the corner of The Strand.

From there, the decaying mustard brick of Full Metal Jacket Surplus blocked the view of the river. To her left, Waterfront Park dappled green and white with ice-cream-eating tourists strolling along the quay and sitting on benches in the sun. In the corner of the park closest to her, another cherry tree puffed pink. A ripple of disquiet went through her. She turned the corner, uncomfortable with the abrupt arrival of spring.

Like most of Old Town, her building dated from the early part of the last century, though the purple-painted brick was only a few years old. Once the home of a company that sold parts to shipbuilders, it now housed three: a vegetarian restaurant called Eggplant — hence the deep aubergine brick — Retro, a vintage clothing store, and her own Legacy Books.

Margo dropped the pile of newspapers with a splat, set the coffee on top, and dived into her purse for her keys.

To her right, a blur of movement snagged her attention.

Half a block away a woman in sharp-toed boots seemed to be eyeing her.

Margo's pulse jammed upward, but the woman checked her watch and hurried away.

Margo swallowed. *Was* she being followed? Or was she being paranoid?

Why even think someone was following her?

Her heart slowed, and she found herself gazing at a belted cotton shirtwaist in Retro's window display. The dress would have looked good on June Cleaver. Couldn't get more real than that.

Paranoid. Definitely paranoid.

Dismissing the incident, Margo returned to her purse for the keys to open the bookstore. While she was digging around, Suzanne, Retro's owner, came out.

"Hey, Margo! How was the trip?"

At twenty-two, Suzanne was ten years younger than Margo, a college dropout with a trust fund who cared more about the clothes she could play in than the business she did. She'd been Margo's business neighbor for three years.

Her platinum hair was short and spiky, and she wore a dress similar to the one in the window. A wide black patent belt cinched her tiny waist, and patent stilettos added four inches to her height. Although the dress blossomed outward over the curve of her hips, the top was tightly fitted. She'd left the first three buttons of the shirtwaist undone and hiked the collar up. Around her neck was a string of white balls that looked too roundly perfect to be pearls. With her wired hair and the old-fashioned dress, she looked like an eerie blend of past and future. June Cleaver, meet Jane Jetson.

The comparison made Margo forget

about the weirdness of the morning. She smiled. "How do you walk in those things?" She nodded toward the heels.

Suzanne shrugged. "No pain, no gain. One of these days I'm going to get you out of those" — she grinned and looked Margo up and down, taking in her comfortable shoes, navy slacks, and blazer — "what do you call that stuff you're wearing anyway?"

"Clothes."

"For a meter maid maybe."

Margo laughed. An old argument. "When's Halloween? You can dress me then."

"You got a deal.. And don't think I won't hold you to it. Here — look at my latest find. This is so cool." She pulled at her necklace and it came apart with a loud "pop."

She giggled and showed the beads to Margo, performing the trick again. "Poppit beads. Is that ever neat? I found a whole bag of them at a yard sale over the weekend. You can make them short, or long, or put two colors together. God, why don't they make stuff like this now?" She replaced them around her neck, popped the beads in place. "So . . . besides the awful getup, how are you?" She frowned. "Wait a sec — aren't you supposed to be away until next week?"

Margo was still fishing around in her purse. "Next week?"

"Yeah, next week. At least . . . well, I don't know." Her voice turned uncertain. "Maybe I misunderstood. Soooo . . ." She dragged out the word expectantly. The smile was back in her voice. "How was it?"

Confused, Margo looked up from her purse. Where were the damn keys? "How . . . how was what?"

"You know . . ." Suzanne made a dramatic circle with her hands. "The great European buying adventure. The elusive Don Quixote, Gypsies, flamenco. Those gorgeous men. Come on . . . give."

Margo frowned. What was Suzanne talking about?

"Oh, babe, you haven't had your coffee yet, have you?" Suzanne picked up the coffee and the pile of newspapers, and dragged Margo into her store. "What are you doing?" she said as she plunked down the stack of papers, "opening a library now?"

Margo looked at the pile uneasily. Why had she bought them? "I —"

"Here, sit down." Suzanne plunked Margo onto a stool in front of a jewelry case stuffed with brooches made of diamonds and emeralds too big to be real.

She pried the lid off the coffee. "Drink," she ordered.

Margo rolled her eyes, and Suzanne slid the cup closer. "Drink," she ordered again, then propped her head in her hands and leaned in. "And then tell me about your trip."

"I think you're the one who needs the coffee. I haven't gone anywhere."

Suzanne looked at her in amazement. "Really? You didn't go to Spain?" Her face fell. "What happened? Where've you been the last month?"

Margo stared at the younger woman. "What do you mean?"

"What do you mean, what do I mean? If you didn't go to Spain, where were you?" Suzanne peered at her closely. "Is everything all right?"

"Absolutely. I just . . ." She shook her head. "I've been here. Right here."

"Margo." Suzanne spoke as if to a two-year-old. "The bookstore's been closed. You were definitely *not* here."

Margo's heart began to thud. The morning came back with vivid swiftness. Her thirst. The trees. The invisible presence stalking her. "We had lunch together yesterday. Greek salads from Tabouli's."

Suzanne frowned and shook her head.

"The last time we had lunch together was the day before you left."

The pounding in Margo's chest grew louder. "All right, very funny, you got me."

"I'm not trying to —"

"Yes, you are." Suddenly, Margo wanted desperately to get away. But she needed her damn keys. "You're trying to drive me nuts. And you know what? It's working." She ravaged her purse again. PDA, pen, cell phone. Frantic, she dumped the entire contents out and scrambled through it.

"Not if you're already there, girlfriend." Suzanne paused to watch what was turning into an insane hunt. "Margo, *what* are you looking for?"

"My keys." There was desperation in her voice, and she worked to eradicate it. "I can't open the store."

"Well, you could just go through the connecting door." Suzanne pointed to the west wall, where a doorway was framed by racks of clothes. "Or" — she tapped a key on the old-fashioned cash register and the cash drawer opened with a ring — "you can go through the front with these." She held up a set of keys, her face lit with a mischievous grin. "Don't you remember? You gave them to me when you" — she gulped — "left."

A pulse beat in the back of Margo's head. The headache returning. Ignoring it, she swiped her keys, thanked Suzanne, and stuffed everything back in her purse.

Suzanne laid a gentle hand on her arm. "Are you sure you're all right? Maybe you should take another day off."

Margo forced a smile and swept up her papers and coffee. "Nothing a little caffeine won't cure." She started for the front door.

"I'm eating late today," Suzanne called. "Puccio's. I'll bring you back a calzone if you want."

"Thanks. I'll let you know."

She scurried out and began to breathe easier only when she'd unlocked her own door and was sitting behind Aunt Frances's huge leather-topped desk.

6

Margo sucked in a breath, driving down the rattle of her heart. She clutched at the smooth cordovan leather. The vines, leaves, and flowers embossed around the edge gave her world solidity and, to keep it going, she focused on the store.

Narrow and compact, it was divided by the desk in front, which acted as a bookish reception area. Floor-to-ceiling shelves packed with books swept above, around, and behind her. Used books mostly, some rare, most not, some nonfiction, most not.

The bookstore's real net worth were the rare, first editions. These one-of-a-kind books were encased in a glass cabinet that had two separate locks requiring two separate keys, both of which hung on the key ring Suzanne had just returned. She glanced at the books fondly. An 1843 *Christmas Carol* with hand-colored illustrations in original cloth. A first-edition *House on Pooh Corner*, signed by the author. A first-edition *Madeline.* And all the Arthur Rackham illustrated books: Hans

Christian Andersen fairy tales, *The Tempest*, *Gulliver's Travels.*

Gazing at the shelves, inhaling the scent of old paper and cloth covers, the real world came back into focus. Suzanne must have been mistaken, that was all.

Margo remembered closing the store yesterday. She remembered going home. She remembered waking up in the middle of last night with a headache. And she remembered her run in the park.

At midnight. How weird was that?

She swallowed. Could Suzanne be right?

Margo flipped the keys around, found the tiny one that opened the center desk drawer, and took out the large, old-fashioned receipt book. Someday she was going to have the business put online, but she never seemed to get around to it.

She flipped open the book to the last page, saw the record of the last sale, and a huge weight lifted. She remembered that sale. A copy of *Pride and Prejudice* to a tourist, who'd mistaken her store for the much more ubiquitous and contemporary Olson Books. She checked the date, then flipped the top newspaper to the front page.

Her hand began to shake. The difference between the dates on the receipt and the paper was as Suzanne said, a month.

She tore through the other papers. The date was the same.

Around her, the books grew menacing, the shelves closed in. Images rushed at her: blurred faces, screams, a gunshot.

Last night. Her dream. The thing that had woken her up.

Her breath hitched and she leaped up and dashed out the door — the back door this time, so she wouldn't run into Suzanne again.

She leaned against the purple brick, breathing hard.

Something was wrong. Something was definitely wrong.

She was hidden from the street by an alley and a blue trash bin. Back here the smells multiplied. Between the restaurant and the Dumpster, the stink of rotting fruit and vegetables was overwhelming. But she didn't care. Couldn't move.

What was wrong with her?

She closed her eyes and stood there, trying to calm down.

A noise butted in. From the store. From inside the bookstore.

She stiffened, her senses suddenly on high alert.

Why? What was she afraid of?

She wracked her brain, had no clue. But her breath was ragged, her skin clammy. She could practically taste the fear.

The sound came again, closer. Footsteps?

Was it a customer?

But people rarely wandered in off the street. Her business was appointment-driven.

The door. Someone was sneaking toward the back door.

Would a customer walk through the store to the back and out into the alley?

She flattened her back against the brick to the right of the door. Carefully slithered out of her blazer. Half her brain screamed overreaction, paranoia. The other half got ready, stance balanced, braced. Slowly, she raised her hands, fingers spread and ready.

What was she doing? She had no idea, but it felt right. Felt . . . safe.

She forced her breathing down. Slow, steady. Easy.

She waited for the exact moment.

A man exited.

In an eye blink, Margo grabbed, whirled, and slammed him face-first into the brick wall. One hand imprisoned his arms behind his back, the other pressed his head into the side of the building.

"Who are you? What are you doing here?"

He grunted. ". . . 's me." His voice strained because his head was shoved into the concrete. "Jake . . . Wise . . . from . . . last night."

7

Inside Margo's head the name clicked: the lawyer with the ankle.

A huge wave of relief washed over her. Instantly, she released him. "I'm . . . I'm sorry."

He turned slowly, gingerly, wiping off his hands. He'd been dressed for work, and his sleek charcoal suit, ocean blue shirt, and burgundy tie were covered in dust. He brushed himself off, staring at her with a mixture of apprehension and admiration. "You are one dangerous woman."

She swallowed. She'd assaulted someone. Not just assaulted, attacked. Competently.

Suddenly, her knees were shaking, and she swayed.

"Whoa," he said, catching her. "I thought I was the one injured here."

He leaned her up against the trash bin, and she stayed there, sweat heating her.

He peered at her closely. "You all right?"

She put a hand over her breasts; her heart was bursting out of her skin. "I guess . . ." She tossed him a wan smile.

"Not so dangerous after all."

"Maybe we should go inside."

She retrieved her jacket and let him lead her into the store. A small bathroom sat at the back. She stopped there, sopped a paper towel with cold water, and smoothed it over her heated neck and face.

Jake leaned against the doorway, watching her. His sharp blue eyes crinkled at the corners. Squint or laugh lines? They creased now, and he wasn't squinting. "Better?"

She nodded.

"Here." He held out a cup of water from the cooler just outside the bathroom.

"Thanks." She swallowed it down, wondering why people thought water was the answer to every upset. Lost your dog? Have a glass of water. Lost your mind? Have a glass of water.

She squeezed past him out of the room and down the hall. Now that she'd made a complete fool of herself, she was swimming in embarrassment.

"Look, I'm really, really sorry," she said when they'd reached the front of the store and her desk.

Arms crossed, he lounged against a bookshelf. "Did you think I was out to rob the Dumpster?"

She grasped for an explanation that made sense, even to herself. Unable to find one, she made one up. "I . . . there's been a series of robberies in the area. I thought —"

"I was the bad guy."

She shrugged. It sounded so lame. "Sorry."

He smiled, and his eyes wrinkled in amusement again. "Hey — my good ankle was feeling too good. Needed a little adjustment."

"Oh, no." She glanced down, horror-struck. "Did I really — ?"

He laughed. "Just kidding. No broken bones, though you get a gold star for originality. It's the first time a woman's attacked me for asking her to lunch."

Did she hear right? "Lunch?"

"And come to think of it . . . I didn't even ask." He cocked his head at her. "So . . . what do you say?"

"About what?"

He checked his watch. "It is the middle of the day. Most people eat in the middle of the day." He paused. "Then again, most people don't go into attack mode at the drop of a hat."

Heat rose up her face again. "I said I was sorry."

He held up his hands. "And I'm the

bastard who keeps bringing it up. So . . . ?"

He looked at her expectantly, and she returned his gaze blankly.

"Lunch," he said.

"Oh." She almost gagged at the thought of food.

"It was going to be my way of saying thank you. For helping me out last night."

She shook her head. "You don't have to —"

"But now I'm thinking it should be your way of making all this" — his nod toward the back of the store indicated everything that had happened out there — "up to me."

"But this isn't . . . I'm really not —"

"Hey, Mar—" Suzanne stopped two steps into the bookstore. "Oh, sorry. Didn't realize you had a customer."

8

Margo wanted to scream. Suddenly it was Grand Central Station in there. "It's all right, come in. He's not a customer."

Suzanne threw Jake a wide smile. "He's not?"

"I'm not," he said. "We're —"

"Friends?" Suzanne supplied.

"Acquaintances," Margo said dourly. She recognized that predatory matchmaker-from-hell look in Suzanne's eyes.

"Really?" Suzanne looked encouragingly from Jake to Margo. "I've never met any of Margo's . . . acquaintances."

Margo flapped a hand between them. "Suzanne DeForrest, Jake Wise."

Jake grinned at Suzanne. "So, Suzanne . . . I'm trying to get Margo here to go to lunch with me. Think she should?"

"Of course," Suzanne said brightly, wiggling her fingers toward the door and mouthing, "He's cute" behind his back.

Margo sank into the chair behind the desk; the recharge from the long night's sleep had deserted her. "I was going to skip lunch. I'm really not hungry."

"What did you have to eat today?" Jake demanded.

"Nothing, but —"

"You almost fainted out there."

"She did?" Suzanne frowned.

"You should get something in your stomach," Jake said.

"I told you to go home," Suzanne said. "I knew there was something wrong."

"There's nothing wrong," Margo said sternly, and boy was that the whopper of the year.

"Come on," Jake insisted, that charming smile pasted all over his face again. "I'll take you both out."

Suzanne quickly shook her head. "Oh, no. You and Margo go. I can't leave the store longer than ten minutes. I was just going to get takeout." She started to back toward the door and stopped only when she backed into someone entering. "Oh, sorry," she said to the newcomer.

Jake hid a smile at the little dance the blond was doing with the newcomer, a chunky black man with tired eyes. A big guy, his wide, squat frame dwarfed the woman's. He edged around her awkwardly with the unhurried moves of someone whose center was low to the ground.

41

When they'd finally disentangled themselves, the man said, "Margo Scott?"

"Uh, no. I'm Suzanne. Next door. Margo is —" She turned to where Margo was perched on the desk.

Margo stood. "I'm Margo Scott."

Suzanne waved, mouthed, "See ya," and slipped out the door.

Margo turned to the man. "Can I help you?"

"Detective Samuel Brewster." He came farther into the store and flashed an ID at her. "I'd like to talk to you."

"We were just going to lunch," Jake said. He really didn't like the way the day was going. First she slept half of it away, making sheer boredom out of his morning. Then the action picked up, but he was the one who'd wound up on the receiving end. Now this joker. He gave a little mental sigh. It wasn't like he wanted much. Just some kind of contact with the woman.

And to figure out why he was watching her.

The detective nodded. "Me too. Won't take long."

"What can I do for you?" Margo asked. She really had a remarkable voice. Low-pitched and deep, almost masculine. In the daylight the fine lines around her dark eyes were more visible. Lines that said she'd seen the world, and it wasn't always pretty. Right now, those dark eyes struggled for patience. Patience and something else. Why *had* she jumped him anyway?

"I'd like to ask you a few questions." Brewster settled into one of the chairs for the long haul, and Jake repressed a groan. What was Alexandria PD doing here?

"It's about Frank Temple."

Jake straightened; his problems vanished. That was the absolute last thing he'd expected the cop to say.

Margo was looking puzzled. "Frank —"

"Temple. That's right," Brewster said, squarely focused on her face. "You don't know him?"

She shook her head. "I don't think so. The name isn't familiar. Why? Who is he?"

Was she lying? Jake observed her closely. If she was lying, she was damn good at it.

"You tell me." The detective took a small photo from inside his jacket pocket and handed it to her. "Recognize him?"

Margo gazed down at it, and Jake wandered over to make sure they weren't talking about another Frank Temple. But the picture contained the familiar angular face with its prominent nose.

She shook her head and handed the picture back. "Sorry, no."

"You're sure? Maybe he was a customer? He had a lot of books in his office."

"Had?" Jake asked sharply.

Brewster sighed. "It'll be in the papers this afternoon. He died last night."

Casually, Jake leaned against a corner of the desk, but his hand gripped the edge until his knuckles turned white. "Accident?"

"Not likely." Brewster turned to Margo. "Sure you don't recognize him?" He slid the picture across the desk again so she could see it.

She glanced at it, then quickly away. "I'm . . . I'm positive. But I'll be happy to look up his name and see if he bought something here. I don't always remember names or faces, especially if it was a one-time sale and not recent." She rose, and Brewster followed her into the back.

Jake stayed behind. He wasn't sure his legs could move anyway.

In the distance he heard the metal scrape of a file cabinet and Margo's muffled words of explanation to Brewster.

Frank Temple dead. Impossible. A shard of grief and panic lacerated Jake. Frank was one of those stalwarts who never retired and never died. At least not on purpose.

Jake sucked in air, his lungs clogged. A sudden memory gripped him. Frank folding his long, grasshopper legs into a patio chair, the sharp blue Cyprus sky cutting into the white wall surrounding the back of the house, the sea beyond it as achingly blue as the sky. Behind him, a squadron of men were helping his mother pack their things, and the keen loss that had shaped Jake's life for the last week turned inside him like a buzz saw honing him down into nothing.

And then Frank, who seemed taller than the trees to Jake's thirteen-year-old self, turned kind eyes on him.

"Your mother says you wanted to see me."

Resentment and fear gripped Jake. "I want the truth. No one will tell me the truth."

"The truth. That's a tall order, son."

"I'm not your son," Jake had snapped.

Frank's response had been calm and mild. "No, of course not."

"Then cut the bullshit. Who killed my dad?"

He'd expected the same glossover that every adult had shoved at him since his mother had told him about the Beirut embassy bombing in a tear-choked voice. But Frank Temple had looked down at his long, tapered fingers, then back up at Jake. And the eyes he turned on him were no longer kind, but flat, even, direct.

"We don't know," he said.

"You don't know? You're the fucking CIA; don't tell me you don't know."

No scolding for the language, no warning to keep his voice down, no acknowledgment of the connection but no denial either.

"It was a big blast, Jake. Windows shattered for miles around. The USS *Guadalcanal* — you know what that is?"

He shrugged. "A ship."

"An aircraft carrier. It's anchored five miles off the Lebanese coast. It shook with the tremors. So I'm not talking popguns here, Jake. I'm talking a massive attack. The embassy lobby is nothing but dust."

Jake swallowed, but set his jaw. He would not cry. "I heard my mother on the phone. They sent the FBI."

"And they're working the scene. But you can't investigate what isn't there. The car and the driver that delivered the bomb were incinerated. There's no trace of the detonator."

"There's always something."

"Not if the bomb makers put explosives inside the device to make sure it's destroyed in the explosion. We haven't even been able to swipe a piece of rubble with trace explosive to analyze the type. Three groups claimed responsibility, but neither Lebanese intelligence nor our own people can confirm they really exist. The truth is, whoever was behind the bombing knew what they were doing. We lost a lot of good people, including your dad. Sometimes you don't catch the bad guys."

It was his first lesson in how the real world worked, but not the last one Frank Temple would teach him.

Now, he tightened his hold on the corner of the desk. Margo and the cop were coming back. Jake had to appear normal. Feel normal, despite the chasm that had opened inside him.

"I'm very sorry," Margo was saying as the two of them trooped back, "but I really don't know the man."

"Well, that's okay. We've got to check out every little thing."

Suddenly every piece of information, no matter how tiny, loomed large and important. Especially anything that linked Frank to this woman. "What little thing connects

Miss Scott to this" — he stumbled over the name — "this Frank Temple?"

Brewster swung his head in Jake's direction with a cold look. "And you would be — ?"

To forestall the wall of authority Brewster was quickly building, Jake stuck out his hand. "Jake Wise. Miss Scott's attorney."

Brewster's brows rose, and he turned to Margo. "You were expecting me?"

Margo opened her mouth — to protest his lie, most likely — but Jake shot her a warning look. He had to get as much information as possible. "I was taking my client to lunch, Detective. Nothing more. But now that I'm here, I'd like to know what the connection is between your victim and Miss Scott."

Brewster shuffled his feet, pursed his lips, then addressed Margo. "You ever been to Warner Park?"

"What does that have to do with Mr. Temple?" Jake asked. God, the sound of the words echoed in his head. *Frank. Dead.*

Brewster ignored him, homing in on Margo. "Warner Park, Miss Scott. Ever been there?"

"I . . . I don't think so. Where is it?"

He took out an envelope from inside his suit coat and removed a folded sheet of paper. Carefully, he presented it to her faceup on the desk. The paper was mostly black, the way photocopies are when nothing is copied. In the center was a small white rectangle.

"Is this your business card, Miss Scott?"

It clearly was. Her name and the store's were obvious. "Yes. Why?"

He took out another sheet of paper from the envelope, unfolded it as he'd done with the first, and showed it to her. The same white rectangle occupied the center of the page, only the printed information was absent. Instead, two words were handwritten along with a time: Warner Park 2:15.

"Is this your handwriting?" Brewster said.

She looked at him, then back at the card. "I don't know. It could be."

"Where did you find this?" Jake said.

"It was in Mr. Temple's wallet." He turned to Margo. "And you still say you don't know Mr. Temple?"

She nodded. "I don't."

"He had your business card."

"So what?" Jake said. "Someone else could have given it to him. Whoever he was supposed to meet at Warner Park.

Doesn't mean Miss Scott had any connection with the man." Oh, but she did. Why else had Frank asked him to watch her? The only question: what connection?

Brewster thought this over. "You're probably right," he said with a tired smile. He turned that same smile on Margo. "I don't suppose you own a gun, Miss Scott?"

"Why? Was Temple shot?" Jake asked. How the hell could anyone sneak up on Frank, let alone shoot him? "Where was he found?"

But Brewster kept his gaze on Margo. "Do you?"

She stared back at him with wide eyes. "A gun?"

"Yes," he said calmly.

She shook her head. "No. I don't own a gun."

"You're sure?"

"Of course I'm sure," she snapped. "I would know if I owned a gun. I own a bookstore. Not a gun shop. I'm sorry I can't help you, Detective. I'm sorry about Frank Temple, but I don't know the man."

Brewster began to gather up his papers. "All right. I appreciate your help. Oh, in case I have a few more questions, do you mind?" He turned one of the photocopies over, handed her a pen. "Would you give

50

me your phone number? I've got the business number, but I'd like your home and cell, too, if that's all right. In this work, you never know when you might need to call."

He held out the pen, and Jake was about to stop her from taking it, then didn't. She wrote down her contact information and handed the pen and paper back to Brewster. "This Mr. Temple. Who was he?"

Carefully, almost plodding through the motions, Brewster folded the photocopy with her phone numbers on it, and being equally careful, placed it inside the envelope. "Washington big shot. Deputy Director, Terrorism Control Force." He returned the envelope to the inside pocket of his jacket and sighed. "I'm gonna have a nice long day." He nodded, calm and friendly, but with a cold center that said he wasn't satisfied. "Enjoy your lunch."

9

Margo waited until Brewster was out the door, then sank into the chair behind the desk and laid her head in her hands. "You can go now," she said to Jake.

"You shouldn't have written your number for him."

Her hands dropped with a thud. "Why not?"

"It's a handwriting sample."

"So? I have nothing to hide."

He gave her a penetrating glance as though he didn't believe her. "This Temple guy," Jake said. "Sure you never heard of him?"

His attitude made her bristle. "Look, I don't know what you thought you were doing when you said you were my lawyer, but you're not. And I have things to do . . ." She looked meaningfully at the door, and he took the hint.

"Yeah, well . . . you're welcome." He gave her a cocky two-fingered salute. "Catch you on the flip side." And he left.

Thank God.

She locked the door behind him and pulled down the shade. She didn't want anyone else barging in.

Forcing herself to stay calm, she went back and sat behind the desk, methodically reviewing her day. She woke, showered, dressed, came to work, had a chat with Suzanne and found out she was missing a month, attacked a near stranger, and was questioned by the police about a murder of a man she didn't know.

Oh, yeah, now that she'd thought it all through, she felt a whole lot better.

She pictured the murdered man's face. Repeated his name in her head. *Frank Temple. Frank Temple.*

"Shit!"

Nothing.

She went through the day again. Wake, shower, dress, work — No, wait. She'd stopped at Starbucks. Bought —

She peered down at the desk. The pile of newspapers stared back at her. Why had she bought so many?

Again, that unsettled feeling stole over her. Was there a story she was supposed to read?

She spread out the papers, skimmed through the front-page headlines, waited for something to hit her. One by one, she tore through the pages. Interest rates, corporate scandal, political quagmire, the war on terror, murder, movies —

Nothing.

Why the hell had she bought all of them? That feeling that she needed to read something. Say something . . .

She swept the papers off her desk in a howl of frustrated fury.

Head in her hands, she bit back another shriek.

Dead end. The newspapers were a dead end. But what about Suzanne and her little land mine?

Suzanne.

In an instant, she locked the bookshop, grabbed her purse, and plunged through the adjoining door into Retro.

The place was empty. Without pausing Margo made for the curtain that separated the front from the back.

"Suzanne?"

"Be right there." A moment later Suzanne swished through the curtain. The smell of microwaved popcorn drifted out.

Margo gagged. Something flashed in her head. A dark-haired woman, smiling. Panic rushed through Margo, fierce and frightening. An instant later the face was gone, but not the dread.

"What's the matter?" Suzanne asked.

Margo rushed for the door. "Can we go outside? Just for a minute? I need to talk to you."

"Why can't we talk here?"

She swallowed. "The popcorn."

"You want some?"

"No!"

"Okay, okay. I didn't want to share anyway." She grinned, gave Margo a you're-acting-very-strange look, which Margo could hardly deny.

Outside, she breathed in a huge gulp of exhaust and smog, grateful that it completely obliterated the other smell.

"So, what's up?" Suzanne asked, and thumbed over her shoulder. "Afraid the store is being bugged? Little microchips in the brooches?"

"Very funny."

"Then —"

Margo pointed an accusing finger at her. "You said I was going to Spain."

Suzanne looked at the finger and up at Margo. "Well, yeah. That's where you said you were going."

"Do you know why?"

"You know, this day is getting weirder and weirder." Eyes narrowed, she gave Margo a close look. "Don't *you* know why?"

Margo raised her chin defensively. "I want to know what I told you."

"What you . . ." Suzanne crossed her arms with exasperated patience. "You're lucky you're my friend, you know that? Okay, let's see. It was something about a book. The kind you like. Old, dusty, falling apart. Worth billions." She cocked her head to one side. "You know, this would look so much better if you just —" She pulled up the collar of Margo's blazer, then stepped back for a critical look.

Margo ignored her. "I was going to Spain to buy a book?"

"*Don Quixote*, I think. At least, that's what you said. Isn't a book why you always go away?"

Something clicked in Margo's head. An unnatural peace. The answer to a puzzle. "Yes. That's why I go away."

Suzanne nodded encouragingly and rolled up Margo's sleeves. "To buy books." She examined her handiwork, nodded, and smiled. "Much better. So what happened to the cutie and lunch?"

Margo blanked.

"The guy," Suzanne said with patient emphasis. "What's his name — Jake something or other. Didn't you go to lunch?"

"Wasn't hungry." She pulled down the

sleeves. How had they gotten all bunched up around her elbows? "Gotta go." She didn't wait for good-bye.

"Are you okay?" Suzanne called after her.

"Fine," she called back.

She left Suzanne standing outside her shop and blindly plowed down The Strand. Around her, people seemed to expand and contract at will; noises boomed beyond their sound. A car horn blared. Brakes screeched. Laughter exploded.

Out of nowhere, a child's scream pierced her brain, and she whipped around to locate the source of the terrified sound. A man in racing gear rode by on a bicycle; two women came out of the vegetarian restaurant talking animatedly with their hands. Another woman walked a child in a stroller across the street at the park. Was that the source of the screams? But no, that child was sleeping.

The screams persisted, anguished, petrified. Margo charged around the corner and up King Street. Her heart was in her throat, her hands were clammy. She stumbled, and someone bumped into her, spinning her halfway around and leaving the tail end of "Sorry" buzzing in her ears. No screaming child anywhere.

She was going crazy. Completely and utterly insane. Breathing hard, she leaned against a wall, closed her eyes. She'd heard screaming before. Last night, in her dream.

Had something happened to her? What?

She'd gone to Spain to buy a book.

No, she was *supposed* to go to Spain to buy a book. She didn't go.

Then where had she been for the last month?

The question thumped inside her, deadly and relentless, and she longed to skitter away to a safe, comforting place. A place with no questions.

Home. She needed to go home.

Her feet picked up, her legs pumped, running. She dodged a couple holding hands, a father with his son on his shoulders. The crowd thickened, and she dashed into the street, weaving around the traffic. Past the visitors' center and the Tavern, the Gap, Banana Republic, and the other chain stores that had turned King Street into a place like any other. She charged around two kids coming out of McDonald's and pushed on. West. Go west. That would get her home.

Finally, she thundered down the steps into the metro station.

The ride was all smudged movement,

the swish of the train white and antiseptic. She closed her eyes, trying to submerge into the sound. But the words came at her anyway.

She went to Spain to buy a book.

She went to Spain to buy a book.

At her stop, she shot out of the station, found the Georgetown shuttle, and endured the short ride. Then it was a few blocks, legs flying, blazer flapping. She fumbled with the keys, slammed the door behind her, and leaned against it, as though it could keep out all bad thoughts.

Sweating, she swiped at her forehead. Her hand was shaking again.

Inside her head, the child began screaming again, but she cut off the sound.

Barb. She'd call Barb. Her sister would know what to do. Wasn't that what sisters were for?

She tore over to the kitchen, yanked the phone off its cradle on the counter, and lifted a hand to punch in the number.

The number.

What was her sister's phone number?

She froze, hands clutched white-knuckled around the phone.

She couldn't remember her sister's phone number.

Blood thundered in her ears. She had to

59

calm down. Just calm the hell down.

Now . . . she would put the phone down. That's right.

She would breathe. Easy. In and out. People forgot phone numbers all the time. No big deal. That's why there were address books. She had an address book, didn't she?

She'd dropped her purse at the door, and now she ran to find it. Dumping the contents on the floor, she rummaged for the PDA, opened it, clicked on the correct link and letter.

There was no listing for Barbara Scott.

With rising panic, she went through every letter in the PDA's address book.

Nothing.

There were no phone numbers at all. The thing was blank.

But that was impossible. Everyone had friends, people they knew. She remembered . . .

What?

What did she remember?

She went to Spain to buy a book.

She sank to the floor, propped heavily against the door.

Where had she been for the last month?

What was happening to her?

10

Jake was only too happy to leave when Margo kicked him out. His brain was on hyperspeed, thoughts swirling. There had to be some mistake. Some gigantic misunderstanding. Frank couldn't be . . .

"Jake," his mother had said, leading him to the couch in the living room after he'd returned from the American School. He remembered how awful she'd looked, hair disheveled, face drained. He knew right away something horrible had happened.

"There's been a terrible attack," she told him. "A bomb. Your father . . ." She'd choked on the words, paused to clear her throat. "Your father is dead, Jake." She'd flung her arms around his neck and burst into tears, holding him in an embrace that was meant to be comforting and only felt suffocating. And he'd sat there, stiff, unbending, trying to make sense of the words.

Since then he'd seen a lot of deaths. But right now he felt thirteen again, with the universe split in two.

He found his car, a black Expedition, squeezed between a minivan and a Lexus. Impatient, desperate to be away, he jerked the wheel back and forth, forward and reverse, angling out of the tight space.

"Goddamn fucking civvies . . ." Finally, finally, he was free.

He went straight up Duke, cursing the red lights. TCF headquarters were in a nondescript office building near the massive Patent Office. No marker announced its presence, but the armed guards securing the mouth of the underground parking garage hinted that this building was different from the others. Jake flashed his ID, parked, and used a coded keypad to get inside the elevator.

Frank had wanted him in deep invisibility, and Jake had already breached it by entering the building. He didn't want to compound the problem by waltzing in and announcing himself. Instead, he got off at the sixth floor and turned right. The aftermath of lunch drew him as he went, the odors getting stronger until he plunged into the commissary and the smell of food surrounded him.

A broad, open space, the cafeteria was brightly lit with a food line on three sides, salad bar in the middle, and tables scattered around the edges. It was closing in on two o'clock, and the place wasn't at its peak occupancy. But people were still scattered around tables, and if something big had happened, they would be talking about it.

He got a tray, absently plunked silverware and a glass on it, all the while scanning covertly for familiar faces. He had a ready excuse, something about a case briefing, but he'd just as soon not run into anyone.

"Baked scrod or Salisbury steak today?"

Jake focused on the giant steam tables behind the glass counter. He pointed to something that looked like meat, declined the overcooked broccoli, and slid the tray past the salads and desserts.

By the time he'd paid for what he hoped looked enough like lunch to pass, he'd spotted a likely place to snoop, and took his tray to a long table, one end of which was filled with three women finishing their meals.

He slid into a chair a few seats down from one of them, a scrawny woman in her sixties whose heavy makeup creased in folds of skin and whose unnaturally black hair was piled on top of her head. She held a compact and reapplied a dark pink smear to her lips. "If they don't let us through soon, I'll have to use the copy machine on the second floor, and that thing is always breaking down." She pressed her lips together, then checked them in the mirror.

"And it doesn't staple," said a shorter, heftier blond.

"I wish they'd tell us something," said the brunette, snapping her compact shut.

"Ours is not to reason why," said the third woman in a kind of reprimand. Older and plainer, she had a pair of glasses suspended around her neck.

"Well, I just wish they wouldn't make it so hard on us while they're keeping us in the dark," said the brunette.

"Hard on us?" said the woman with the glasses. "What about poor Dottie." She lowered her voice. "She found him. Can you imagine? First thing, too. I hear they sent her home."

In the sober silence that followed, Jake stuck his fork in the mound of gravy-covered meat and pushed it around his plate. His mouth had gone dry; Dottie was the name of Frank's longtime secretary.

"I don't understand how this could have happened," said the blond. "Here. With all this security."

"My God," said the older woman. "Frank

64

Temple is an institution around here."

"Was," said the blond.

A small chill went up Jake's back. His fingers lost their volition and his fork clattered to his plate. Quickly, he picked it up again, stuck a piece of meat in his mouth, and swallowed without tasting it.

God almighty.

One by one, the women stood up, cleared their trays and left. Jake waited half a minute and did the same. He took the elevator up to the tenth floor, but a cop with an Alexandria PD insignia was waiting when the door opened.

"Sorry, sir. This floor is closed."

Jake peeked around the cop's shoulder. Investigators, some in white clean-room suits, some in plain clothes, were crawling all over the hallway. "Any idea when it will be clear?"

"No, sir."

Jake stared at the cop, a brawny Slav with a square face shadowed by beard, and the cop stared back, an unwavering line beyond which no one was going to cross.

Jake was supposed to be lying low, and a fight would draw too much attention. He retreated, went down, found his car, and called information. It didn't take him long to find out what he needed.

11

Dottie MacKay lived two blocks off Mt. Vernon Avenue in Del Ray, just as she had when Jake knew her during his TCF training. The northern Alexandria neighborhood, originally built for railroad yard workers, was still in transition from decay to rejuvenation. Mattress warehouses and hole-in-the-wall taquerias vied for space with gourmet coffee bars and cheese shops. New brick town houses were going up, and the Mt. Nebo Baptist Church looked like it was thriving.

The residential sections were a warren of constricted, winding streets dotted with small homes, some derelict, others renovated with loving hands and lots of money. Dottie's house appeared to be neither. A well-maintained original, it was the only one on the block of stone and brick. Like the woman herself, it stood tall and firm, its dignified façade formidable with pitched slate roof and sharp, pointed gables over stone-trimmed windows and an arched door.

Jake rang the bell, hoping the gossips were right and the police had sent her home. And if so, that she wasn't knocked out with a sedative. The Dottie MacKay he used to know was made of stronger stuff, but it had been six years since he'd seen her last.

She opened the door herself, an elder stateswoman with a straight back and graying hair pulled tight into a neat bun. The lines in her brown face appeared deeper than he remembered, time or sadness weighing them down. He felt the pull of those lines himself, like a heavy load of loss on his shoulders. He'd known Frank for twenty years; she'd been Frank's secretary for nearly as long.

"Yes?" Her warm voice was fruity and round, and the sound came back to Jake like an old melody. Before he could explain why he was there, the whites of her red-rimmed eyes widened, and she placed one hand on her ample breast. "Jake? Jake Wise?"

He nodded, and spoke low. "Are you alone?"

"Dear Lord, I don't believe it." She stepped aside to let him in. "How did you get here so fast? It only just happened." Her eyes filled with tears, and she dabbed

67

at them with a tissue already clutched in her hand.

He hesitated, not knowing how much, if anything, she knew. But sometimes he had to give a little to get a little. "I've been in town a couple of days. A small job for Frank."

Something clicked behind her eyes as she closed the door behind him.

"You knew about it?" he asked.

She shook her head. "I had no idea. But he mentioned you last week. Out of the blue, or so I thought."

A ripple of pride mixed with sorrow sneaked up on Jake. "Yeah? What'd he say?"

"He told me about your first training exercise."

Heat suffused Jake's face, and Dottie smiled through a fresh well of tears. "Did you really bring back —"

"The sarin capsule? Yes, I did," he said with dignity.

She laughed, the sound full-throated and rich. "You not only brought back the capsule, he said you brought back the package."

Jake's throat tightened with grief, remembering. Frank had hidden the thing inside a cow pie. It took Jake a day to track it to the right field and two more to find the right piece of cow shit. He knew Frank wanted him to put his hands on every piece of crap in the field, and he'd had to comply. But when he finally found the cold capsule masquerading as sarin, he stuffed it back inside the pie, plopped the excrement in the sample case he'd been supplied with, and dumped the whole thing on Frank Temple's desk.

Dottie dabbed at the corners of her eyes. "He always had a soft spot for you, Jake."

Jake nodded, acceptance still warring with denial. "Yeah, I liked the old man, too."

They stared at each other. Jake didn't know what to say and neither, it appeared, did Dottie. Her eyes filled with tears again.

"Come on, sit down." He led her to the nearest seat, an armchair in the living room. "You shouldn't be alone," he scolded, sitting opposite her.

She waved his objections away with a flap of the hand holding the tissue. "My daughter is coming after work. She teaches at the school. Mt. Vernon. She'll be here soon. I'm fine. Fine." She leaned back in the chair and sighed. "I just can't believe . . ."

"What happened?" Jake asked quietly.

She sniffed and shook her head. "Don't know. I came in this morning and he was lying there. Just lying there." She shuddered. "Never saw so much blood."

"Was he shot?"

She shook her head again, and the tears welled up once more. "His throat . . ." Under her chin, her hand moved horizontally.

A wave of nausea shook him. He stared into space, his vision blurred. Jesus Christ . . .

His voice had gone jagged, and he cleared it. "Can you tell me what he was working on?"

She gave him a look of schoolteacher reproach. "You know better than that."

"Okay, but . . . anything particularly dicey? Arguments? Tension?"

She laughed. "You've got to be kidding. Didn't a day go by without an argument. Especially since 9/11. Every agency has come under intense pressure, and the TCF is no exception. Plenty are looking for scapegoats. Frank's been around for fifty years. He was an easy target."

Did she mean that literally? A turf war gone bad?

"Look, Dottie, I know you kept his secrets for many of those years, but this thing he asked me to do. I need to know if there's a connection."

She shrugged. "I'll tell you what I can, but the lines are still there. Clearance is clearance."

"I understand." He looked down at his hands, trying to figure out the right angle of attack. But when he came down to it, what was the point of sidling up? So he just came out with it. "Did he ever mention a Margo Scott?"

The soft brown skin on her high forehead furrowed. "Margo Scott?" She thought about it. "I don't think so." She shook her head. "Why? Something to do with that job for Frank?"

He shot her a sly grin. "You know better than that."

She grunted and gave his knee an affectionate push. "You watch yourself, Jake Wise."

A car door slammed outside. Dottie rose and went to the window. "It's my daughter."

"Okay. One more thing, and I'm out of here."

She turned expectantly.

"A key to Frank's house. I know you have one."

"You going to get yourself in trouble?"

"Not if I can help it."

71

She examined him, then sighed, left the room, and returned with a battered gold key on a thin wire. "It's to the back door." She handed it over with a look of grave concern. "You be careful now."

"I will. And Dottie."

"Yes?"

"Thanks." He bent, gave her a peck on the cheek. Her skin was soft, and she smelled of powder. "Take care of yourself."

He went out the back, circled around to his car, and drove off, the sound of Frank Temple's dry voice echoing in Jake's head.

It was the end of the sarin test, and Frank had finally stopped laughing. "You like shit, Jake?" He'd come around to the front of the desk and perched on the edge, his long arms crossed over his concave chest, legs crossed at the ankle.

"Yes, sir." Though Jake wasn't in the army anymore, he'd stood at attention.

The corner of Frank's mouth twitched, and a gleam appeared in his eyes. "You come work for me, you'll be in shit all the time."

"Whatever it takes, sir."

Frank had laughed again, and pumped his hand. "Your dad would be proud, son. Real proud. Welcome aboard."

Now, sitting in his car after the visit with

Dottie MacKay, Jake gazed out the window, not seeing anything. The Beirut embassy bombing had never been solved. No one had ever been tried, sentenced, or hanged for murdering his father.

Jake clamped down his jaw. Not this time. This time, he'd find the piece of shit responsible.

Whatever it took.

12

Jake knew where Frank lived; years ago, during the long hours of training, he had crashed there twice, sleeping in the tiny bedroom that had been Frank's home office. Grim and determined, Jake drove straight to McLean. When he got there, Feds and cops were still swarming over Frank's house. Jake drove by the wooded property slowly, rubbernecking the way most people would. He knew a back way in and even in daylight could get in without being seen, but the chances of staying unnoticed were slim.

He reined in impatience, circled around, and headed out.

Half an hour later, he was in upper Georgetown, the less-congested and slightly less-pricey part. He drove up Foxhall, passed Margo's house, turned right and right again into the narrow alley behind her house. The Expedition was a tight fit, and he slowed to avoid a couple of badly placed trash cans. He left the car in a white-clapboard shack with peeling paint that seemed as if it had been through a couple of world wars but responded readily to his remote. Two lots farther down sat an equally decrepit-looking shed in the back of Margo's yard.

Well-placed shrubs obscured the side of the shed facing the house, but the alley side was clear. He pushed away a stream of ivy covering a fuse box, keyed open a lock on the box. Inside was a keypad. He punched in the code, the shed door slid silently open, and he stepped into a small foyer in front of a flight of downward-facing stairs.

The door closed behind him and he hurried down the stairs, his head back at McLean. Would the cops find something there? What?

Undoing the top couple of buttons on his shirt, he absently stripped off his tie, stuffed it in his suit jacket pocket. Striding through the tunnel that led to the back of Margo's house, he let himself into the surveillance room, flicked on the light. The illumination showed banks of live monitors, counters with audio insets, headphones, computers, and an endless array of switches and buttons. A cot lay against one wall, his army duffel zipped open at the foot.

He tossed the jacket on a hook near the door, turned up his sleeves, rolled over one of two chairs. Turning it backward, he straddled the seat and stared at the monitor bank. The central image showed a view of the front hallway.

Margo Scott was on the floor, her back against the door like a trapped animal. Her face was drawn and white, her eyes hard and staring straight ahead. A sagging sack of a purse lay beside her, and strewn all around was what looked like its contents.

So. Margo. Dark, mysterious Margo. Where did she fit in?

He studied her carefully, cold to the distress in her expression. Using the chair like a skateboard, he pushed himself off the counter and rolled to the other side of the room, where he stopped himself with his hands. Running fingers over the toggle switches, he found the right one, set the date and time to the evening before, and waited for the data spool to rewind.

When it hit the correct time, it clicked to a stop and started forward. On the small monitor set into the counter, he watched Margo enter her house wearing the running clothes of the night before. She jogged up the stairs and disappeared from view. He repeated the same reset and rewind procedure with another camera, saw her go from the top of the stairs to the bedroom. Switched to a third camera, then a fourth, then back to the third, as she went from the bedroom to the bathroom and back to the bedroom.

He watched impassively as she slid out of her clothes and into bed. He couldn't help noting that he'd been right about her body — she was trim and toned, high-breasted and curved in the right places — but he set that aside. She wasn't a woman; she was his target.

And she might be a murderer.

Then again, maybe she had nothing to do with Frank's death. He supervised a lot of cases. Any one could be the reason his throat was cut.

Out of the corner of his eye, Jake saw movement on the central monitor. Margo shifting position. One eye on the present, one eye on the past, he remained vigilant. In one monitor, the picture remained static from the night before: Margo unmoving in bed. In the other, she slid on her knees, fished around the junk on the floor, and came up with a cell phone.

He pushed himself off the counter, spun backward to the other side of the room, flipped a switch up, and rolled to his first position as the audio came through.

". . . St. Louis," she said into the phone, that deep almost masculine voice reverberating over the microphone. "Barbara Scott."

Ordinarily, he'd make a note of the name and report it to Frank that night. Now, he didn't know what to do. Was he supposed to continue? Desist?

Had Margo killed Frank? Had he asked Jake to watch her because she was dangerous?

If so, Jake had done a piss-poor job and Frank was dead because of it.

That thought rolled over him like a deadweight. He fisted a hand, lightly punched the counter. On his watch. It had happened on his watch.

But Jake hadn't gotten the sense that Margo was a threat, not from any of the conversations he'd had with Frank.

Then again, he hadn't gotten the sense of anything from Frank.

Cursing, he found his surveillance notebook and jotted down the name Margo was repeating, just in case.

"No . . . no address," she was saying. Her voice was strained and tense. Barbara Scott. A relative?

Christ, he wished he knew more about

her. Frank had purposely been vague. He'd wanted a favor, and Jake could never say he didn't owe him. He'd have done it anyway. Out of boredom and the pure joy of working for the man, but it also cleared the books. He had needed help more than once. Frank had never let him down.

So he put in for some long-neglected vacation time and drove from Manhattan, where he was based, down to DC.

"Just for a couple of days," Frank had said. "A week at the outside. Just until I can straighten something out."

Had he? Or had whatever the twisted thing was that needed straightening killed him?

In the current monitor, Margo was scavenging around for something to write on. "Hold on," she said, and dashed out of frame.

Shit. He rolled across the floor, scanned from monitor to monitor, picked her up in the kitchen, flipped the audio switch, and glanced back at the picture from the night before.

It was 1:45 a.m. She was still in bed.

"Okay, go ahead." She was writing on a piece of paper towel in the kitchen. "Thank you." She disconnected, and immediately punched in one of the numbers she'd just received.

"Barbara?"

He fast-forwarded the image from the night before, watching the static picture. All the while, Margo's voice from the kitchen monitor sounded around him.

"It's me, Margo." Pause. *"Your sister. No, I'm not kidding. It's not a joke. Oh. I see. I . . . must have the wrong number. Sorry."*

There. He pressed STOP, rewound and stopped the image again. Right . . . there.

"Barbara Scott? Do you know when she'll be back? Look, I know this sounds strange, but does she have a sister named Margo?"

At 2:10 a small flare occurred, like a burnout, and the image disappeared. No bedroom, no Margo, no nothing.

Damn . . .

It wasn't the first time equipment had failed on a surveillance job. A storm kicks in a power surge, a switch decides to be twitchy. Bad batteries, bad luck. They were the great and powerful U.S. of A. and yet the simplest things could screw up a job.

He checked the cables and tested the buttons. Found a loose connection and examined it. Had it been tampered with? He couldn't see that it had, but he didn't like the coincidence.

He noted the time of the glitch and fast-forwarded again. In the background, Margo was still making calls.

"I'm looking for my sister, Barbara Scott."

"I'd like to speak to Barbara Scott."

"Barbara Scott, please."

Out of the black field on the monitor, Margo's bedroom popped into view again. He stopped, rewound, and played forward at normal speed. Margo was in bed. Asleep. Again, he noted the time — 8:00 a.m.

"Do you know if she has a sister? Is her name Margo?"

He gazed at what he'd written. If Dottie found Frank first thing this morning, that meant he could have been killed at any time between their conversation last night and eight-thirty in the morning. And from two until eight, he had no idea where Margo Scott had been. Six hours would have given her plenty of time.

To do what? Slice open Frank Temple's throat?

Fury wrenched his chest tight, and he took a moment to let it pass. He stared at the woman in the kitchen. Margo's elbows were on the counter, her head in her hands. It looked as though her fingers were yanking her hair out of her scalp.

It took power and hate to work a man's neck. Or pure detachment. She didn't look detached. Not now, at least.

But he hadn't forgotten her reaction at the park the night before. Or how fast she'd moved on him this afternoon.

"No, that's okay," she was saying. "Thank you."

The question was why. Did she discover Frank was having her watched? Did he, Jake, do something to tip her off? His stomach crawled with the thought.

But if she knew, why was she still there, in front of the cameras?

And if she didn't know, why kill Frank?

She hadn't looked like she was lying in the bookstore when she told Brewster she didn't know Frank. Jake had plenty of interrogation experience; he would have sworn on a stack of Gideons she'd been telling the truth.

Despite her denial, there had to be a connection between her and Frank. What? Did it have anything to do with his death?

And just as disturbing, what had happened during those missing hours of video?

13

Margo fled from the kitchen into the belly of the house. In the living room, a narrow, antique-looking writing desk sat in the corner. She flung open the drawers, but only found a stubby pencil and a dry ball-point in one, a few scraps of blank paper in another.

She turned around wildly, looking for all possible hiding places. She upended the cushions on the couch and turned the armchairs upside down. Bookshelves lined the walls. She attacked them, taking out books one at a time, shaking them for whatever might be stashed between the pages, then throwing them on the floor. She swept each shelf carefully.

Nothing. Not a single hint as to what was going on.

She ran back to the kitchen and attacked it in the same way. Red-and-white cans of Campbell's soup landed on boxes of Kraft macaroni and cheese. Pots clanged on the floor, silverware clinked, a plastic lid rolled. Breathing heavily, she ripped off her blazer. It fell forgotten to the floor. She up-ended every drawer and emptied every cabinet and shelf. Still nothing.

She left the mess where it lay, took the stairs two at a time, and made a similar assault on the upstairs bathrooms and the three bedrooms.

When she was done she was surrounded by chaotic clutter, but had found nothing. No family photos, no worn-out address book, no yearbooks, scrapbooks, or postcards.

Exhausted, she sank onto the bed.

Maybe this was all a dream.

Maybe she was going crazy.

She was Margo Scott. Her parents were Tom and Eleanor Scott, now deceased. She had a sister in St. Louis, where she'd grown up, named Barbara. After her mother died, her great-aunt Frances had filled in. When she died, she left her house and bookstore to Margo. She traveled the world to buy books. Rare books. Expensive books.

The facts came easily, each one a stepping-stone in Margo's life.

Why couldn't she find proof?

Worse, why did she need it?

From a distance came the sound of a phone ringing. She leaped off the bed and scrambled down the stairs. Maybe whoever was on the line knew her. Could tell her why she couldn't find her sister. Why she couldn't remember what she'd done for the last month. Why she could tackle a man with ease and why she'd want to.

She'd left her phone in the kitchen and swiftly swiped it off the counter.

She punched a key. "Hello? Hello?"

She clutched the phone tightly, glaring at it.

As with everything else on this weird and frightening day, there was no answer.

14

Jake left the surveillance room with the monitor showing Margo staring up at her ceiling. He'd watched her frenzy with interest, wondering what the hell she was looking for. Since she came up empty-handed, they were both in the dark.

When she'd subsided, collapsing like a deflated balloon on top of her bed, he changed into sweats and a long-sleeved T-shirt, both black for concealment. Double-checking the equipment, he made sure the video timers were correct and the audio set to record. He sheathed his Night Raider and strapped the knife under his left sleeve. His SIG he stowed under his shirt at the back.

Exiting the way he came, he left the shed and crept down the alley to the shack where he'd stashed his car. He backed out and headed for the bridge. Traffic was heavy, so it took him an extra ten minutes to get to McLean. By the time he got to Frank's house, most of the police cars were gone. A CSU van was still parked at the bottom of the long drive near the house, so he drove past, exited the neighborhood, and parked in a bank lot half a mile away.

Then he waited.

He pictured Frank's house. Set back from the road, it was a wide and rambling farmhouse with a creek in front and lots of barely budding trees around it. No sidewalks. No place to hide a car.

So when darkness descended, he left the Expedition behind the bank and quietly hiked back, cutting through the bank lot, around the street at its rear, and into the neighborhood of large homes. He slithered through the properties, sticking to the outer edges. Some were newly built monstrosities of stucco and brick that gleamed stark against the old trees surrounding them. Others were smaller, settled and lived-in.

A new home was being built behind Frank's house. The foundation hadn't been poured yet, and the site looked like a wound sliced into the land. But it made sneaking in easier. The earthmovers were as motionless as dead giants, and he slipped by them, weaving around trash bins and tarp-covered woodpiles. A hedge separated the site from the back of Frank's house. He slipped through it.

Dodging trees and shrubs and scrambling over a stone wall that terraced the back, he tramped down the slope to a brick patio with a gas grill that looked like it was rusting in place, and a couple of moldering plastic chairs.

Jake couldn't help a small smile. He and Frank had shared beers on that patio. Frank had confided that he'd never used the grill, it had come with the house. And he'd carped about the upkeep on the place and castigated himself for buying it because he was rarely there and it was big enough for a small tribe. And Jake remembered him saying with self-deprecating humor, "Watch out for vanity, kid. It'll get you every time."

Grief and loss tightened in the back of Jake's throat, and he fought against it, screwing down his resolve.

At the back door, he tugged on a pair of paper-thin black gloves that molded to his hands, and using the key from Dottie, let himself into the kitchen. Traces of carbon dust still blackened the interior door, especially near the knob, and on the drawer and cabinet pulls. Some of the drawers in the kitchen hadn't been closed all the way, and a cabinet under the sink had been left partially open.

Slowly, he moved inward, reaffir... general impression of sterility and c... Then again, when Jake knew him, I... had lived in his TCF office, a haven fo... ports and files and piles of paper that c... gregated there like it was Mecca, clogg... up shelves and cluttering the furnitur... Frank refused a desk, substituting a tabl... in the center of his office. He liked talking to younger agents, and that arrangement encouraged them to come in and hang out. How many hours had Jake spent in that office, running case ideas by Frank? A pang ran through him. Too many. Not enough.

Unlike his TCF office, Frank's house was navigable. Spotless. Because, as he'd said, he was never really home. A carpeted hallway off the living room led to the home office, where Jake had slept, and here he found the Frank he remembered: piles of paper strewn haphazardly, books stacked on the floor, old magazines vying for space with certificates of merit, service awards, and framed snapshots, all of which sat in arbitrary positions, bookends more than display items.

He picked up one of the photographs. Frank grinning like a goofball in his navy whites, the tall, gangly guy who towered over his two buds.

Jake spent the next hour sifting through the papers and files. He found little of value and nothing needing clearance. A shopping list on a scrap of paper showed Frank needed tuna, mayo, and shoe polish. There were lots of personnel items, things like disciplinary reports and job evaluations. Things he could take home and work on safely. Sighing, Jake looked around to make sure he hadn't missed anything.

Leaving the office, he went down the hall to Frank's bedroom. A long closet took up one wall, and the CSU technicians had left the doors open. A row of suits hung on the rod, as limply as they would have from Frank's bony shoulders. A line of size 13 black shoes sat on the floor, all long, narrow, and well worn.

His throat working overtime, Jake carefully closed the closet, feeling as though he were sealing up Frank's grave.

Turning to face the room, he skimmed over the bed. It had been tossed, and someone had made an effort to put it back together. But the spread was still rumpled and the pillows askew.

White dust ringed the knobs around the nightstand, and more decorated the dresser. He scanned the framed pictures

that sat on top. A smiling Frank with the first President Bush. Frank shaking hands with another suit and receiving some kind of award. Frank with a woman behind him, her arms thrown around his neck.

Jake blinked. He'd never seen Frank with a woman. He moved in to pick up the photo. Stared at it, his gut grinding in disbelief.

Not just a woman. Margo fucking Scott.

15

Margo leaned outward from her bedroom wall, arms braced, back to the room. The place looked like holy hell, but the thought of cleaning up made her want to vomit.

A low growl rumbled up her chest and came out her throat in a roar of frustration. She punched the wall, shredding her knuckles and leaving an indentation in the plaster.

"Goddammit!" She sucked the knuckles, feeling stupid.

She had to calm down. Had to just . . . calm down.

Her running clothes from the night before lay in a heap near the chair in the corner. They called to her.

She flung off the tailored blouse she'd sweated through, peeled off the confining slacks, and slipped on the shorts and the tank.

God, she could breathe again. The air swirled around her bare skin, and her muscles ached to be stretched and abused.

She dashed down the steps, ignoring the

overturned chairs in the dining room and the jumble of books on the floor of the living room.

At the front door, she heard a distant beeping that signaled a message on her cell phone. She swerved, headed for the kitchen, and grabbed the phone.

The pen and paper towel were still where she'd left them on the counter. She turned the paper over, obliterating all the numbers for Barbara Scott, and jotted down the information on the message ID line: Argyle Towers and a phone number. She listened twice. Both times the woman on the other end said the same thing.

"This is Dana calling from Argyle Towers. We've run into a bit of a problem, Miss Scott. I hope everything is all right. Please call at your earliest convenience." And she left the phone number Margo had already written down.

Margo stared at it, her heart suddenly racing. What and where was Argyle Towers? What did it have to do with her? She punched in the number but got an answering machine message saying the office had closed for the day.

A hasty scan around the kitchen revealed drawers and cabinets hanging open, contents spewing out. No phone book or Yellow Pages.

She got the address from information and stuffed the paper towel on which she'd written it in the pocket of her running shorts. Taking her phone with her, she went into the hallway, gathered up her keys and the contents of her purse, which were still scattered on the floor, and sprinted out the back like a prisoner escaping. Her run would have to wait.

Racing down the walk to the alley, she looked for her car. A dark blue Taurus sat on the cement slab next to an eyesore of a shed. Was that it?

Of course it was.

The vague thought that she should tear down the useless shed ran through her, but she was quickly distracted by a neighbor carrying a plastic trash bag to the can behind her house. Margo changed course and dashed over to her.

The pudgy woman had a round, pumpkin face framed by short gray hair. She looked up at Margo and smiled. "Yes? Can I help you?"

Margo hesitated. What could she say anyway? Do you know where I was for the last month, because I don't?

From the politely blank look on the

woman's face, Margo already knew the answer, but she plunged on anyway. "I'm . . . Margo Scott."

"Yes, dear, it's nice to meet you. I'm Betty Halpern."

"I live next door."

"Yes, I saw you come out of the house." She dumped her trash in the can and glanced toward her own front door, clearly eager to retreat inside.

"Did you . . . did you know my aunt Frances?" Margo nodded in the direction of her house. "That used to be her house."

"Oh. No, I'm afraid not. We've only been here a few months. Keep to ourselves mostly."

"So you haven't" — Margo's face heated — "haven't seen me around the neighborhood in the last few weeks?"

"Well, I'm sure I have, dear." Betty Halpern moved around Margo and headed home. "Apologies for not being more neighborly." She continued up the path and slipped inside.

"No problem," Margo said, but only to herself.

She let out a shaky breath and gazed at the rest of the houses. They snaked along the alley, their backs cold and uninviting, an entire row of strangers.

She thought about knocking on every one: "Hello, do you know me? I've lost my mind. Have you seen it?"

"Ms. Scott?"

Margo whirled. A uniformed officer approached her. "Yes?"

The cop was a woman, shorter than Margo with a thin, Appalachian face and light hair pulled back under her cap. The nameplate above her shirt read SCOFFIE.

She murmured into a radio on her shoulder. "I got her. Round back." Then she turned to Margo. "Would you come with me, please?"

Margo looked at her warily. Younger and slighter than Margo, even with the extra bulge of the vest she wore beneath the uniform shirt, Scoffie would be easy to overcome. In an instant Margo knew how she would do it.

Before she could move, a police car zoomed down the alley and stopped on a squeal of brakes.

Scoffie gestured to the car. "Please, ma'am."

Margo's gaze flicked to the cop at the wheel. Male. Thirty-five maybe. Rapidly she calculated the possible number of weapons and the risk of having them discharged at her.

She held back for more information. "Why?"

"Detective Brewster would like to ask you a few questions."

Brewster. The police officer at the bookstore earlier today. It seemed like it had happened a century ago. "Is this about Frank Temple?"

"Sorry, ma'am, I don't know." She shifted her weight, quartering her stance so her left foot was in front and the right behind, a move intended to protect her gun side and give her better balance in a fight, should one occur. Margo recognized the move, though she didn't know why.

"Ma'am?" Her hand went to her ASP baton, which hung on her utility belt, and her eyes locked on Margo's. "We can take you there."

The driver got out of the car and stood. "Problem, Scoffie?"

She responded, but kept her gaze on Margo. "We're coming, Terillo." And she smiled at Margo. "Aren't we, Ms. Scott?"

Margo made herself smile back. "Sure, whatever you say." If the police had questions, maybe she'd get answers.

16

Jake skirted the borders of Frank's house and returned to his car. First thing, he checked on Margo's whereabouts, hoping whatever meltdown she'd experienced had left her too enervated to leave the house.

No such luck. The map he pulled up on the GPS screen showed her in a different place. He pressed the location button, waited for the various possible addresses to flash by and finally settle on one.

Shit.

So the police had also figured out her lies.

He flipped the device closed and sped away. Not enough time to go back and change into his lawyer garb, so he hoped the clothes wouldn't be too telling. He left the SIG and the Night Raider in the car just in case there were metal detectors.

They'd already put her in one of the interrogation rooms. Brewster opened the door with methodical care, a trait Jake was beginning to think defined him. This wasn't a guy who would blurt out much or act on impulse. He was deliberate. Measured.

"Your lawyer is here," he said to Margo, whose only sign of surprise was a small widening of her eyes that she quickly masked. For a murderous bitch she was certainly cool.

"About time," she said, and that husky voice shimmered through him again.

He looked her over. He thought the run last night was a one-time thing, some kind of manipulation of Frank's. But seeing her here, now, in her running clothes, he wondered if maybe that was her regular routine. She wore the same dark blue shorts and tight gray tank that neatly outlined her breasts. Her long legs were crossed under the table and her bare shoulders showed the curved shape of muscle. She was beautiful the way a panther was. Sleek. Dark. Dangerous.

Brewster looked between the two of them. "She call you from the cruiser?"

Jake took a chance. "That's right. I came as fast as I could."

Brewster grumbled something about rookies, and Jake said, "I'd like to talk to my client. In private. Someplace where you can't listen in."

Brewster shot him a hostile look but led

the way to a small break room that wouldn't be wired for sound and left them. A table to one side held a coffeepot and the paraphernalia that went with it — foam cups, stirrers, the powdered stuff that was supposed to taste like cream and left an oily film on your tongue. The smell of burned coffee permeated the place, but Jake poured two cups anyway and slid one in front of Margo, who eyed it as suspiciously as she eyed him.

"How did you know I was here?"

"Second sight." He sipped, nearly gagging on the acid taste. The pot must have been made last week. "What did you tell him?"

"Who are you?"

"Your new best friend. What did you tell him?"

"You're not a lawyer, are you, Jake?"

"I'm whatever you need me to be." He sent her a direct and pointed stare, the words that followed slow and sharp with emphasis. "What did you tell him?"

She pursed her lips, then gave in with obvious reluctance. "The truth."

"Which is?"

"That I never heard of Frank Temple, that I don't know why my picture is in his house."

Jake watched her watch him. Her eyes were level and straight, her simple, unemotional words held the ring of truth. Then again, she'd have to be a damn good liar to get to Frank. He'd seen that picture.

"Your picture?"

"Yeah. Everyone seems to be working up a theory that casts me in the roll of rejected lover." Her face said the idea was ridiculous, but he pushed her anyway.

"Were you?"

"Not my type."

"And what's your type?"

"Someone a little younger than my grandfather."

His hands clenched beneath the table, fingers yearning to squeeze the breath out of her.

"Can you alibi out?" He was curious how she'd lie her way out of that.

"Not unless dreamland is an alibi. I was in bed last night. Sleeping."

"Are you sure?"

She gave him a lethal look. "What's that supposed to mean? Maybe I killed him in my sleep?"

He ignored the silent daggers. "Do you have a history of sleepwalking?"

"No." Her tone was short and resentful, and he switched gears.

"Were you alone?" He knew the answer, but her lawyer wouldn't, and it seemed natural to ask.

"Not that it's any of your business, but yes, I was alone."

"And you've never been in Frank Temple's house or his office?"

Her jaw flexed. "For the nineteen-thousandth time, before today I didn't even know who the man was."

He ran a finger around the rim of the foam cup and observed her. She was good. Very good. She stared back, dark, brooding, and silent.

And a seed of doubt sprouted. Why would she kill Frank? In all the years he'd known the man he'd never had a steady lover. He couldn't see Frank starting now.

Then again, who knew what flattery and sex did to men at that age.

But Frank wasn't "men." Frank was better than that. Smarter than that.

Yeah, right. Jake recognized the hero worship. Was any man too smart for Margo's lethal combination of intelligence and exotic looks?

Maybe that's why Frank hauled Jake down to DC. To check on his lover.

Jake wouldn't believe it. Couldn't.

Then why?

He pushed back his chair, still not knowing what to believe. "Okay." He left to find Brewster.

The cop was at his desk, his jacket on a chair, his tie loosened, and his shirtsleeves rolled up. Above his thick neck and broad shoulders, his round face was concentrating on a pile of papers. He rose when he saw Jake and met him outside the break room.

"You in this alone?" Jake asked him. "Where are the Feebies? The Feds are in on this, aren't they?"

Brewster barely hid his irritation. No man liked another agency telling him what to do. "They're running the case, if that's what you mean. You want to talk to them, I'll put you in touch."

"I want to talk to whoever's in charge." Jake noticed the wrinkled shirt. Another long day for the detective.

Brewster scowled. "They get the national-security stuff. We get the locals."

"You going to charge her?" Jake asked.
"Maybe."
"But not tonight."

Brewster shrugged and reluctantly admitted, "We're still deciding."

That was bullshit. A stalling tactic. "Sure you are." He smiled and leaned against the wall. "Any physical evidence tie her to the scene? Fingerprints, hair, GSR?"

Brewster shook his head. "No gunshot residue, but it's been almost twenty-four hours. She's smart. She could have gotten rid of it."

"Bottom line, you have no trace evidence at all."

"The handwriting samples match."

One more line anchoring her to Frank.

"That's not trace evidence. And it doesn't prove she was at the murder scene."

"We got that bullet."

Jake quickly covered his surprise. "What bullet?" Dottie had said Frank's throat was slit. "He was shot?"

"It's not what killed him, but we found a slug. We're still looking for the weapon, but if it traces to a gun owned by your client . . ."

"She said she doesn't own a gun."

"She also said she has no knowledge of the deceased. Why lie if she has nothing to hide?"

He wanted the answer to that himself. "Maybe to avoid this inquisition."

"The killer was right-handed. Your client is right-handed."

"So are ninety percent of the world's population."

"She own a six-inch blade?"

"I'm sure she does. For chopping celery." He looked around. "Anything else?"

"Not yet," Brewster admitted, albeit reluctantly. "Doesn't mean we won't find more."

"Yeah, maybe. But not tonight. I'm taking her home."

There wasn't much Brewster could do about that, so he kicked her loose.

"Stay close," he warned her on the way out. "No trips to Brazil. Department can't afford to pay me to haul your ass back here."

17

"You didn't tell me they matched the handwriting samples."

Margo stared out the car window, streets whizzing by in a blur. "You didn't ask."

"You're a real hardcase, aren't you?"

She ignored his bitter amusement, sticking to the facts. Or at least the facts as she knew them. "I don't know Frank Temple."

"Yeah, you don't know Frank Temple, but they found a business card with your handwriting in his pocket and a picture of you in his house. Next they'll match the bullet they found to the gun you don't own."

Margo ground her teeth. That summed things up neatly. Now if he'd only toss in the month she was missing and the sister she'd lost, he'd have the whole sorry mess down pat.

"You never did say how you knew where I was."

He shrugged. "Police scanner. I heard your name, thought you might need help."

"What are you — an ambulance chaser?"

"A friend in need . . ."

"Look, Jake, whatever you think you're doing —"

"Helping you out —"

"Glomming on to me for profit and who knows what else —"

"What the hell is that supposed to mean?"

"You know damn well what it means —"

"I got your butt out of there —"

"Yeah, well, whatever." She drew in a breath, trying to calm down. "Look, just stay the hell away from me. My life is beyond weird right now. Trust me, you don't want to get sucked in."

"Thanks for caring, but I'm a big boy. I'll take my chances."

She bit down on her lip. She had enough on her plate without adding him. "You can drop me off here. I'll take the metro."

He didn't stop. "I said I'd take you home."

She was too tired to argue. "Fine. Make a right here."

She directed him to her house, and fifteen minutes later he pulled into her street and past a Crown Vic with a man inside. The occupant turned his head away as they zoomed past.

"You got company," said Jake.

"Yeah," she replied softly. She swiveled around to look. The man had also turned back and was staring after them.

Clearly, the police were not convinced of her innocence.

Was she?

She swallowed the jolt of fear that bucked inside her. She had not killed anyone.

But the child screaming, the blood, the man falling.

A dream. She was allowed to dream. She clenched her hands together, hoping to hide their tremor.

Two houses down she said, "Here. Pull up." Jake was already slowing. He stopped in front of her house, and she got out. "Thanks for the ride."

"I owed you one."

"So we're even now."

"Sure you don't want me to come in?" He thumbed over his shoulder in the direction of the Crown Vic. "Given the neighbors."

"No thanks."

"Your funeral."

"Let's hope not."

She waited until he sped away before jogging to the door and letting herself in.

Then she took the stairs two at a time.

She did not own a gun. She did not know Frank Temple. She had not killed anyone.

And yet . . .

She plunged into her disordered bedroom, tore through the clothes on the floor.

Where the *hell* were her jeans?

She rifled through the clothes hanging out of drawers and heaped at the bottom of the closet. Nothing but gray slacks, navy slacks, black slacks.

Howling, she flung a pair across the room. She couldn't even get dressed without a major crisis.

Forget it. She had no time for this. She had someplace to be.

She pulled on the first pair of pants her hands reached, ripped off the tank top, and shrugged into a blouse. She buttoned it up as she ran down the stairs and out the back.

The Taurus still sat on the cement slab, and she still felt a moment's doubt looking at it. But she fumbled for the keys in her purse, saw what looked like a car key, and inserted it into the lock. It worked. Relief coursed through her.

She slid in, turned the engine on, and

pulled away. She turned the corner into the street, then left down Foxhall. In the rearview, the Crown Vic pulled out after her.

Damn.

She drove carefully, keeping the tail in sight. Three blocks ahead, a traffic light controlled the intersection. It changed from green to yellow. A flick at the rearview. Did she have enough time? Luck was with her; the road up to the light was clear.

She floored the gas, tires squealing, and ran through the yellow light just as it turned red. Her shadow tried to follow, but cross traffic cut him off.

She smiled. Finally, something was going her way.

The address she'd gotten for Argyle Towers led her over the Key Bridge into Rosslyn and Pentagon City. Massive clusters of towering apartment and office buildings loomed against the night sky. Shops and restaurants huddled together and curled around Army Navy Drive. The bars were open, neon screaming in the darkness.

Two minutes later, she left the lights below and entered a quiet, apartment-lined street: Arlington Ridge Road. The street followed a sharp incline, and at the top of the hill sat a cement-and-glass apartment building. Argyle Towers was written in black script and lit with tiny spotlights near the roofline.

From there the road made a hairpin curve down the ridge. Nothing but woods lined that part of the road. There were no sidewalks, no parking places. A small park bled into the apartment property, and she pulled up to the green space to examine the building.

Twenty stories, one entrance. Going up the ridge, she'd passed an underground garage cut into the slope, what must have been the back of the apartment. Which meant a second entrance from the garage.

The building and park were well lit, but both appeared deserted. She got out of the car.

A historic marker named the place Prospect Hill. Once the site of a brickmaker's mansion, it offered a vast view north, east, and west. From the heights it overlooked I-395; traffic hummed and buzzed, headlights dazzling the night with constant motion. Across the way, white headstones in Arlington National Cemetery gleamed like bleached bones in the moonlight. Through the naked branches of trees to her right, the Pentagon's enormous wedges claimed dozens of acres on the flatland below. Across the river and far in the distance, the District sparkled and sputtered, some areas dim, some bright. The tiny glow from inside the Lincoln Memorial lit the dark shapes in front of it. Treetops, she thought.

The view was breathtaking, the heart of the country spread out before her. It made her shudder with something she couldn't name. A heaviness settled in her chest, like some forgotten duty. Out of nowhere, pictures flashed into her head. Boats in the water. A tarp-covered cargo. The smell of fish.

A pulse leaped in her throat. She couldn't see the Potomac in the dark, but looked to where it should be. Was that where she'd been the last month? On the river? Why? What could she possibly have done there?

She searched her memory, eager for any hint, any clue to where she'd been and what had happened. But even the brief flashes she'd just had were gone.

She bit down on a scream of frustration. What did all this have to do with her? Why couldn't she remember?

She whirled around, dared the apartment building to answer, but it remained hulking and silent.

Leaving the view — and the questions — behind, she jogged to the entrance. The front door opened onto a vestibule big enough for a single person. The tiny room was separated from the interior by a second glass door. Through it the lobby was lit in low, soothing light. Fat floral arrangements centered dark wood tables. A tasteful composition of carpet and upholstered furniture led the way in.

Who lived there? Why were they calling her?

She tried the door. Locked. A narrow box like a credit-card swiper stood off to the side. Keycard. She'd need a keycard to get in. The same was probably true of the garage entrance.

Retreating to her Taurus, she laid her head back against the seat and closed her eyes. The office said it would reopen at eight. It was going to be a long night.

18

From the woods on the downslope of Arlington Ridge Road, Jake yawned and checked the GPS screen. Margo was still where she was an hour ago, still in her car, still bleeping steadily away.

He picked up his NOD and watched her through the night-vision minibinocs. From his position behind the trees, he thought it looked like she was sleeping, head lolling back against the seat. He groaned inwardly. A bed, even the damn cot in the surveillance room, was a whole lot better than this.

Yes, he was cranky. He'd been following her ass all night. Who wouldn't be?

Worse, it felt familiar. Too familiar. The lying, the tough-guy routine. He'd seen those looks on the face of another woman, and she was dead now.

He growled, not wanting to think about Dani again.

What the hell was Margo doing in Arlington anyway?

Waiting for someone seemed the most

logical explanation, but she'd already been there a couple of hours. Whoever it was, if there was anyone, he was way overdue. And why wait in the middle of nowhere, with her butt parked practically in the middle of the street?

He was about to put down the NOD when she twitched. He focused, his attention sharpened. Not just a twitch, a jerk, as though some invisible hand had squeezed her whole body. Again, and again.

Rapidly he scanned around her car. No tracers, no laser sights. Nothing. No one.

The answer hit him: she was dreaming.

Well, slitting a man's throat was a bloody business. It could give anyone nightmares.

He watched her lurch awake, breathing heavily, shoulders heaving. The door flung open; she staggered out. One hand clutched the door as if she might fall otherwise. She looked around, and for the first time he saw her face. Eyes wild, sweat-soaked hair clinging to her forehead. He'd seen her frenzied change out of the running shorts, but expected she would have straightened up by now. But the shirt was still untucked and only half-buttoned, and that half crookedly done.

For all her professed calm in the car on the way home from Brewster and his crowd, Margo Scott was falling apart.

Did that mean she was guilty or innocent? He observed her coolly, professionally. Maybe he should throw her in the Potomac and see if she floated.

She slammed the door closed, leaned against it, head down, arms braced.

That's it. Breathe, girl. Just breathe.

She wiped her forehead, swallowed, got herself under control, and checked her watch. Back in the car, she drove away.

He followed her down the ridge to a bar called Eastlake's. Shoved into a corner a few blocks from the apartment, its dark windows showed off a couple of neon Miller Lite signs that were a bitch to see through. He didn't think he could sell her on another excuse for showing up, so he couldn't blindly follow her in. But he was damned if he'd spend a wasted night in his car. If she was meeting someone, he wanted to see who.

He sprinted around the corner, found a back entrance. It led through a small kitchen that was closed for the night, but Jake had a good view from the window in the swinging door and located her at the bar up front.

He crept out, took a seat at a table in the back where he could see her. A tired-eyed bar girl with too much makeup took his order, and he sipped a beer while watching.

The seats around Margo remained empty. She spoke to no one, and no one spoke to her. Hunched over a drink — scotch maybe, or whiskey, straight up — she seemed to turn inward. He caught a single glimpse of her pinched, white face. Her dark eyes looked haunted.

19

"I come here often?" Margo said, accepting the drink the bartender slid in front of her without ordering.

The guy might have given her a wry smile at the way she'd twisted the old pickup line, but her face was too serious for the question to be a joke. Instead, he gave her a curious look. "Often enough."

"You know my name?"

He raised his brows and crossed his arms. "What is this — a test?"

"That's right." Margo sipped the drink. The scotch slid down smooth and easy, and released the knotted ball in the center of her chest. "Gold star if you pass."

"Okay." He grinned. "I'll play." She toted him up: late forties, grizzled hair going gray, strong Irish face going soft. Was he the Eastlake above the door? She'd heard someone call him Pat.

"Let's see," Pat said. "Your name is Margo. Don't know the rest because you keep it to yourself. Which is fine; we don't pry here." He nodded at her glass. "You drink single-malt scotch — Glenlivet mostly, but Macallan 18 if you're in a really good mood and just got paid. You come once, maybe twice a week for a month or two, then we don't see you for a while, then you come back." He leaned against the bar, and whispered, "I think you travel." Another grin. "So, how'm I doing?"

She took a sip. "One gold star coming up."

He stood and laughed. "Bartenders. Best observers in the world."

"You ever see me in here with anyone else?"

Pat thought about it, shook his head. "Come to think of it, no." He winked. "I can fix that if you like."

She shot him a hard look, and he held up both hands. "Just kidding. Don't shoot me, Officer." He tapped the bar. "Let me know if you need anything else."

He moved on to another customer, and Margo huddled over her drink. When she'd stumbled out of the car, she hadn't known she was coming here. Some instinct had guided her. Now she knew why.

He knew her. Tears stung the backs of her eyelids. God, he knew her.

It was so good to find someone who did.

To know she wasn't a ghost in her own life.

She sipped at the scotch, the hand holding the glass quivering. She set it down with a thunk, the downside fighting the up.

She was a regular. She disappeared and came back. Travel or blackouts? Legitimate or *Three Faces of Eve*?

She downed the rest of her drink, nursed a second, then a third, and ended up closing down the bar.

Staggering into the night, she leaned against the bar front and inhaled deeply, hoping the air would clear the fog. Then she blew it all out, hoping it wouldn't. She needed the fog. Drink fog. Mind fog. Any mist would do. As long as her brain stayed on hold.

She should go back to Aunt Frances's house. Go to bed in a bed.

But going back meant facing the mess, and the mess meant facing the questions she couldn't resolve. Better the night and the car and the possibility of answers first thing in the morning.

So she crawled inside the Taurus and sat there, needing sleep and scared to give in to the need. But the body was weak, and the scotch was strong. She drifted off.

A car horn jerked her awake. Pale sun

filtered through the windshield. She sat up, rubbed the sleep from her face, and checked her watch. Eight-fifteen.

She found her phone, groaned as stiff muscles uncramped. Whose idea was it to spend the night in her car anyway?

She ran her tongue around the wool in her mouth, wishing she had a bottle of water with her, and cleared her throat loudly, priming it for speech.

Refreshment would have to wait.

Retrieving the mashed-up paper towel from her pocket, she punched in the number she'd written down. "This is Ms. Scott. I had a message from Dana."

"Oh, yes, Ms. Scott. This is Dana." She had a light voice with a slight Virginia drawl. Margo pictured baby blue encasing middle-aged spread. "Thanks for calling back so soon."

"You said there was a problem?"

"Well, yes." Dana laughed nervously. "It's the rent."

The rent. Margo focused, her body tense.

"We . . . well, we haven't received it," Dana said. "We've never had a problem in the past, and I wanted to make sure it hadn't got lost in the mail."

Fog lifted, sleep over, Margo's brain

worked rapidly. "I've been out of town. I thought I sent you a check before I left, but I was in such a rush . . ."

"Well, bless your heart. I know how that is." Again, Dana giggled.

"How about I come by later and drop it off?"

"That would be fine."

"Remind me again where the office is."

Dana told her, and Margo hung up.

She leaned back against the seat, closed her eyes for half a second, trying to shape up for the day. It didn't seem as if it was going to wait for her to be ready.

She drove back to the apartment, remembered too late the lack of parking from the night before, and had to circle around the ridge, find a real street where her car would go unnoticed, and park there. She walked the rest of the way, slipping into the garage at the back of the building.

She'd been right about the second entrance, and right about the security. She stood near a car pretending to look through her purse for keys. Every few minutes the back entrance flashed as someone stepped out, suited and polished for work.

None of it looked familiar.

But if she was paying rent on an apartment there, it should.

She licked her lips. Would Dana think it strange that Margo didn't know her apartment number?

Bless ole Dana, she probably would.

Grimly, Margo called information and got the number for the electric company.

"My name is Margo Scott," she said when someone from billing got on the line. "I've had some trouble receiving my bill and I want to double-check the address."

"Do you have an account number?"

"Sorry, no. I'm at the office, and the old bills are at home."

"Can you spell the last name?"

Margo did and heard the distant click of the keyboard, like the flap of an insect scurrying across linoleum.

"I have a Scott, Margo at 1025 Arlington Ridge Road."

"That's it. Do you have apartment 10C on it?"

"No, it's 20B."

"Oh, see, no wonder I haven't been getting my bills. They should be going to 10C. Can you fix it?"

She said she would, and Margo hung up. She looked over at the door, thinking about cruising to the top floor.

One more obstacle. The keycard. But that meant a trip to the office and a conversation with Dana. Margo really wasn't in the mood for a chat. Her fingers were twitchy, her chest hollow, her lungs working overtime. She had to get inside that building.

A woman in heels exited. It was morning; traffic in and out was brisk.

Margo crossed the garage and planted herself near the glass door. On it, ARGYLE TOWERS was lettered in gold. Within ten seconds, someone came out, and Margo slipped in.

20

The door to apartment 20B was locked, of course, but Margo had keys. The keys she hadn't remembered giving Suzanne to hold. The keys now clenched in her fist while she held her breath, daring her hand to be anything but steady.

She closed her eyes briefly, then forced her fingers open. One by one, she moved each key aside: car, store, house. Three were left, one too tiny to open the apartment, the others equal possibilities. The first didn't fit the lock. The second slid home.

Her heart rammed her ribs. Slowly, she pushed open the door.

Down the hall a door slammed, and she jumped.

"Sorry." A man came toward her: suit, briefcase. "Hey — haven't seen you around lately."

She blinked. Tried to smile, but her mouth wouldn't work that way. "Uh . . . been out of town. Just got back."

"Welcome home."

He continued on his way, the encounter

125

polite, impersonal, and she watched his back, desperate for more.

"Wait!" She chugged after him, catching up at the elevator. "You know me."

He punched the down button and gave her a puzzled look. "What do you mean?"

"I mean . . . you know me. You've seen me in the building."

"Uh . . . sure. You live down the hall." He shuffled his feet, looked uncomfortable. "Everything all right? You look kind of . . ." His gaze swept her clothes, and she looked down. Her shirt was wrinkled and buttoned crookedly.

Quickly she crossed her arms. "I know this is strange, but bear with me. Are we . . . friends?"

His face blanched, and he held up a hand to forestall her. "Look, I'm getting married in the fall," he said nervously. "Marsha, Marcy, right? You're in 20B. I'm in D. We see each other, you know, in the hall, taking out the garbage."

"That's it?"

"Well, yeah." The elevator arrived and he leaped in. "Hope you, uh, feel better."

The door closed, leaving her staring at it.

Talk about your anonymous living. He lived down the hall and didn't even know her name.

And she sure as hell didn't know his.

She thought back to Betty Halpern. She hadn't known Margo either. And last night at the bar, Pat said she never came in with anyone.

She was getting a picture here, and it wasn't pretty.

Retracing her steps, she returned to the apartment, gulped a breath, and made the move she had to make: inside.

Cream rug, chrome and black-leather armchair slung supple and low. Off-white couch, black pillows. Chrome lamps. Bookshelves. An entire wall of drapes, white and cold.

Not cozy and inviting, that was for sure. Nothing like Aunt Frances's house. *Spare* was the word that came to mind. Spare and simple. And very empty.

"Hello? Anybody home?"

Silence.

She moved in farther, a soldier stalking enemy territory. In the kitchen, an unopened bottle of Glenlivet sat in a corner of the counter. The refrigerator was empty, the ice in the freezer shriveled. She hadn't been here in a while. Cabinets held cans of soup, a few spices, a box of water crackers. Didn't look like she cooked much.

The glass dining-room table had four

chairs with wrought-iron backs. A two-spout, terra-cotta pitcher sat in the center of the table. She picked it up and turned it over. *Hecho en españa.* Made in Spain.

A chill ran down her spine.

Shoring up her resolve, she pushed the implication away, and moved into the hallway. A closet held towels, cleaning supplies. Wedged between a box of Tide and a pile of washcloths sat a package wrapped neatly in brown paper. Ready to mail, it was addressed to a Peggy Ballinger on 18th Street in the District.

Margo lifted the package, stared at the name. If this was her apartment, the package came from her. She must know Peggy Ballinger. Which meant — her heart gave a little jump — Peggy Ballinger would know her.

She brought the package to the dining room, slid a kitchen knife through the mailing tape. The paper fell away revealing four . . . no, five books. Picture books. She frowned at the collection: *Curious George Flies a Kite, Amelia Bedelia, Harold and the Purple Crayon.* Kids' books.

Why was she sending Peggy Ballinger a pile of books? Well, she was a bookseller, wasn't she? Maybe Ballinger was a customer.

Or maybe . . . Again, that tiny electric jolt of her heart. Maybe Ballinger was a relative and the books a present for her kids. If that were true, if Margo discovered a cousin, an aunt, a friend . . . someone who knew her, who could tell her what was going on . . .

She found her cell, punched in the number for information with eager fingers.

The automated system transferred her to a live operator. He informed her there was no Peggy Ballinger on 18th Street.

She closed her eyes, refusing to believe this was happening again. She was not going crazy. She found a package with an address. That was real. Solid.

She'd just have to check it out. But not now, not yet. There was still the rest of the apartment to explore.

She pushed the panic aside, left the books on the table, and continued down the hallway. Past the closet were two bedrooms, a master with bath, a smaller bedroom without.

She examined the smaller one first. Queen bed, slate blue spread. A mostly empty dresser, except for the bottom drawer, which contained sheets. Inside the closet were lightweight clothes in technical fabrics. Black and gray microfiber pants and shirts. On the floor, heavy-duty work boots and a couple of pairs of Nikes.

She backed out of the bedroom and down the hall to the larger room. Another queen bed, another slate blue spread. She opened a dresser drawer, found jeans, T-shirts, tank tops.

So far, no skirts, dresses, or heels.

Guess she liked to dress up as much as she liked to cook.

She turned to the closet, a double-door affair that was larger than its companion in the other room. She opened it and stared.

A blur of black, olive drab, and khaki stared back at her. She blinked, and the colors dissolved into distinct shapes: multipocket vests, backpacks, harnesses and belts with pouches and holders — all of which looked way too serious for hiking. One shelf held medical kits. Another, bent metal piping — some kind of tool.

Finally, on the third shelf, a metal case. She stared at it, heart thudding. She closed her eyes, took a breath, flipped up the clasp and opened the lid.

Two rows of wicked-looking knives greeted her, each embedded in custom-cut foam. From a three-inch blade to a twelve. Single-edged. Double-edged. Serrated, smooth. A stiletto.

The dream came rushing back, the smell of blood, the thump of a man falling, a terrible scream. Her fingers loosened, and the case lid crashed down.

She backed away. Away from the closet and the answers she didn't want. All the way out the bedroom door, down the hall, and into the living room. She sank into the leather chair, mind racing.

Maybe this wasn't her apartment.

Maybe she rented it for a friend. For Peggy Ballinger. Then why was she mailing books to her at a different address?

Maybe Margo was covering for someone else.

Maybe she *was* someone else.

Yeah. A crazy, wacko loony with a knife collection.

Her stomach lurched, and she bolted up. The scotch from the night before came up out of nowhere and threatened to spew out of her mouth. She careened out the door. The exit stairway seemed a mile away. She flew down all ten flights of stairs, ran out of the building, and gulped fresh air like she was oxygen starved.

21

Jake had stuck with Margo all night. Now, he stood hidden around the corner on the twentieth floor and watched her fly out of the apartment and down the stairs as though pursued by ghosts. Seconds later, the locator showed her at the foot of the building, hanging there. He watched closely, waiting for her to make a move. She didn't budge.

Half a second of debate: should he or shouldn't he? But all he needed was five minutes. Just enough time to see who or what had spooked her.

He slipped around the corner and ambled down to the apartment. She hadn't even closed the door behind her.

He peeked in. No one visible. The place smelled empty and unused.

"Hello? Anyone here?"

Silence hung heavy. Quietly, he stepped inside.

Was this where she lived? If so, she was damn neat. She liked straightforward, clean lines, nothing fussy or girly. No cutesy little cat pictures or Home Sweet Home embroidered on cloth.

He scanned the layout: kitchen, living room, dining room. The only thing out of place was an open parcel on the dining room table. Books. Kids' books. He fingered the glossy covers. These were new, not used like the rest of the books in her store. But they were hardly exceptional or upsetting, especially for someone who sold books.

Farther in, he passed one bedroom that looked like it hadn't been lived in for a while. A dresser drawer was slightly ajar. He opened it wider. Sheets.

The second bedroom was bigger and the closet open. He moved toward it and stopped when he saw what it contained. Packs, tactical vests and thigh rigs, rifle slings, mag and grenade pouches. She had a set of fence climbers, several holsters, both belt and shoulder, and a nicer set of blades than he had, including a six-inch combat knife.

He fingered the gear. It was used and all in good shape. Well cared for. The knives were sharp and clean.

He turned his back on them, his mouth thinning.

Bookseller my ass.

* * *

Margo wiped her mouth with the back of her hand. She'd gotten her pulse down to something resembling normal. The vomit was staying down, the panic under control. No point hiding outside. Or pretending she hadn't seen what she'd seen.

She closed her eyes and laid the back of her head against the building. The morning air cooled her heated skin. A few minutes, and she straightened, swallowed, and having had the presence of mind to prop the building door open, marched back inside. She was sick of running away.

Upstairs, the apartment was wide open. Had she left it that way? Probably. Stupid, out of control . . . She couldn't afford to lose herself like that again. Not if she was going to make sense of any of this. She closed it carefully, engaging the lock.

The click set off another question: did she want to make sense? Maybe she should just stay insane. What's the old saying? What you don't know can't hurt you.

She headed toward the master bedroom. She was dirty, sweaty, she'd spent the night in her car. There were clean clothes here. She'd shower, see if she could breathe easier.

Just outside the room she heard a small

shuffling sound. The back of her neck prickled, and she stopped midstride.

Was someone inside the apartment?

Her heart jacked up. She flattened against the hallway, slid toward the bedroom. A rapid peek around the doorjamb: empty.

Paranoia in overdrive again?

Crouched and low, she entered cautiously.

A blur in the dresser mirror. Someone *was* here. Between the room and the corner bathroom.

She didn't think, she pounced. Rushed the corner, grabbed an arm, swung it around. But instead of disabling the intruder, she found herself smashed against the wall instead.

"Not this time," the man growled.

He inserted a knee between her legs, spreading them. The cold bite of steel pricked the skin at her neck.

"Did you kill Frank Temple?"

She recognized the voice now. That bastard, Jake Wise.

"No." Her mouth was wedged against the wall, and the word came out smeared.

"Don't fuck with me, you murdering bitch."

"I didn't —" She bucked back, but it

135

only made him press her deeper into the wall. He had three inches on her, a lean, muscled body, and his entire weight was keeping her immobile.

The knife stung her neck. "Did you kill Frank Temple?"

"No."

"Say it again."

"No!"

"Who are you?"

She almost laughed.

"Who hired you?"

"No one hi—"

"You're pretty geared up for a bookseller. More knives than a butcher. Frank's throat was slit. Did you do that?"

Blood was dripping down her neck.

"Did you?"

God.

"Did you?"

"No!"

"No?"

"I don't know!"

"No one likes a liar, Scottie." He grabbed her by the hair, pulled her head back, and slammed her forehead into the wall. "How the fuck can you not know?"

She gritted her teeth. "I don't remember!"

"You don't —"

"Remember. I don't remember!"

He seemed momentarily stunned, and in the wake of that surprise, his grip loosened. It was infinitesimal, but all the chance she'd get.

She thrust back with everything she had, used a leg to trip him sideways. He stumbled a step, giving her more room. She whirled, ducked the knife, gut-punched him, and when he doubled over, she chopped the back of his neck.

The knife fell out of his hand, and he went down with a grunt. A knee at his back kept him down. Now it was her turn to play with knives. She held the blade to his throat.

"Who are you?"

"You know who I am."

"An ambulance-chasing Georgetown lawyer? I don't think so."

"Fuck you."

"Not in this lifetime. What do you know about Frank Temple?"

"I worked for him."

That set her back, and he knew it. He pushed her off, rolled, and was on his feet at the same time she was. Like her, his legs were bent and braced, his hands ready. They edged around each other, chests heaving.

His gaze went from her face to the knife and back again. A quick assessment of her skill and his own, same as she was doing. He had weight; she had speed. A toss-up as to who had the advantage.

But she wanted answers more than she wanted blood. Slowly, oh, so slowly, she lowered her knife arm. Another beat and she tossed the weapon out the door into the hallway.

There were plenty more in the closet, and he was closer to them than she was, but she hoped disarming herself would persuade him to maintain the balance of power.

She straightened, walked back until she hit the dresser, then leaned against it, her now-empty hands in plain sight. "You work for Frank Temple?"

He nodded, face still wary.

"That means you're what — a federal agent?"

"That's right."

A shock of fear. What the hell was a federal agent doing with her?

"You want to explain that?"

"You first," he said. "What did you mean when you said you don't remember killing Frank?"

"Look, if we're going to have this little

chat, get the assumptions out of your head. Especially the one about me killing Frank Temple."

"I thought you don't remember."

"Whether I did it *or not*. It's the 'or not' I'm focused on."

He whistled in cynical admiration. "That's the weirdest bullshit I've heard in a long time."

"Welcome to my world."

He scratched his chin with his thumb, watching her, taking his time to think things over. "Can we sit down? Take this outside?" He nodded over her shoulder toward the door.

Was he making a move or a genuine peace offer? She searched his face, and he held up his hands. "Look, Ma, no toys."

She nodded. "Okay." Backing out, she stood in the hallway and waited for him, one foot on the discarded knife.

Equally cautious, he came forward and, at the doorway, turned to face her. They walked down the hall to the living room like that, him backward, neither one taking eyes off the other.

22

Margo took the chair, leaving Jake the couch. But she sat at the edge and leaned out over her knees, as though ready to leap away should she need to.

"My house, my rules," she said. "You first."

"Is it?"

"What?"

"Your house."

She opened her mouth, closed it again. Uneasiness shifted inside her. "I don't know," she said at last. "Maybe. I have a key." She eyed him. "Which is more than I can say for you."

He didn't deny the implication or even acknowledge it. Only paused as if silently debating what to say. "Frank Temple asked me to keep an eye on you."

A slap of surprise. "He what?"

"Under the table. Nothing official and only for a few days. A week at the most, he said."

"Why?" The tiny word couldn't come close to expressing her astonishment.

He lifted a shoulder. "I don't know."

That was her line, not his. "You get what you pay for, Wise. You hold back on me, I'll only do the same."

"I'm not holding back." He let out a breath. "I don't know why. He wouldn't tell me."

Well, that sucked. If she believed him. "And this all started — ?"

"The night I met you running."

She counted back. Night before last. "So that was a setup?"

"Frank told me you'd be at the park."

"How did he know that? *I* didn't even know that." She remembered the overwhelming urge to get outside and felt betrayed by her own body.

"I don't know."

"You don't know a helluva lot, do you?"

His lips thinned in anger, but she ignored it. "The mission?"

"Make contact, check you over. He seemed concerned about your physical state." He sent a sharp look her way. "Been sick?"

"Does losing parts of your life count as sick?"

"Only if it's Alzheimer's."

"Yeah, well, I haven't been to the doctor

lately. I woke up one day, and it was a month later."

His brows quirked, the expression just this side of contemptuous. "A month?"

"That's right. I go to bed a happy little bookseller, I wake up a raving lunatic who can't remember where she's been for the last month, what she's done, or, if we're being honest here, who the hell she really is."

He stared at her, then laughed. And it wasn't the laughing *with* you kind. "You gotta be kidding. You think I'm stupid? Come on, you can come up with something better than that. Alien abduction maybe?"

She glared at him. "Fuck you, Wise."

"Not in this lifetime."

Damn her for flushing. "Look, why would I make something like that up? It's patently ridiculous."

"You got that right."

"So why —"

"I don't know why." His voice hardened. "Why is the sky blue? Why do the birds sing? You're a whack job. Who knows why you do what you do."

Her glare deepened into a scowl. "I can't *make* you believe me."

He nodded sagaciously. "This is true.

So why not cut the crap and —"

"I'm not —"

He stood, his voice rising over hers. "Your picture was in his house. They matched the handwriting on the back of —"

"My business card." She jumped to her feet. "I know. I was at the police station, I heard —"

"He was killed with a six-inch blade." He stepped forward. "You own a six-inch —"

"I just found that stuff an hour ago!" She also stepped forward.

"You don't seriously expect me to believe —"

"It's the truth!"

He took another step closer. "Lady, you wouldn't know the truth if it bit you on the ass."

She moved toward him, too. "Speak for yourself, asshole."

They were nose-to-nose now, drill sergeant and recruit, only she wasn't sure who was playing what role.

She shoved him. "Look, if I did kill Frank Temple, I'd want to know as much as you."

Jake let himself be pushed. "Not likely."

"You think I enjoy wandering around not knowing who I am, where I've been, or what I might have done? Would you, would anyone?" No one could fake the anguish he heard in her voice. She slumped back into the leather chair. "I don't know what it is for you. Justice, a job. For me, it's my sanity."

The face she turned to him was white and bleak. A small cut had opened in her forehead where he'd slammed her into the wall, smearing blood into her hair. He'd nicked her throat, and blood had dribbled into the collar of her shirt. She hadn't complained or taken notice, which meant she'd been in pain before and could handle it. But he'd caused both wounds, and that rankled.

But only if he forgot the set of Ginsus in her closet.

"Okay" — he waved a hand in the air, forcing himself for the moment to set aside the gleaming steel — "let's say, purely for argument's sake, I'm talking hypothetically now, that you are telling the truth and you do have some kind of partial, alien-induced amnesia —"

"It's not hypothetical."

He noticed she didn't protest the alien-induced crack. "Fine, whatever. What's the last thing you do remember?"

"Closing up the bookstore. Going home. Bed." She leaned forward over her knees, staring at something he couldn't see. "I woke up with a headache. Saw my running clothes. Had an overwhelming urge to put them on." She met his gaze. Her eyes, he'd noticed, weren't black as he'd originally thought, but blue. Dark, dark blue. They were troubled now, puzzled, trying to sort everything out.

"Some kind of subliminal suggestion?"

She shrugged. "You said Frank knew I'd be there."

A little mental shudder ran through him. Could Frank do that? Mess with someone's head like that?

"When did you realize you'd lost a month?"

She told him about her conversation with Suzanne, about her supposed trip to Spain, the discrepancy between her last sale and the newspaper date. She moved on to her inability to find any trace of her sister and her discovery of this apartment. The story became more fantastical as she progressed, and his mistrust of her grew in direct proportion. And yet, she was convincing on one level: her own. She believed it. That much was obvious.

He eyed her with suspicion. "That's a very bad, very weird couple of days. It's asking a lot to believe it." Her face tensed with resentment. "Then again," he continued, playing it out to see where else she led him, "no one could make up crap like that. It's too Twilight Zone." She didn't disagree. "So, what do we know? You are —"

"Margo Scott. My parents are Tom and Ellen Scott. I have a sister, Barbara."

"Who you can't find."

She raised her voice, overriding his objection. "I have a sister, Barbara. I'm from St. Louis. My aunt Frances left me her house on Foxhall Road, where I live, and her bookstore, which I run."

"Yeah? Well, we'll see if that checks out."

"It will."

She was so definite. A little too definite. Bordering on desperate, like clutching at straws.

"What about Spain?"

She spread her hands, a gesture of doubt. "I don't remember going. Doesn't mean I didn't. I don't remember killing Frank."

"Doesn't mean you did," he said flatly, and found himself wanting her face to soften, to lose the tension and relax, if only for a moment. She had such an interesting face. All bones and hardness, with that wide, supple mouth splashed across it.

"Thanks," she said.

He said nothing, not ready to acknowledge the moment. Or the trust it implied. He rose, shaking off the momentary compassion. Frank was dead, and she could be responsible. Feeling sorry for her was beside the point.

"Ever been to Spain before?"

"Possibly."

There was an edge to her voice. His instincts sharpened, and he rounded on her. "What's that supposed to mean?"

She gestured with her head toward the dining room. "The vase thing on the table. Made in Spain."

He crossed over, picked up the vase and examined it. "You could have bought it in Pier One just as easily as Madrid."

"If I bought it at all." She joined him. "See these?" She pushed at the parcel of books. "I found them here, wrapped up and ready to mail."

"So? You sell books."

"Not new ones. Besides, there's no one by that name at that address. I checked information. And this place." She gestured around her. "I don't even know if it's mine. How can I live here and also at Aunt Frances's house?"

He could think of a couple of reasons, but until he knew more he'd keep them to himself. Along with a few other pieces of 411, like the true nature of Aunt Frances's house. "You said someone called you about the back rent here. Why don't you pay it and find out?"

She nodded. "Yeah, I was getting to that. But I had unexpected guests." She pulled a set of keys from her pocket and headed for the door.

He caught her before she got there. "Hold on."

"What?"

He pointed to his forehead. "You might want to clean up. Don't want to scare the neighbors."

Her formidable black brows came together in a puzzled frown.

"Here." He marched her by the shoulders down the hall and into the bedroom, placing her in front of the mirror on top of the dresser. "I got a little carried away," he said.

She stared at the wreck of her face, at the bloodstained shirt that was still buttoned wrong. Her fingers probed the head wound, and she winced.

"Then again, it's not every day a friend is murdered," he told her.

"Yeah, I'll bet." She met his gaze in the mirror. "Watch your back, Wise. I owe you one."

Yeah. And payback was a bitch.

23

Margo showered and changed, and afterward felt better than she'd felt since this whole nightmare had started. The jeans she found in the closet fit perfectly, as did the black tank she found in the dresser. Inside them, she felt more . . . herself, though she couldn't say why or even what herself was.

The clothes were one more confirmation that the apartment was hers, which was eerie but also okay. It meant she was making progress. She might be heading toward a cliff, but at least she was moving forward.

She towel-dried her hair, checking the cut in her forehead. It was small and had stopped bleeding. She'd have a bruise there, but nothing she hadn't had before.

She stopped toweling off in midstroke. *Nothing she hadn't had before.*

She thought back, desperate for a memory, any memory to validate that thought. But the past was a broad, blank sea. All she knew for certain was she'd been knocked around and survived.

Then again, she was plenty able to knock someone else around. Handle a knife, a man, a fight.

Panic shuddered through her as the dream images rose up: the blurred body, the scream. Was the body Frank Temple? If he was killed with a knife, was it one of hers, and was her hand wielding it? Was it a dream or a memory? Phantom or real?

She'd go crazy if she didn't stop thinking about it, so she willed the images away. Far away.

But not so far that her hands stopped trembling. She clutched the towel to her, gripping it tight, waiting for control to return. After a few minutes, she was able to hang the towel in the bathroom. Another breath, and she could head out. On her way, she noticed the drawer in the nightstand by the bed.

She hesitated, blood roaring in her ears. What would she find there?

Every discovery was a potential land mine.

But also a vital clue. A crumb in the Hansel-and-Gretel trail that could lead home, if only she knew where home was.

She opened the drawer fast, as if it might explode.

Relief swept over her.

Condoms. A box of Trojans.

She stared at the style: Her Pleasure. Lubricated.

Well, at least she had a sex life. And not just with herself.

An image of Jake rose in her head, moonlight streaking his broad naked chest on the trail around Rock Creek. What would it feel like to touch that body, to hold it and stroke it, to have strong arms around her?

But he'd had his hands on her, and he'd only drawn blood.

She closed the drawer. No way was she letting him get that close again.

She hoped some miracle had happened while she was in the shower and Jake had left. No such luck.

He was standing in the living room, in front of what had been a wall of drapes. He'd opened them, and now his tall, rangy body was outlined by the light streaming in from the floor-to-ceiling glass.

The view stopped her just as it had the night before. It stretched forever, smeared by haze but still gold and green in the sun. The needle of the Washington Monument, the spires of the National Cathedral, the remote horizon.

The Potomac was visible now, a slick, silvery line that twisted and curled around the land. Bits of fluff she took to be trees in blossom dotted the banks.

Apprehension sifted inside her again. Flashes of memory popped like cherry bombs. Water, a pitching boat. Men.

There were men with her.

She gasped, tried to focus on their faces, but the images in her head dissipated.

"Amazing, isn't it," Jake murmured, still looking out the window.

She said nothing, rocked by those hazy pictures. What did they mean? What was she doing?

"So . . ." He turned at last. "Feel better?" Something sparked in his face when he saw her.

Appreciation, maybe.

Ah, he liked the jeans.

She could use that. She'd done it before.

Another troubled wave rippled through her. What else had she done before?

True concern and sympathy appeared in his face, and against her will she responded to it. Like a flower turning to the sun. It beat agonizing over something she couldn't grasp or hold on to anyway.

"I feel much better," she said.

"Look what I found." He handed her a

framed photograph from the bookshelf. "Recognize anyone?"

She took it eagerly. A picture meant faces, connections.

Answers.

But the only answer she got was herself. "Me." She gazed at her younger self dressed in army camouflage and white T-shirt. Her dark hair was pulled back tight, her grin restrained, as though dragged out of her.

"You look like someone was holding a gun to your back forcing you to smile."

She shrugged. "Maybe I'm wound tight." Or was, or will be again.

"So you were in the army."

"Looks like."

He looked at her thoughtfully, and behind his eyes doubt lingered. "You don't remember?"

"No. But isn't that par for the course? At least as far as alien-induced amnesia goes."

He gave her a cocky grin. He had a taut, tanned face with thin, sensuous lips. The grin split the hardness in two, softening it.

She didn't want to think about the appeal of that smile, so she tapped the frame, focusing on the picture and what it implied. "If I was in the army, wouldn't there be a record somewhere? Paperwork?"

He nodded. "I'll see what I can dig up."

She set the picture down where it had been, between a row of books. They caught her eye and she ran a finger over the spines. *Kidnapped* by Robert Louis Stevenson, illustrations, N. C. Wyeth. *Little Women*, leather-bound with raised gilt letters. An Arthur Rackham Fairy Tales. More children's books.

"Who's Arthur Rackham?" Jake asked.

"Early-twentieth-century illustrator," she said without hesitation, then stopped to exchange a glance with Jake.

He shrugged. "Maybe you *are* a book-seller."

"Or a superhero with a secret identity," she said grimly. "Bookseller by day, fighting the forces of evil by night."

Or robbing someone blind. Thief, hired killer. More likely *she* was the forces of evil.

Darkness crowded in, fear twisting cold in her veins.

A fat, oversize volume sat next to the Rackham book. She checked the title and blanched. "Oh, God."

"What?"

"*Don Quixote de la Mancha*," she read off the spine. The panic started to bubble again and she couldn't breathe. "The elusive *Don Quixote.* That's what Suzanne said. Why I went to Spain. The book I was supposed to buy."

Mouth dry, she pulled the book from the shelf.

Except it wasn't a book.

It was a lockbox made to look like one. She stared at it blankly, her mind not working.

"Here." Jake led her to the couch. "Bring it over here." He pushed her down and took the box from her, setting it on the glass-and-chrome coffee table.

She poked at it, turning it around so she could see all sides. It was a clever piece of work, cloth-bound, with a real spine and a tiny lock embedded on the cover.

"Do you have the key?" Jake asked.

"I have keys," she said, running to get them. "Don't know if it's *the* key."

She brought back the key ring, fumbling for the smallest. It looked like a luggage key, but it turned the lock cleanly.

Breath held, hands sweaty, she opened the box.

Inside was a fat pack of money, several passports, a stack of snapshots rubber-banded together, and a gun.

A gun she'd sworn she didn't own.

24

Jake disconnected his call to Brewster and turned to Margo. Her face was hard and blank, but he sensed the struggle to keep it that way. Better put her out of her misery.

"Ballistics on the bullet in Frank came back. Brewster says it's a nine. Probably from a SIG Sauer nine millimeter." He picked up the gun from the box. "This is a .44. A Glock."

She licked her lips, the only sign of the relief she was probably feeling. She was right; she was wound tight. But that could be guilt as easily as anything else.

"So it's mine." She nodded uneasily in the direction of the Glock. "I own it."

"It's in your possession."

"Maybe I'm just holding it."

"For a friend?"

She nodded. He could see she wanted badly to believe that, but it wasn't likely. "You holding the rest of the gear for your friend, too?"

She flushed.

Too bad he had to burst that little

bubble of hope, but that's how things were stacking up. "Don't be surprised if a few more weapons show up. You have a rifle sling in there."

Her jaw tightened; she was bracing herself to accept that possibility. "So I'm what — some kind of assassin?"

He pursed his lips. It was one way to go. "Maybe. But Brewster also said the knife used on Frank had a single edge. Yours is double."

She looked relieved. "So I'm off the hook?"

"As far as what's in your closet. Doesn't mean you couldn't have used another one and tossed it. You have the skills, I can testify to that."

Her lips compressed into a grim line. She didn't like what he'd said, but it was true.

"And someone hired me to kill Frank. That's what you think, isn't it?"

He shrugged. "You could also be law enforcement. Or military. Could be a badge bunny."

"A what?"

"Badge bunny. Cop groupie. You know, hang around in cop bars, impress them with your . . . equipment."

The look she gave him was narrow-eyed and cold.

"Yeah. Didn't think so. Maybe you're a collector."

"Maybe I'm not."

"The gear's used. Well cared for, but definitely used." Abruptly, he tossed the Glock at her. She caught it expertly. "That's a big gun." He watched her wrap her hands around it. She checked the safety, held it up, sighted through it. "Feel comfortable?"

She nodded, and he could tell from the look on her face that she wasn't happy about it.

"Guess I'm a big girl." She continued to stare at the gun as though she couldn't believe it was real.

"You know, the nine didn't kill him. The shot was made postmortem."

Her head snapped up. "They shot him after he was dead? What kind of sicko would —" She paled, and he knew what she was thinking. Same as him. Maybe *she* was the sicko.

She set down the Glock, and it rattled against the coffee table.

Several passports and identity cards were bundled together, including ones from Canada, Britain, the U.S., and Argentina. None were in her name, though they all showed her picture.

"What about these?" He indicated the banded photographs, and she unwrapped them, then handed them to him one at a time. They all showed views of a house. Back, side front, rear, roof. Stucco walls, cobbled streets.

"Recognize it?"

She shook her head. "Europe?"

"Could be."

The obvious answer hung between them. "It's Spain, isn't it?"

"It could also be a million other places."

"And I have them because . . ."

"Could be surveillance photos. Except if they are, they're typically taken with a long lens. These look like tourist shots from an instant camera. One-hour-photo stuff."

She turned one over. "Calle Gitana, 44." She looked up. "Gypsy Street."

He gave her a sharp look. "You speak Spanish?"

"No," she said automatically. Then more slowly, "Yes." She covered her face with her hands. "I don't know. I think . . . *sí, hablo,* yes."

Man, this was weird. Maybe she *was* a lunatic on the loose.

Is that why Frank wanted her watched?

Damn that old man for keeping secrets.

"Okay. I'll check it out. You have a computer here?"

"Not that I've seen."

He stood. He had a lot of stuff to do, and it would be faster to do it where the equipment was state-of-the-art. That meant the surveillance room. "Look, you take care of the rent. See if you can find out how long you've been here, whether your signature is on the application, any other personal information."

"Oh, goody, and then — what? We meet back here with the rest of the gang and put on a show?"

His jaw tightened at her sarcasm. "You know, you are one ungrateful —"

"Why are you helping me?"

Her tone was rough, her face wary, and despite himself, he admired the way she cut through the crap. She shouldn't trust him. Not if she was smart.

"Why, Jake?"

Because he had a thing for black-haired ball busters. Because she was in trouble. Because . . . He sighed. She'd asked straight, so he gave it to her that way, even knowing he was holding so much back.

"You said if you killed Frank, you want to know. So do I."

160

25

Before heading to Georgetown, Jake retrieved his laptop from the trunk of his car. He'd been right when he told Margo she could jump either side of the good-guy/bad-guy line. For one, her gear had looked too random for military. Not enough of a uniform look. That left what? Mercenary? High-tech thievery? CIA?

He'd done more than explore the bookshelf while Margo was in the shower. He'd also rummaged around her purse. The checkbook he'd found was tied to a post office box; her driver's license was non-existent. Was Margo Scott even her real name?

He booted up the laptop, punched in his access codes to lock on to a satellite feed. Then he did a quick database search.

He came up with squat. No military history, no arrest record, no library fines, *nada.* The woman didn't exist on paper. He checked for a Tom and Ellen Scott in St. Louis with two female dependents, Margo and Barbara. Nothing again.

Only two ways that could happen. Margo Scott was a false identity created by an underground organization for all the wrong reasons. Or she was the genuine article, and her records and background had been scrubbed for all the right reasons.

The former required a deeper dig, for which he had neither the time nor the resources at the moment. That would have to wait for the equipment in the surveillance room.

The latter . . .

He punched Dottie MacKay's number into his cell phone. Had she gone back to work? Someone would have to clean up the horrific mess left in Frank's office. He hoped it wouldn't be her. And if it was, that she'd have time to get some distance before facing it.

He was in luck; she picked up on the third ring. "This is Dottie MacKay." Her authoritative voice was strong, but he wasn't deceived by it. He remembered her red-rimmed eyes, the easy way they welled up.

"It's Jake, Dottie."

"Well, I'm glad to know you're still with us."

"I am. And I need a favor."

She humphed. "If memory serves, you already owe me one."

"How about we start a tab?"

She chuckled in her usual rich, musical tone. "I'm warning you. I don't come cheap. What is it you need?"

"How well do you know the head of DCO?" Deep Cover Operations was the black ops side of the TCF. Shrouded in mystery, it was as underground as it gets, and as difficult to penetrate.

"Bill Connelly? Not the kind of man who talks to the help, if you catch my drift. Why?"

"I need to see him."

She paused, smart enough not to ask why. "Well, I do play bridge with his secretary."

Bless the god of bridge. "Even better. Can you get me in to see him today?"

"Today? Not even the angels in heaven could do that. But I can probably get him to take a phone call. That do?"

While he waited for Dottie to call back and confirm she'd talked to Connelly's secretary, he did a satellite search for Calle Gitana. After a few minutes he got one hit. The picture was two months old and too high up to get crisp resolution on his laptop, but the location was clear: Seville, Spain.

Had Margo been there? Or had the

163

snapshots been taken by someone else and sent to her? He stared at the blurred image shot from two miles up. If she'd been there, why didn't she remember?

The question of the year.

He input a third search for Warner Park. Came back with several possibles: Nashville; Chicago; Madison, Wisconsin; and a stadium in St. Kitts.

Jake stared at the search engine list on the screen. If he were meeting someone at a park he had to take a plane to, would he write it down the way it had appeared on Margo's business card — a simple "Warner Park"? Seems like he'd do that if the place was local. If everyone knew it as a matter of course. Otherwise, he'd likely add the location: Warner Park, Tennessee. Or Warner Park, St. Kitts.

His phone rang; it was Dottie.

"You're all set up." She gave him the number. "Just mention me to Melva — that's his secretary — she'll put you through."

"Okay. Thanks."

"Oh, don't thank me, Jake Wise. You just pay up when I call in your marker."

He smiled. "One more thing. You ever hear of a Warner Park?"

She thought about it. "There's a Water

164

Park in Manassas. Never been, but my daughter's taken the grandson there."

Water. Warner. Similar yet not. Could Margo have written it down wrong?

"Thanks, Dottie. I'll check it out."

"You be careful, now." Her voice had turned sober; that was the second time she'd told him that. "I need you alive to collect."

26

It didn't take Margo long to scope out the Argyle Towers office. Dana proved to be a middle-aged cheerleader type with a smile a little too eager and a dress a little too tight.

In ten seconds Margo found out that the original rental agreement was in her name — Margo Scott — that she'd been renting the apartment for five years, that her previous address was a post office box, and that she owned her own business, Legacy Books.

Two steps forward, one step back. The apartment was hers. But the rest — nothing she didn't already know. Disappointed, she left Dana a check for the rent, got a new keycard, and left.

She took the bridge into the District and headed for 18th Street with hopes high for a better outcome. On the passenger seat the pile of books swam in a ragged lake of brown mailing paper. She imagined Peggy Ballinger greeting her with the hearty smile of a long-lost friend.

But when she got to the address on the mailing paper she found a home, only not the kind she expected.

She pulled to the curb and stared at the drab, mustard brick building. A sign in front said ROLAND CARROLL CHILDREN'S HOUSE. Giant cutouts of fruit and vegetables decorated the long front windows. They were colorful and gay, meant to liven up the façade, but they hit her like a forced laugh — overbright and phony.

Disappointment already sneaking into a corner of her mind, she parked in the lot at back and headed up the ramp to a back entrance, clutching the books and paper. She didn't know why the place depressed her so, but it did.

A teenager with a bad case of acne was passing through the hall. Margo stopped and asked for Peggy Ballinger. The boy pointed the way and wiped out one of Margo's misgivings. At least Ballinger was a real person. And the fact that this was clearly a work address explained why there'd been no listing under her name.

She shored up her confidence. She and Peggy could still be friends. As her friend, Peggy Ballinger could still set Margo's mind at ease. Tell her she was as she seemed, a normal woman from St. Louis.

Sister of Barbara, daughter of Tom and Ellen. A bookseller.

But when she entered the office marked DIRECTOR and Peggy Ballinger saw her, no recognition lit her face. And when Margo showed her the books and explained why she'd come, Ballinger only looked thoughtful.

She was a small woman with cropped hair and an aging, elfin face. Her eyes squeezed shut when she smiled. "Sit down," she said kindly, gesturing from behind her desk to a threadbare armchair. "Please. Would you like a cup of tea?"

Margo declined. She wanted answers, not tea.

The older woman seemed to sense her impatience because she wasted no more time. "Well, books like these arrive every month. They've been a wonderful addition to our library, but there's never a note or a return address."

The disappointment that had already begun to percolate rippled through Margo. "Never?"

"The donations have been completely anonymous."

"So . . . you've never seen me before?" It was a ridiculous question, but she asked it anyway.

"No. I'm sorry."

Margo felt like collapsing in a puddle. Instead, she focused on the shabby couch in the corner, the worn-down rug. "What is this place?"

"It's a group home. For children who have lost parents or come from dysfunctional families that can't take care of them, children who might otherwise have nowhere else to go. We depend largely on private donations. The books have truly been welcomed. I can't thank you enough."

Margo accepted the woman's thanks, not knowing whether they were owed to her or not. Or if they were, whether they were deserved. If Margo did donate the books, was it out of altruism or guilt? A chance to give back, or a chance to make up for something?

Back in the car, she tried to push the questions aside. What was one more dead end in a never-ending string of them? She leaned back against the headrest.

What now?

She thought about the river and, wanting to get as far away as possible from Roland Carroll Children's House, drove to Old Town. She parked in the lot next to Full Metal Jacket and crossed the street into the quay along Waterfront Park. It was a warm, sunny day with a high blue sky, and the river was so bright it hurt her eyes to look at it.

She conjured up what she could of the memory flashes. Looked out at the serene Potomac. On the distant shore, the District shimmered in the sun.

Something was wrong. Different.

A chaste white cruiser jetted into the middle of the silver-blue stream. Picturesque, like a postcard.

And it hit her. What was wrong. In the flashes there was no sun, no gleam off water.

Because it was dark.

Night.

Her heart began a rapid dance. Wherever she'd been, something had happened at night. The knowledge was like a little explosion inside her. If she could figure that out, she could figure out the rest. That meant it would come back. Her memories would all come back.

The guns and knives and tactical gear rose up in her mind. The scream, the child's scream, began wailing in her head. What if she'd done something horrible? What if she *was* something horrible? Terror shot through her. She stumbled and clutched the railing at the edge of the cement walk. The river wavered, the view fluttered before her eyes. Dizzy. Her head was swirling.

"Hey, Margo!" Someone ran up to her. Her eyes focused. Vision sharpened. Suzanne. Suzanne was grinning at her.

"Wondered if you'd show up today. Feeling better?" She did a double take. "You must be. Where did you get those jeans?" She looked Margo up and down, then walked around her. "And those wicked curves. Why have you been hiding them?"

"What are you . . ." Margo swallowed. "What are you doing here?"

Suzanne waved away the unspoken concern. She looked very Marseilles today. A clingy shirt in black-and-white stripes with a boat neck that showed off her shoulders. She'd wound a red scarf around her throat, and a black beret perched at a jaunty angle on her spiky white hair. "It was too pretty to stay inside. God, look at it." She gestured dramatically toward the river and the park. "It's so gorgeous. And I didn't have a single customer all morning." She giggled and twirled. Literally twirled and flung her arms wide as if to embrace the day. "I closed for lunch. Look." She dragged Margo onto the grass by the shipbuilder's statue. He stood tall and stern, a spyglass in one hand. "I'm having a picnic. Want to join me? I mean, as long as you're playing hooky, too."

She'd spread a blanket over the grass, a brightly colored tablecloth printed with old-fashioned drawings of apples and cherries that looked like something her grandmother might have used. Or Aunt Frances. Take-out containers were scattered over the blanket. The food set Margo's stomach roiling.

And there was something else, something . . . God, she didn't want to be around people. Normal, everyday people who knew what they were. And what they'd done.

"Thanks, but . . . I've got to go."

Suzanne pouted. "Really? Well, okay." She brightened. "But take my advice. Burn the rest of your clothes and live in those." She nodded toward Margo's legs.

Margo shifted uncomfortably. "They're just . . . jeans."

"Girl, those legs are not 'just' anything." She held up a container of bloodred berries. "Sure you don't want some?"

Margo shook her head. "I'll . . . I'll see you." She backed away, turned, practically fled.

"Hey! Margo! Wait a sec!" Suzanne hurried after her. "I almost forgot." She caught up with her on the corner. "Someone came by after you left yesterday."

Margo's heart thumped. "The police?"

Suzanne shot her an amused glance. "Why, are they after you for your crimes against fashion?"

She wished. "Something like that."

"Well, it wasn't them. Some guy in a suit. Caught him peering in the window and stuff. Thought he was snooping around, but he said he was a, you know, a collector. Wanted to talk to you."

Margo nodded, tried to smile, but she couldn't think about the book business now. "Okay, thanks."

Suzanne stood on the corner and watched her leave. Margo looked back once and Suzanne waved, her gesture big and broad and gay, a beacon of light against the dark hole slowly swallowing Margo up.

173

27

Before leaving Arlington, Jake checked Margo's whereabouts. It wouldn't have surprised him to discover she'd run; if she was going to split, now would be a good time.

But the flashing dot put her in Old Town. Since the bookstore was there, she hadn't taken off for parts unknown. And since she wasn't at the Foxhall Road house, he'd have full access. He put the car in gear and drove to Georgetown.

Traffic was light, as light as it ever was around the District, but he still got stuck on the lead-in to the bridge. Seemed like everyone and their mother was going to lunch on M Street.

Since he was at a standstill, he punched in the number Dottie had given him.

Officially and for public consumption, Bill Connelly was Assistant Director of Case Investigation. What that meant on the outside was anyone's guess, but everyone inside knew the division by its more descriptive name: Deep Cover Operations. What Connelly did and the kind of teams he ran was never openly discussed, but if you moved in those circles, it was no secret either.

On the surface he was an odd choice for black ops. A small man with an accountant's face, balding and innocuous, he was a far cry from the black-leather-and-Uzi set that Hollywood had embedded in the public mind. Totally anonymous in a crowd, there wasn't a speck of glamour about him, which was what made him so useful in the shadows.

A story circulated about him, a kind of legend that to Jake's knowledge had never been confirmed or denied. Years ago, while working on heroin production in the Golden Triangle, a DEA agent had been captured by a warlord with ties to the local Burmese military commander. They sent Connelly in on a covert, and he kidnapped the commander's fourteen-year-old daughter, strapped explosives to her body, and held the rest of the commander's family hostage. The agent was released.

Twenty years younger than Frank, the two men were bureaucratic equals, both ADs under the Director of TCF. Connelly was a professional generation ahead of Jake, though, and they'd only met a couple of times years ago during Jake's training before Connelly had been promoted to Frank's level.

Calling him was a long shot. The force had to know Margo had been questioned in connection with Frank's murder. Daily briefings, case reports — Jake was sure they'd been apprised of any movement in the case. If she worked for DCO, the agency would have intervened — if only to sit in on the interrogation and make sure no state secrets were spilled.

Then again, deep cover meant just that. Hands off, government deniability. If she was involved, the stain would run all over the *Washington Post* and the *New York Times.* The DCO — and Connelly — might wash their hands of her.

Not to mention the fact that the job for Frank had been sub rosa. If Frank hadn't trusted TCF with whatever was going on, why should Jake?

All of which meant Jake couldn't come out and ask if Margo was one of Connelly's agents. Given DCO secrecy, he'd only deny it. So Jake had to find another way of fishing for the information.

The call went through, and Connelly picked up. Jake identified himself, gave rank, agent code, and clearance level, then thanked him for taking his call.

"What can I do for you, Agent Wise?" He had a high Midwestern twang that made him sound harmless.

"It's about Frank Temple," he told Connelly bluntly, and to forestall the expected objections, rushed on. "Look, I know the protocols, and that you're not going to want to talk to me. I also know TCF has probably launched its own investigation. I'd like to help."

"Speak to Command." The direct response was meant to stop the conversation cold, but Jake had other ideas.

"Field Op Command isn't plugged in. Not the way you are." They both knew what he meant, though neither said so: underground, under rocks. "I can't get much out of them."

"That's because you're not in the loop, Agent. That's the way it works."

"That's fucked, sir, if you'll excuse my frankness. You must have already developed a scenario list. Let me work on one."

"I admire your enthusiasm, but procedure is in place for a reason. You have to go through channels." It was a typical bureaucratic response, one Jake had to cut through.

"You know that channels will take a

while. Maybe more than a while. I'm ready now, sir. I'm on vacation. On my own time. And I'm in town. I'll do whatever it takes. Frank Temple wasn't just a colleague or my boss. He was with my dad in Beirut in '86 and helped get us out after the bombing. He was a close family friend. My mother is devastated."

"I appreciate that, son, and I'm sorry." He was all soothing bureaucrat now. "We all are. This has hit everyone hard."

"I just want to catch the bastard that did this." And that was no lie.

"Your fervor is admirable. But this investigation needs a cool head, not a personal agenda."

"With all due respect, sir, it is personal. For all of us. Frank was one of our own."

Jake had made himself all gung ho marine: hit 'em hard and keep on coming. Now he paused, hoping the bash-your-head-in energy was working.

"All right," Connelly said slowly. "Let's say I could bring you in. Where would you start?"

"I hear they questioned someone today. A woman. Scott. Margo Scott. Who is she? What do you know about her?"

Silence. Because Connelly wanted to contain information from the investigation? Or because he knew her and wanted to keep that quiet?

"Look, I just want to make sure the piece of crap who did this pays." He didn't have to fake the truth of that. "Who is this Scott woman?"

"Owns a bookstore," Connelly admitted at last.

"A bookstore? What's the connection to Frank?"

Connelly gave him what Jake already knew: the business card, the photograph.

"That's it?"

"That and the fact she evidently lied about it."

"He was killed in his office, right? How the hell could some civvie get in there anyway? Unless . . ."

"Unless what?"

"She's not a civvie." He let that sink in a bit, then pushed a little more. "You do a background? Watch lists, alerts, stuff like that?"

"We're working on it."

"Anything come up yet?"

"No."

Jake inched his way onto the bridge, the same way he was inching toward his real purpose with Connelly.

"Look, sir . . . could she be one of ours?"

A beat, no longer than a breath. "What are you implying? That she's some kind of rogue?" A hint of fear crept into Connelly's voice. Jake could hardly blame him. The agency's worst nightmare was to have one of its own, someone they trusted, turn on it.

"A mole, double agent. I don't know," Jake said. "Just thinking out of the box here. Covering all the bases."

"Keep those thoughts to yourself, Agent. We haven't gotten that far. Until we do, there's no need to doubt ourselves."

"Yes, sir." He didn't think he could take the subject much further. "Cases, then. What was Frank working on?"

Another small silence.

"Look, sir, you need help, I can help. But you've got to let me in."

What was Connelly thinking? "All right," he said at last. "I'll see what I can do. How can I contact you?"

Jake gave him his phone number.

"How much longer will you be around?" Connelly asked.

"Couple more weeks. More if I need it."

"If I can work something out, I'll be in touch."

By the time Jake disconnected, traffic had loosened up. Five minutes later, he drove over the bridge and proceeded to upper Georgetown.

If Connelly was smart he was already pulling Jake's file. He hoped he liked what he found.

Just in case the Crown Vic was still there, he avoided Foxhall Road and came the back way. He pulled the Expedition into the narrow alley behind the house, reviewing the conversation.

Connelly didn't claim Margo, that's for sure.

But then, lying was endemic to his profession.

That worked for Margo, too, though more and more he didn't want to admit it. The truth was, he wanted to believe her. Believe in her. The haunted look in those midnight blues tugged at him.

But the picture in Frank's house, her gear, the knives, her skill — concrete evidence kept the doubts alive. He'd believed the look in a woman's eyes once before, and it had ended in the worst possible way.

The SUV bumped over the road heading for the dilapidated hut that would hide his car. He hit the remote and while waiting for the door to open, he checked on Margo. She was on the move, but still in the vicinity of Old Town.

Brakes squealed. Jake looked up.

A car bounced into the alley. The Crown Vic.

And it was roaring down at him.

28

Jake rammed his foot on the gas, careened backward out the opposite end of the alley from the looming Crown Vic. But a second car zoomed down that end, blocking his escape.

Trapped, he grabbed his weapon from the console and dived out the door.

Two men were already scrambling out of the second car before it came to a complete stop. Another two were racing toward him from the first.

A rapid glance at the shed. Too late to punch in the code and get inside.

He darted toward the house, but there were four of them. When he dodged one, another obstructed his route.

He aimed at the guy on the right, but he was armed and returned the favor.

Jake pivoted. The guy behind was armed, as were the guys in front and to the left.

The circle of men closed in, all four weapons pointed right at him.

Shit, shit, double shit.

Had Margo sent them? Fuck that bitch.

Perfect opportunity, and what a cretin he was for giving it to her.

He wheeled in every direction, no way out. The four were uniformly swarthy, one tall and thin with a huge Saddam Hussein mustache, two shorter with more bulk, one with thick, black-rimmed glasses, the other without. The fourth was this side of an offensive tackle, stubby but mammoth, with huge arms and meaty hands. Jake kept a careful eye on him; he didn't want to get sucked under that bulk.

"My name is Jake Wise." He pivoted slowly, keeping eye contact with each of them in turn. "I'm a federal agent with TCF. Identify yourselves."

Instead of complying, Mr. Mustache nodded to Glasses, who peremptorily relieved Jake of his gun. The Offensive Tackle grabbed Jake's arms, and Mustache approached.

"Where is the woman, Margo Scott?" His voice was heavily accented.

Jake hid his confusion. If Margo had sent these clowns, why would they be asking about her? "What woman? I don't know who —"

Mustache slapped him. "The Scott woman, where is she?"

"I don't know —"

OT hit him in the belly. Jake lost his breath and doubled over. Jesus, that guy could punch.

"You want more?" Mr. Mustache asked. "Come, we take you inside." He said something to the others. Christ, was that — Jake's Arabic sucked, but it sure the hell sounded like Arabic.

Before he could puzzle it out further, OT was shoving him toward Margo's house. The back door loomed closer, and Jake's stomach took a nosedive. He knew what waited inside. Knives, kitchen stove, boiling water. A whole host of makeshift torture devices that would work just as nicely as the real thing, thank you very much.

He dug in his heels. Time. He had to buy himself time. If he could get to his car . . .

But OT had him firm. Jake struggled, if for no other reason than to make the big guy's job hard. Mustache said something, which made the other three laugh. They sauntered ahead, apparently confident that the fourth stooge could handle whatever Jake dished out.

Unfortunately, they were right.

No Glasses punched out the window in the back door, reached through, and opened it. OT hauled Jake into the kitchen.

The wreckage of Margo's wild war still lay scattered over the room. Cans and pots and boxes of food on the floor. Cabinets hung open, and drawers gaped wide.

"Not a neat creature, Miss Scott," Mustache said.

"The hobgoblin of small minds," Jake answered in a screw-you tone. "Or is that consistency? I never get it right."

In answer, OT heaved Jake into a chair and stretched a beefy arm around his neck to keep him there. A trickle of sweat leaked down Jack's back.

Mustache gave No Glasses some foreign-language instruction, nodding toward the rest of the house. Gun at the ready, the man headed toward the living room while Mustache issued another order to Glasses, who vanished outside again.

Silence, while Mustache waited for the men to return. Jake tried not to listen to the hammer of blood in his ears. Instead, he focused on the sound of No Glasses rooting around the house, stomping up and down stairs. Searching — for Margo, he guessed. Minutes later, the man returned shaking his head: she wasn't here.

Mustache put a fatherly hand on Jake's head. "Too bad for you."

"Look, this is crazy. I don't —"

Glasses burst through the back door with rope and a heavy chain. They tied him in and handed the chain to OT. Glasses and No Glasses split, one to the back, the other to the front, leaving him alone with Mustache and his pal.

Lucky guy.

At a nod from Mustache, OT lifted the chain over his head and whirled it like a lasso, faster and faster, until the metal links hummed in the air. He grinned as he did it. It was not a nice grin.

"The woman," Mustache said calmly. "Where is she?"

"I told you. I don't know."

The chain smacked the side of Jake's head. Oh, Christ. He yowled in pain.

"She returns when?"

Jake locked his jaw. The chain sliced across his face, cutting his cheek and lip.

"We do not wish to hurt you," Mustache said.

Yeah, right. "Coulda fooled me."

Another slash ripped across him. He sucked in a scream. "Get fucked," Jake replied, licking blood.

Swirl, CRACK! His head lurched back. He groaned and tried not to pass out. "Listen, you dickhead, I don't know where she is or when she's coming —"

WHACK! upside his head.

"We wait then," Mustache said.

WHAM! Jake couldn't keep his head up anymore. Everything was a blur.

"We have time," Mustache said. "Do you?"

29

Margo didn't particularly want to go back to Aunt Frances's house. But the dread simmered just below the surface; if she let it, the panic would erupt and boil her alive. She had to do something, go somewhere, act, not just stew. She'd left the house a mess, but in that mess . . . maybe she'd missed something. One small simple thing that would unlock everything else.

At the last minute, she remembered the Crown Vic, and though she couldn't exactly say why — what did it matter if the police knew she'd come home? — she took the long way around.

Everywhere she looked, ubiquitous cherry trees reminded her of time lost. Two days after she'd woken to discover they'd bloomed overnight, the trees were already balding. In places the blossoms were so thick on the ground they carpeted the sidewalks pink.

A metaphor if she'd ever seen one. Soft blossoms masking brute strength underneath. She sent books anonymously to a children's home, yet owned enough equipment for your average assassin. What else was hiding inside her?

A parking space opened up a few blocks from Foxhall Road. Leaving the car there, she came on foot to the back of the house. She rounded a bend behind the neighbor to the west and stopped short.

The Crown Vic perched in the alley like a vulture waiting to peck.

Quickly she ducked back, took cover behind a row of bushes, and conducted visual recon.

Three cars blocked the alley behind her house. She peered closely at the Crown Vic. Empty.

"The Scott woman, where is she?" A man's voice. Coming from the yard behind her house. Some kind of accent. Looking for her. Why?

"I don't know —"

Her heart lurched. That was Jake.

She crept to the border between the houses, careful to stay hidden in the shrubs, and peeked out. Someone slammed a fist into Jake's gut.

A rapid scan of the scene: three men, all armed. A fourth pinioning Jake.

Automatically her hand went to her thigh.

She looked down at the jeans she was wearing and the hand searching for a gun that came up empty.

Her reflexes were taking over.

What reflexes?

A weapon. She was supposed to have a weapon. She should always have a weapon.

The thought sank heavy inside her, no time to probe it. Another quick glance at the men in the backyard: Jake had lost his sidearm to them. They were dragging him toward the house.

She waited, tense and still. Who were they? What did they want with her?

Glass tinkled in the distance: they were breaking in.

Then what? What would they do to Jake?

She didn't want to know. She should leave. No one knew she was here; no one would know she'd gone. There were four of them and one of her. And they had guns.

One of the men dashed out again, went to a car, opened the trunk and retrieved what looked like rope and tire chains, then ran back to the house.

A third man exited and stood outside the door.

Sentry.

Silently, she sidled along the shrubbery

191

until she could view the front of the house. Another sentry stood guard there.

That left two in the house.

What did she owe Jake anyway? She didn't even know if he was on her side. And just in case he wasn't, he'd be out of her hair. Better to let him take whatever the men in the house were dishing out.

Even if it was meant for her.

Scanning the ground, she picked up a rock and edged closer to the border.

God, she was a fool.

She tossed the stone a few feet. An old trick, but it worked. The guard turned toward the sound. She threw another rock, and he left his post to check out the disturbance.

Now, said a voice in her head.

The guard had crouched down to examine the place where the rocks had settled, leaving his back exposed. Three fast, stealthy strides, and she landed a vicious kick to his head. He went over without a sound.

For half a second she stared down at the man on the ground, confused. How did she know to do that?

Get him out of sight, the voice spoke again.

Grunting, she dragged the guard by the

feet around the side and out of view from the street. Her gaze caught on his gun, and after a second of hesitation, she lifted it. It felt right in her hand. Instinctively she knew what to do with it: check the mag, pull back the slide to chamber a round.

Do it, the voice whispered. *Don't think about it.*

Creeping back the way she'd come, she scouted the guy at the back. Shooting him would be the most efficient way to take him out.

Could she?

Instinct said, yes.

Did she have the will?

That she was less certain of.

Jake screamed, and she raised the weapon.

Damn. Her hand was shaking.

She gritted her teeth and screwed her courage. Aimed.

Her hand was still shaking.

And a gun would make noise. Too much noise.

Relieved, she pulled her arm back and shoved the pistol into her waistband. Working the same trick she'd used out front, she lured the back sentry toward the cars, then cut him down with a merciless blow to the back of his head.

Breathing hard, she stood over the downed man. She could smell her fear, a sour, sticky sweat. And beyond that a feeling of power, of accomplishment that she didn't want to acknowledge. As though some distant part of her was pleased. She'd taken two men out as though it were nothing. As though she did it every day.

The scream inside her head started to wail, but she shuttered it tight. She had to. Jake was still inside the house, and there was no one to get him out but her.

Someone had knocked out the backdoor window. Inching closer, she heard the sound of metal striking bone and Jake's howl of pain.

The chains. They were beating him with the chains.

Fury tightened a screw in her chest.

They were in the kitchen. Could she scope out the field from the back door without them seeing her? Not likely.

She scrambled around to the front, carefully let herself in and slithered to the kitchen without detection.

The man with the chain was huge and the weight behind every arm swing massive. He swung the chain around his head again, but this time, Margo lunged and grabbed it, pulling the big man off-balance.

"Drop it," she said, still yanking at the chain.

The men whirled, but they were too late. Her gun was already aimed dead center at the boss man's chest.

"Drop it," she repeated, and the boss nodded. The end of the chain the bigger man was holding fell to the floor with a heavy clang.

The boss smiled. He had yellow-edged, tobacco-stained teeth beneath a bushy mustache. He chewed an unlit cigarette. "Ah . . . you are here. Now, we can let your friend go."

"Shut up," she said. "Your weapon. On the ground."

He hesitated.

"Now, now! On the ground now!"

Slowly, he obeyed. She kicked the gun over to Jake. Out of the corner of her eye she saw him cover it with a foot.

She relieved the big man of his weapon, too. "You." She gestured to the far end of the kitchen table. "Over there."

"We will have our revenge." The boss man's calm voice belied the fiery conviction in his eyes. "You cannot escape."

The language was cheesy and melodramatic, but the intent behind the words was deadly serious. She forced herself to ignore it.

"Sit," she ordered. "Hands on the table where I can see them."

Disarmed, they did as she commanded. Half a second later, she freed Jake. He was tempted to shoot them where they sat, but Margo stayed his hand. "I've got enough bodies chasing me."

He kept the gun on the men until she'd trussed them and stuffed half a dish towel in each man's mouth. They left the chain wound around the big man's neck.

Outside, Margo gulped air like she was a heroin-starved addict. The man's words reverberated in her mind: *We will have our revenge.*

She'd done something terrible. The screaming child inside her head echoed it. The man's words confirmed it.

Whatever it was, she was no longer sure she wanted to know.

30

Jake's car was still barricaded in by the other two vehicles, and the alley was too narrow to maneuver around them. Forced to hike back to Margo's Taurus, he cursed and bit down on a moan of pain. The car ride was little better. Every bump and jostle went through him like a blade.

Beside him, Margo drove fast and steady.

"Anyone following?" He held on to his ribs to keep the impact of the car's motion at a minimum.

"No."

Thank God for small miracles.

"There's a hospital five minutes away," she said.

"No. Until we know what's going on, we stay under the radar."

"Yeah, but you haven't seen your face yet."

And he wasn't looking forward to it.

She didn't argue, though, and took him to Argyle Towers, where she parked in the underground garage and helped him toward the elevator.

Once inside the apartment, he took a few moments to rest against the front door while Margo disappeared down the hall toward the bedrooms. A groan and a shallow breath, and he pushed off, plodding on to the hallway bathroom.

He faced the mirror.

She was right; he did look a mess. His lip was split, and a cut near his eye looked interesting and would probably puff up. His cheek and jaw were raw, as was the skin on his neck. He didn't bother looking at his back and shoulders. They'd probably turn all sorts of nice colors. Oh, he was going to be pretty.

But it could have been worse. If Margo hadn't shown up when she did, it could have been a whole helluva lot worse.

And wasn't that a kick in the teeth?

He found a washcloth, turned on the faucet, and was dabbing at the blood when Margo came in with a medical kit.

She sat on the toilet and opened the kit on her lap. "I should have known I'd need this sooner rather than later."

He grunted a reply, concentrating on not hurting himself more than necessary.

"Who were they?" she asked, watching him work.

"Don't you know?" He flicked a glance

at her. "No, of course not." He applied an antiseptic to the cuts and winced at the sting. "Well, they didn't introduce themselves."

"But they were after me."

"That's what they said."

"The leader. The skeleton with the mustache. He said something about revenge."

"Looks like you pissed someone off. Big-time."

"Who, why? God, Jake, what did I do?"

Her voice was low but anguished. He glanced down at her. She was staring hard at the cross on top of the medical kit, clutching the metal box like a life preserver. A cord of compassion tugged at him, and he knelt in front of her.

"I don't know." He wished he could offer more comfort. "I guess we'll have to find out."

"We?" Her dark blue eyes lifted to his. They were filled with worry and wonder. "Haven't you had enough?" Her fingers fluttered lightly over the slash near his eye, then slid down to his mouth, gently tracing the cut there. Her touch sent a ripple of unexpected heat through him.

Whoa. Down, boy. Step away, move back. She just saved your ass, and you're one grateful s.o.b.

Yeah, right. That wasn't gratitude he was feeling.

Rising, he took the kit from her, rummaged around, found a small bandage. He laid it carefully over the cut near his eye. It was deeper than he would have liked, but short and narrow; he didn't think it needed stitches.

He sighed and twisted the water off with a jerk. "Patched. Best I can do."

"Jake," she said quietly. "Why didn't you tell them where I was?"

He turned away from the mirror, leaned against the sink. "Why didn't you leave me there?"

She could have. He knew damn well she could have. She'd be free of his suspicions, his doubts, of him. And her hands would have been clean.

"I thought about it."

The corners of his mouth turned up, and he winced in reaction. "Yeah? Well, I thought you'd sicced them on me. And don't make me laugh. It hurts."

"I told you to stay out of my life."

"What can I say? I'm a guy, I don't listen."

"Got yourself beat up for me." She shook her head. "How stupid is that?"

"That's what you do for your teammates, Scott."

She searched his face, the look doing things to his breathing no grown man should allow. "Are we a team?"

Were they? Slowly, he nodded, not able to look away from the penetrating blue of her dark eyes. "Sort of. The losing, come-from-behind kind."

She seemed to take that in and turn it over, not quite sure what to do with it. And who could blame her? He didn't know what to do with it either.

The truth was, any feelings of . . . comradeship were dangerous. She could still be Frank's killer. He couldn't forget that. Easy to do in a haze of attraction.

He'd just have to keep that dog leashed.

She stepped away and busied herself with closing the medical kit. Somewhere along the way, her hair had come undone, and as she fiddled with the box, it slid over her bare shoulder, a thick, dark blanket against her pale skin.

That hot pulse began to hammer through him again.

Why shouldn't he grab what she offered, if she offered? He could still take her down if he had to.

Because using her would be shitty.

Yeah, but it could work. He could soften her up, make her trust him . . .

"So anyway . . ." He pulled the hair back from her neck, and it was as plush and heavy as he imagined. "Thanks."

She jumped a foot at his touch. "For what?"

"Getting me and my butt out of there."

She snapped the lid shut, suddenly all business. "You've got a nice butt, Wise. Wouldn't want it damaged."

He followed her out of the room. "You think my butt is nice?" His gaze lowered to the similar body part in front of him. Encased in the tight jeans, it swayed sweetly ahead. "I gotta return the compliment."

She spun around, walking backward. "Hands off."

He raised both of his, wincing, as the action set off the bruises. "I didn't touch a thing."

She narrowed her eyes, the amity of a few moments ago replaced by suspicion. And man, he was so much more comfortable with that.

"What were you doing at my house anyway?"

She ducked into the big bedroom, and he followed, leaning against the doorjamb while she replaced the kit on a shelf in the closet. He knew this would come up, and he'd already got his answer ready.

"Checking you out."

She closed the closet and faced him, frowning. She didn't like that answer, but she'd like the truth even less.

"You still think I'm lying?"

"I'd be a fool not to learn as much as I can about you. Since you're so . . . vague on the topic."

She stalked past him and out of the room.

"Teammates trust each other, Wise," she called over her shoulder.

"Well, we're still gelling."

He followed her to the living room, where she was standing in front of the bookshelf and staring at the photograph of herself. The drapes were open, and the panorama was spectacular. The crosses in Arlington popped keen and white from their bed of deep green grass, a sharp reminder that death had brought them together.

"For example," he said, "you have no arrest record."

"Thank God for small miracles."

"And your military records are non-existent."

She pivoted, transferring that intense gaze to him. "How is that possible?"

"Maybe the picture is a Halloween stunt."

"A costume?"

"Sure, why not?"

But she didn't seem to like that explanation any more than he did.

"And I talked to Connelly." He watched her for signs of recognition, but her face remained blank.

"Connelly who?"

"Bill Connelly. Head of Deep Cover Ops. Sister branch of Field Ops, what I do."

"What's the difference?"

"DCO is black ops. Heavy-duty secrecy. If-you-get-caught-we-don't-know-you kind of stuff. I thought maybe you worked for them. You've got the gear for it."

"But?"

"Connelly didn't seem to know you."

"Would he tell you if he did?"

"He might." He shrugged. "Might not. What'd you find out about the apartment?"

"It's mine. I also tracked down the person the books were addressed to."

He listened while she told him about the donations to the Roland Carroll Children's House.

"Well it's nice to know you're so philanthropic. Too bad it didn't lead anywhere." With a groan, he eased into the leather chair in the living room. "There's no

Warner Park in the greater DC area, but I found your street. From the pictures."

Her whole body seemed to still. "You've been busy."

He grunted. "It's in Seville."

She swallowed, her slim white throat working hard. "So, I did go."

"You've got the pictures. Doesn't mean you took them."

The info dump had been nonstop, and she suddenly seemed to have had enough. She threw her arms in the air. "You know what? I'm tired and hungry. I can't remember the last time I ate. I'm going to get a sandwich, and I'm going to think about something besides this nightmare I'm in."

He started to rise, thought better of it. "Want company?"

She looked at him balefully. "Not particularly."

"I could tail you."

"You could, but you won't. You look like Godzilla back from the dead. The last thing we need is attention, and that face, well, it's not exactly low-profile. Stay here. I'll bring something back."

She was probably right. But could he trust her enough to let her out of his sight?

After her rescue of him, he was a little more likely to.

Besides, he had the locator, so she couldn't exactly disappear.

"Okay." He thumbed over his shoulder toward the bedroom. "If you don't mind, I'll lie down."

She scowled at him. "Don't you have a home to go to?"

Not unless he wanted to hike to Manhattan. And the cot in the bowels of Aunt Frances's was out for the time being. "Not one I want to chance going to."

She sighed. "Whatever," she said and headed for the door.

"No mayo, hold the ketchup," he called.

The door slammed.

Man, she was one cranky female.

He fished the locator from his pocket and opened it, watching the dot flash her position. At least the four stooges hadn't searched him and found it.

Speaking of the four stooges . . .

He debated whether to call Manhattan and institute a database search on them. He still remembered that Frank hadn't trusted TCF with any of this, so he was loath to go through official channels. But channels was also the fastest way to get an ID. That meant pictures, though, which meant getting back to the surveillance room, where he'd have access to plenty.

He closed his eyes. Suddenly the bedroom seemed too far away, let alone a house on the other side of the river.

31

Suzanne DeForrest wasn't particularly detail-oriented. She often forgot to turn off her shop lights, and once she even forgot to lock the door before going home. But Margo was a different story. Even cracking up — and knowing Margo's crisply controlled personality, Suzanne wasn't ready to concede that Margo was — she didn't forget the details.

This is what occurred to Suzanne when she dropped her bag of poppit beads just before closing. She hadn't been open long; the sun had seduced her into staying away for most of the afternoon. She was still feeling the effects of the gorgeous day, so instead of being annoyed when the beads bounced and rolled, she laughed and got down on her hands and knees to collect them.

As she crawled around the floor, she popped the beads together in one long, randomly colored chain that she wound around her neck. The chain was in triple strands when Suzanne noticed several beads near the connecting doorway between her store and Margo's. She scrambled over to them, and as she absently popped them onto the chain, she observed the light streaming from beneath the doorway.

She sat back on her haunches and stared at the thin strip of yellow.

Had the lights been on all night and all day?

Margo had gone home yesterday. Suzanne had seen her dash down the street. The bookstore had been closed all day. A dart of worry speared Suzanne: maybe Margo *was* cracking up. Those jeans she had on were proof. Forgetting to turn the lights off was definite proof.

There must be another explanation.

Could Margo have come back?

Suzanne shook her head and rolled her eyes.

Of course, Margo could have come back. That's what happened. She came back.

"Margo?" Suzanne rose and knocked on the connecting door. "Are you feeling better?" She listened briefly and when there was no answer, knocked again. "Margo?"

Suzanne sighed. Something was not right.

She giggled, thinking of the Madeline

books, and cast herself in the role of Miss Clavel waking in the middle of the night. Smoothing down her black slacks, which clung to her hips and thighs, she tried to imagine the angular, not to mention chastely habited, Miss Clavel in skin-hugging pants, a black beret, and poppit beads.

Feeling foolish — after all, Margo could certainly take care of herself, and if she hadn't been acting so strangely Suzanne would have finished picking up her beads and gone home — she went to the cash register, depressed the NO SALE button, and when the drawer opened, rummaged around for the key to the connecting door. She didn't use it very often, so Suzanne had to scrounge, but eventually found it wedged in the back left corner below some old credit-card slips.

Returning to the connecting door, Suzanne noticed the strip of light was no longer there.

She paused.

Had she imagined the light earlier?

No, that was ridiculous. A light had definitely been on.

Another flicker of worry ran through her. She remembered the man snooping around the other day. He said he was a collector, but he had those dark glasses and evil beady eyes . . .

One of her displays showed a mannequin in rolled-up jeans, tight white tank, and a hot pink silk baseball jacket. She'd thrown in a bat as a prop. Now she tiptoed over, got the bat, and unlocked the door into the bookshop.

"Margo?" Suzanne stepped in and looked around. The place was dark. It had an eerie, empty feel. "Margo, are you here?"

She headed for the back. Margo had a small office there; she could be doing accounts or some other boring business chore. She probably turned off the lights in the main part of the store when she went to the back. "Hey, Margo," Suzanne called, "what are you doing?" She opened the door, but the office lights were out. A huge shape loomed out of the darkness. "Margo?"

Something pushed her. The bat fell to the floor with a thud. It was the last thing Suzanne heard.

32

Jake was asleep in the living room when Margo returned. She stood in the doorway, watching him. She still couldn't grasp why he hadn't given her up to the men at Aunt Frances's house.

More important, why hadn't she left him to his fate?

She remembered the electric leap when he'd touched her hair in the bathroom. Was that why she'd rescued him?

Friends could be dangerous. Lovers even worse. Why, she didn't know. She searched her brain. Had she been betrayed? Cheated on? No memory surfaced, but deep inside, like a foundation buried under fathoms of water, that truth was bedrock. Alone was better. Safer.

And yet . . .

She admitted it: she could use the help. Given that she was wading through mud in a dark tunnel, turning down a light, a guide, was not only ungrateful, it was unwise.

And there he was, stretched out in her

chair, his lean, powerfully muscled body bruised because of her. A smart man would have turned her over to those men. A smart man would have protected himself.

But maybe Jake was more decent than smart. Too decent for his own good.

Could she trust him? Had he proved himself? She still wasn't sure. *Honor* was an old-fashioned word, but he'd acted honorably. And she was tempted to believe in what he'd done for her.

She let him sleep and ate her sandwich alone, brooding at the walls and wondering when the men at the house would come for her again. Would they find the apartment? Would Jake be there to stand between her and them again?

Her stomach twisted, and she pushed the food away. The meal sat in her belly like sludge, slowing her down. She yawned.

She needed a hundred hours of sleep, but she didn't want to close her eyes. Not yet. Too much escaped in the darkness, too many voices she couldn't control.

Along with the food, she'd brought back a pile of newspapers. Again, she didn't know why she'd felt compelled to buy them, but something beat at the back of her brain — if only she could remember it.

From front to back, she went through every page of the *Post*, then started on the *Times-Daily*, and then through five others.

Once again, nothing clicked or jumped out at her.

What was it? She pounded her head. What couldn't she remember? A wail started deep inside, the child screaming, and she bit her lip to keep from giving it voice.

She checked on Jake again, more out of something to do than any real concern. He was still passed out, so she went into her bedroom.

Her eyes went immediately to the nightstand. The condoms inside the drawer shouted at her. God, sex would be good right now. An escape, a chance to run into pure black sensation. To pretend, even for a moment, that she was connected to someone.

But the only someone nearby was out cold.

She could do it herself. Wouldn't need condoms for that.

She shivered. Sex with herself. How lonely was that?

Too lonely. Too pathetically alone.

She buried the thought and noticed a book on the shelf below.

A swift, anxiety-filled surge.

How to Kill with Knives?

She held her breath, pulled it out. No how-to-kill manual. No manual at all.

The Illustrations of Arthur Rackham. Well-worn and thumbed. ST. LOUIS PUBLIC LIBRARY was stamped in faded letters across the edge of the pages.

A flutter went off in Margo's chest. Some kind of . . . what? Warmth, maybe? Something inside her, something just out of reach, but there, faraway and distant. Something good.

Intrigued, she sat on the bed and opened the book. It unfolded naturally to the middle. Between the pages sat a tiny snapshot. Old folds crisscrossed the surface, as though the picture had been crumpled, then smoothed out.

A pulse in Margo's throat sped up. Another picture of the house from the *Don Quixote* box? Another time bomb primed to explode into her life?

She fingered the photograph. It was round but unevenly shaped, awkwardly cut as if by a child from a larger picture.

A woman's face stared up at her. She had long dark hair and a smile on her face. Margo peered at the photo. The folds had created white lines across the

215

image, so it was hard to see clearly.

Who was it?

Sister, aunt, mother, cousin? Was it a picture of herself? It looked like her. Was it herself in another life?

A flash burst in Margo's head. A kitchen. The smell of popcorn. The raw taste of terror.

She gasped and dropped the photo. The images vanished, and slowly the rush of panic subsided. But the questions remained.

Who was she?

Why did popcorn freak her out?

She sank back onto the pillow, aching to know the answers. But all she found inside herself was a vast cloud of sadness. She tried to build a wall against the sorrow, but like smoke, it couldn't be controlled. The grief expanded. It lengthened and stretched until it filled every crack in her soul. Tears welled up, and before she could stop them, they overflowed her cheeks.

She curled into herself and softly, silently, cried.

33

A cry penetrated Jake's sleep-induced darkness. For half a second he thought he was
back in Kosovo, the screams of a UN
bombing raid overhead and Danika beside
him.

"Down!" his mind screamed. He lurched
to cover her, to roll them both off and
under the bed. His eyes shot open. Instantly, he remembered where he was.

Margo's living room. He must have
fallen asleep in the chair. Jesus Christ. He
groaned, checked his watch; it was close to
midnight.

Mouth dry, blood pumping, he fought to
steady his heart. The cry came again, and
he bolted upright. What was that?

Ignoring the rip of bruises, he hurtled
down the hall and charged into Margo's
room.

She was bucking in the bed, tossing the
covers, fighting a phantom opponent.

The sharp edge of pity tore through him,
and he watched her for a moment, not sure
what to do. He moved forward, but his foot

hit a book lying on the floor as if it had fallen off the bed. Another fairy-tale book. He picked it up, set it on the nightstand.

Feeling at sea, he sat, hesitated, then shook her gently. "Margo. Wake up."

She slapped at him, hands flying. Something fell out of her fist. A woman's face in a snapshot, crudely cut out. He put it on top of the book and ducked her flailing arms.

"Margo!" He shook her harder. "Wake up. You're dreaming." And then, because he didn't know what else to do, he lifted her up and held her. "It's okay," he said. "It's a dream. Just a dream."

Her breasts were squashed against his chest, her spine was sharp and pointed. Soft and hard, like she was herself. He rubbed her back, wishing he could rub the ghosts away. "Shh. You're okay."

She jerked and stilled. Pushed at him.

"What . . ." She swallowed, her voice sleepy and hoarse. "What happened? What are you doing here?"

He eased away. "You were screaming. A nightmare."

She sat back. She was wearing the black tank top. In the dark, with the black shirt and the dark hair and her fathomless dark blue eyes, she looked mythical, an inky goddess of night.

A rush of desire hit him.

He watched her dig the heels of her hands into her eyes. "What was the dream about?" he asked.

"I don't . . . nothing. I don't remember."

He let that evasion slide. "This isn't the first time, is it?"

Her face hardened. "I don't know what you're talking about."

He couldn't tell her about following her to the bar, watching her jerk and tremble inside her car until she staggered away with haunted eyes. "You don't seem surprised."

Her hair tumbled thick and wild over her shoulders, and he wanted to lift it, push it back, touch her. *Soften her up, make her trust him.*

She ran a hand through her thicket of hair, let out a huge breath, and relented. "No," she said grudgingly. "I've had them before."

"Bad memories?"

Suddenly, her eyes welled up. She looked away, the bedclothes bunched in a tight fist. "I don't know. Dreams or memories . . ."

He felt as if a tiny hand had clamped around his heart and twisted it. "Want to talk about it?"

"No."

She didn't look like she could handle any more badgering, so he rose to leave, kindness getting the better of him. "Who's this?" He fingered the picture on the nightstand.

She looked, seemed to withdraw even further. "Not sure. It was in the book."

He tapped the oversize volume. "You have a thing for kids' books. What's that all about?"

"Wish I knew," she said gloomily.

He picked up the photo, studied the woman behind the creases. "Could be you."

"In another life."

"A relative?"

"Possible. Like I said, I don't know." There was testiness there, a rim of anger. She closed her eyes. "Sorry. Didn't mean to snap."

He shrugged. "It's the middle of the night. You're entitled."

He turned to go. He should probably leave. Grab a motel if the Georgetown house seemed too risky. Then again, he didn't want to let her out of his sight. The second bedroom would do nicely. "Catch you later."

She reached out to grab his arm. "Wait." Surprised, he turned back, looked down at her. Her face was open, vulnerable. "Please." The whiskey tones of her low voice vibrated inside him. Her hand slid down to grasp his. Her long, slim fingers wound around, stroking, seductive, their invitation plain. "Stay."

Dani's image flashed in his head, that last confident smile before she got in the car that never came back. Why was he such a sucker for endangered women?

He let her pull him onto the bed. God, this was *so* not a good idea.

And yet, so irresistible. Besides, wasn't it what he'd already decided to do? Take what she offered and use it?

Briefly, their eyes met. He saw need and hunger in hers, and if there was also a hint of desperation, he ignored it. How could he help it? Her breasts were crushed against his arm, and her mouth was coming fast.

The kiss was deep and erotic. Her tongue slid in and wound around his own, licking, sucking, pulling him under.

Whatever qualms he'd had vanished in a haze of heat.

He wrapped his arms around her and they fell together on the bed. She tugged at his jeans, scuttled out of her panties. She found a rubber in the nightstand drawer and rolled it over him. He shuddered with the touch of her hands.

Who was using who? He no longer knew. Or cared. She was on her back, open to him. "Go," she panted, her hips raising to meet his. "God, go. Please."

He didn't need a second invitation. He stabbed into her, and she sighed with something close to relief. His ribs hurt, but the pleasure swiftly outraced the pain. He didn't think about it, he could hardly think at all. She was wet and ready, a soft, fluid fist that encased him in velvet.

Margo worked her hips, frenzied with need. Her hands pressed against his butt, pushing him in, controlling the thrusts. She was desperate, hunting for that click, that peace only mindlessness brought. When she wouldn't care who she was or why she couldn't remember.

She didn't worry about pleasing him. His harsh breathing and moans of pleasure told him she didn't have to. He tried to kiss her. She didn't want him to. Kissing was not what this was about. This was about that one burning place stinging with pleasure. Pleasure that could flood her brain and drown everything out.

He winced once, and she remembered

his injured ribs. She rolled them over, straddling him.

Through a sex-infused blur, she saw him below her, face thick with passion, neck taut, chest flat and wide. He was beautiful. Bruised but strong, a hard, potent guardian. Her guardian.

Her body responded, her breasts so tight the nipples were like bullets. He crushed them, his long fingers working the erect buds, and she cried out and moved faster, swirling her hips to please herself.

A black abyss of sensation opened up, and, grateful, she fell in. Heat climbed, reckless, wild, the pleasure tightening inside her until she thought she would burst.

And then she did, and the exquisite, pumping fulfillment filled her brain and her heart and her mouth, and she thought nothing, nothing. Only felt.

And somewhere, far, far away in the distance she heard a stuttering groan, and knew he had finished, too.

She shuddered. Her breathing slowed. Bit by aching bit, the world came back. But the edges were softer now, sleepy. Not so fearsome. She collapsed on top of him, her eyes closing.

Unthinking, Jake slipped his arms around her. His heart came down from the ledge it had leaped to. He stroked her. Held her. Realized it was what he'd wanted to do since he saw her thrashing in bed under the sway of her demons.

Hold her. Shield her.

God, was he in trouble.

They lay there, sweet and warm, for a few minutes.

Then she was gone, leaving his chest cold and empty. She lay beside him, an arm flung over her forehead. Her eyes were closed.

"You okay?" he asked.

"Mmm." She brought her legs up toward her chest and curled away from him. In minutes, she was asleep.

He lay beside her, dismissed, and stared up at the ceiling.

So she'd used him. So what? He got his rocks off. No complaints there.

And yet he felt curiously empty.

He leaned over and brushed hair off her face. She looked peaceful finally.

A good fuck. Better than a sleeping pill.

Lying back, he ran a hand down her spine. She murmured, but didn't wake. His hands roamed left and encountered a ridge on her hip. He rolled off the bed and opened the blinds over the single window to let the moonlight in.

Back in bed, he found the ridge again. A scar. There was another on her thigh, and a third on her left shoulder. That one was a bullet wound. The other two? He couldn't tell. Knife wounds, maybe.

Badges of war.

What war? Whose side had she fought on?

The mystery fascinated him. Fuck it — say it. *She* fascinated him. And that was the pure honest to God's truth.

He spooned himself around her scarred body. He didn't know why he did it, she clearly was interested only in the comfort of his dick, not his arms. But it felt good to hold her. She was a woman who needed protection. From the men who wanted revenge on her. From him. From herself.

Dawn was still an hour away when his cell phone woke him. He'd slipped out hours ago and brought it into Margo's bedroom, along with the nine they'd taken off Chain Man. Now he untangled himself from Margo's arms and legs, which had twined themselves around him in the night, and answered it.

Detective Brewster's voice boomed in his ear. "Wise? That you?"

He pulled the phone away from his ear.

"Yeah, it's me." He yawned. "What time is it?" He checked his watch. Four-thirty.

"Where the hell is your client?"

He brushed a strand of hair off Margo's face. Her dreams hadn't haunted her for the rest of the night, and she'd slept through the ringing of the phone. The beginnings of a smile graced his lips. Amazing what sex can do. He rolled off the bed and tiptoed into the hall, closing the door behind him. "It's four-thirty, Brewster, where the hell should she be?"

"I know what time it is. And she's not home. Where is she?"

"Why? What's so important you need her before the sun is up?"

"We found another body."

34

"We've been trying to get in touch with you, Ms. Scott. Where have you been?"

Margo pulled her shoulders back. She was standing in front of the bookstore. Crime-scene tape marked off the entrance and stretched across Retro as well. A swarm of uniforms and other functionaries milled around outside, entering and exiting at will. Police cars blocked the street, blue lights circling. More cars lined the curb. A CSU van was double-parked next to an unmarked.

Margo's gaze flitted over the area. Deep inside, the terrible drumbeat that had started when Jake woke her began to throb again. "What happened?" Her voice came out hoarse, and she fought to clear it.

"Cleaning crew found her," Brewster said bluntly. "Name's" — he checked an open notepad — "Suzanne DeForrest."

She shook her head stiffly. "No."

"We found her in your office," Brewster said. "Her throat was cut."

"No!" She surged forward, shoving him

rudely away, and lurched toward the building. "I don't believe it. Where is she?" A phalanx of cops massed to block her way. She plowed into them. "Let me see her. Let me see her!" Two uniformed bruisers had her by the arms, and she jerked and twisted to dislodge their hold.

Jake rushed to free her. "Let her go," he ordered the men. "Let her go!" His arm slipped around her. "I got her."

"No." Her voice cracked on the word, and she broke Jake's hold, feeling brittle enough to splinter at the slightest touch.

She stumbled to a streetlight and braced her hands against the post, arms rigid, head down. Her chest was heaving as though she'd run a hard mile.

Brewster called over to her, "Where were you last night, Ms. Scott? Around six."

"Give her a second," Jake said.

"I don't have a second. Ms. Scott?"

Margo didn't respond. She couldn't move.

Jake answered for her. "She was with me. We had dinner."

"Where?"

"In her apartment."

Brewster frowned. "Her apartment? I sent a car to the home address. No one there. The place had been broken into,

228

ransacked. My guy said it looked like there'd been a fight." He shined a flashlight at Jake. "What happened to your face, Mr. Wise?"

Jake shielded his eyes, as much to buy time as anything. Did Suzanne know Frank? Was there a connection between his death and hers? Or was the only link standing a few feet away, drowning in grief or guilt?

Not knowing what was secret and what wasn't, Jake lied. "Fender bender."

Brewster's expression flattened. "Pretty big fender to do all that damage."

"You should see the fender."

Brewster pursed his mouth, not buying any of it. But he seemed to evaluate Jake and come to the conclusion he wouldn't get far there.

It didn't matter anyway because by now Margo had herself under control. Straightening, she put her back against the lamppost and cradled protective arms in front of her. She looked used up, but Brewster didn't seem to care. He waddled over to her, a grizzly on the prowl.

"When was the last time you saw Ms. DeForrest?"

She sighed. "Yesterday. Over there." She nodded in the direction of the park. Jake remembered that Margo had been in Old Town yesterday. She hadn't mentioned seeing Suzanne.

"Time?"

She waved a limp hand in front of her. "I don't know. Noon. One o'clock maybe."

"What was she doing in the park?"

"Having a picnic." Margo smiled ruefully.

"In the middle of the day? What happened to the shop?"

"She closed it."

He humphed. "Not much of a work ethic."

"Free spirit," Margo snapped, protecting her friend's reputation.

Jake had only seen Suzanne for a few minutes, but that's exactly how he would have described her. Frothy. Lightweight. Not someone who'd have much to say to Frank.

Then again, it was the perfect cover.

Could she have been watching Margo, too?

"How long did you stay?" Brewster persisted.

"A few minutes."

"And then?"

"I left."

"Back to the bookstore?"

"No."

Brewster observed her closely. "You didn't go back to work?"

"I . . . I wasn't feeling well."

"And yesterday afternoon?"

"I told you," Jake said, "she was with me. We had lunch."

"*And* dinner?" Brewster looked between the two of them. "I hope you're on an expense account, Wise. So you were together all afternoon?"

"That's right." Jake didn't bother adding that he'd been asleep for most of it.

"And evening?"

"That, too," Jake said.

Brewster's pointed stare said what words didn't. Jake grinned.

Brewster humphed again. "I assume that means you weren't *awake* the entire time."

"Awake enough."

"And somewhere between lunch and dinner you had this . . . fender bender." He nodded toward Jake's face.

"That's right."

But if Jake thought Brewster was going to give Margo a break and concentrate on him, he was mistaken.

Brewster turned, looked to her. "So where'd you eat?"

She paused. Something flickered across

her face. Fear? Guilt? "I . . . I went to get sandwiches."

"By yourself?"

She nodded, and Brewster homed in on the one loophole in her alibi. "Where?" he demanded.

"Daily's. Pentagon City."

Brewster looked accusingly at Jake. "So she wasn't with you the entire time."

"Except for the sandwiches, and I'm sure that will check out."

Brewster wrote it all down in his notepad, tore out a sheet of paper, and handed it to a passing detective. "Rainy, you know Pentagon City. Find this sandwich place."

Margo gave him approximate times and the details of their order. When the other cop left, Brewster snagged a uniform. "Get someone from CSU out here with a swab kit." He turned back to Margo.

"Why didn't you open the bookstore yesterday?"

"She didn't feel well," Jake answered quickly.

"Dammit, Wise, let the woman answer for herself. Ms. Scott, why didn't you go into the store yesterday? Were you expecting trouble?"

"No," Margo said. "I . . . like I said, I wasn't feeling well."

"You were well enough to take a . . . a meeting with Mr. Wise."

A woman wearing a pair of latex gloves came out of the bookstore carrying a small box. "What do you need, Sam?"

Brewster nodded at Margo. "Can we see your hands, Ms. Scott?"

"What for?" Jake asked.

Brewster screwed up his face in irritation. "We can hold her in place until we get a court order. Refusing now will just prolong the inevitable."

"It's all right, Jake," Margo murmured. "I want to know, too."

Brewster gave her a pointed look. "Want to know what?"

"Whether the earth will end in ice or fire. Look, she's confused. Shocked. Nothing she says right now will make sense. Let's just get this over with so we can go."

While the CSU technician worked, Brewster eyed Margo suspiciously. "Did Ms. DeForrest have any enemies? Anyone who might want to hurt her?"

"I . . . I don't know."

"How about you, Ms. Scott?"

She hesitated, and Jake was sure she was thinking about the thugs at the house. "I . . . I don't know."

Brewster's brows rose. Again, he looked from her to Jake and back again. "You don't know? Well, if you don't know, who would?"

A uniform trotted up. "M.E. wants to see you," he said to Brewster.

"Be right there."

Jake saw an opening. "Look, Brewster, how about I take Ms. Scott home and give her a chance to let this settle. If you still have questions, we'll come down to the station in a couple of hours."

"Detective Brewster!" a uniform called, beckoning him into the bookstore.

"I'm coming, I'm coming!" To Jake he said, "All right. We might even have some of the test results by then. But you be there, eight-fifteen sharp. I don't want to have to send a squad car after you."

Jake held up two fingers. "Scout's honor."

Brewster harrumphed. "You a Boy Scout? What is this world coming to?"

Brewster stomped away, and Margo turned dark, horror-filled eyes on Jake.

"Jake, did I . . . did I do this?"

35

"Not now. Do you want someone to hear you?" Jake slid an arm around Margo's shoulder, and she stiffened against the embrace, not sure she deserved the support.

"I don't care. I want to know."

He dragged her back to the car. "You'll care when those steel bars clang shut behind you."

She drew a sharp intake of breath. "So you do think I could have —"

"Keys." He held out a hand, palm up.

She set her chin. "My car. I drive."

"You want to fall apart or drive? Can't do both."

"I'm not falling apart." But she handed him the keys. Once inside, he slid the key home and got them away as fast as possible.

Margo squeezed the top of her head. It felt like it might explode. "I don't remember. I just don't remember."

"What? What don't you remember?"

"Coming here. Doing . . . anything."

"What *do* you remember?"

"Going to Daily's. Ordering the food. Bringing it back."

"No blackouts?"

"Would I remember if there were? Isn't that why they're called blackouts?"

"How long were you gone?"

"An hour or so. But you only have my word on it." She felt cold and tight and leeched of blood.

"That doesn't give you enough time to get over to the bookstore, kill someone, then hightail it back to the ridge with the food."

"It might."

"Yeah, if you're the Flash." He paused, looked at her. "You aren't, are you?"

She hit her head against the back of the seat as if pounding sense into it. "I don't know." She glanced bleakly out the window. "He said . . ." God, she couldn't even get the words out. "He said her throat was . . . Same as Frank Temple. If I" — she closed her eyes — "If I did one, I could've done two."

He reached over with one hand and squeezed hers. "Yeah, and someone else could've done both."

She exhaled a huge breath. "God, I'd like to believe that."

"Me too." He shot her a fast look. "Especially after last night. I hate it when the woman I'm sleeping with is a murderer."

She scowled. He loved watching those black brows mass together like angry caterpillars. "We're not sleeping together. We slept. Once. Doesn't mean we're going to make a habit of it."

"Oh, yeah, absolutely. I hate habits."

"And I'm not a murderer."

"You seemed pretty sure you might be a minute ago."

He gave her a small, encouraging smile, and she stared at him, realizing what he'd done. Made her believe in herself again.

A ripple of warmth rolled through her. Another act of random kindness from Jake Wise, unasked for and unexpected.

"Why would Suzanne be in your office? Did she ever come there?"

"I —" She wracked her brain. Could come up with nothing solid. "I'm not sure. Maybe. To talk. Hang out when she had no customers and was bored."

"You remember?"

"I . . . no." She felt so stupid and out of control. "Not really. Just a feeling."

"You ever get a feeling that she'd been there alone?"

She thought about it. Came up with nothing. "No."

"So if she did come to your office, the only reason would be to see you."

"But the store was closed yesterday. I wasn't there."

"Maybe she thought you were."

They exchanged a look. Could someone have been in the store last night?

"She said a man had been asking for me."

"A man?"

"A collector."

"Description?"

She shook her head. "I didn't ask. Didn't think it was important." If she had, would Suzanne be alive? A flood of remorse filled her.

He shifted in his seat. "Hold that thought. We got company." He nodded up toward the rearview mirror. "Dark blue midsize."

She was smart enough to look at him and not at the tail. "Mr. Tire Chain and his friends?"

Jake shook his head. "Two white guys in suits."

"Police?"

"Could be."

She hadn't given the police the Argyle Towers address, mainly because at the time, she hadn't remembered it. Now she wanted to continue keeping that secret. So far, the apartment was her only refuge. "Can you lose them?"

In answer, Jake sped up, dodged right, and zoomed across King Street. A bathrobed man was walking a dog outside an apartment complex, but besides that the streets were mostly deserted this time of morning. No traffic to speak of, no one to hide behind. He checked the rearview. The blue car was gaining.

Jake was familiar with many types of surveillance. The Dolphin technique put out a team you couldn't miss and that didn't let go for days. Then they'd disappear for a day. After a while you began to see ghosts. Waterfall surveillance tailed a target by heading toward him, not away. When the tracker had passed the rabbit, or target, he'd turn a corner where a van would be waiting. A change of clothes, and the van would drop him off ahead of the rabbit, where he'd pick up the tail again.

But this didn't look that complicated. A couple of guys. A single car. In any moving surveillance there were times when the rabbit was out of sight. It was unavoidable. He just had to choose his time.

Jake spun left onto Oronoco, and they lurched into a block of row houses. The scream of tires followed. The blue car was right behind them. He turned again, taking the corner like the Indy 500, but the tail not only stuck, it closed in.

"What are they doing?" Margo had to shout over the rumble of the engine, but the car butted into their rear, so the answer was obvious. "Would the police do that?"

"I think we made them mad," Jake shouted back, and streaked through a stop sign, whipped right and then left and they hit North Washington. A six-lane highway in both directions, it was broad enough for the car behind to not only catch up, but pull alongside.

Through red lights. Through stop signs. Past an Exxon and Wendy's and some kind of urban mall that shouted Talbots. Both cars were racing in reality now, zooming side by side. Close enough to see their pursuers.

"You recognize anyone?" he bellowed at her, hands gripping the wheel, desperate to outrun them. But her car wasn't made for speed, and he couldn't get enough traction to pull away.

Margo shot a glance at the pursuit car. The driver was leaning over the steering wheel giving the passenger access to the driver's side window. Braced over the driver's back, the passenger raised his arm. He was holding something.

"Gun!" she screamed, and ducked as Jake rammed their car into the blue one, throwing her brutally against the door, but also messing with the shooter's aim.

The back-side windows exploded.

"Jesus!" Jake rammed the other car again, and this time, it spun away and smashed into a parking meter at the curb.

Jake hurtled down the street, and she whipped around to see what had happened. The two men in the tail car were running into the middle of the street. Each took a shooter's stance and fired.

"Down!" she screamed, but the shots fell short. They were out of range.

Jake straightened, got the car under control. He spared her a swift, violent look.

"Who the fuck was that?"

36

Heart pumping out oxygen, Margo leaned back heavily against the car seat.

Before she could reply, Jake said, "Wait — don't answer. You're only going to say —"

"I don't know."

"— You don't know," he pronounced at the same time. "Yeah, what I thought." He turned down another street, bumped over a set of railroad tracks, and found himself in Del Ray again, not too far from Dottie MacKay's. He pulled into the side streets, drove around the block, and back out to Montgomery. The blue car was gone.

Margo closed her eyes, her erratic breathing still not under control. "Why would the DC police try to gun us down?"

"No reason. They need you to build their case. And besides, last I looked, murder was illegal."

"And it wasn't our friends from Aunt Frances's house."

"Didn't look like them."

"So what does that mean?"

"That you are one popular chick."

Yeah, but with whom? And why? She tried to push through the fog of confusion. "What do we know? Can you check on the guys who were at the house yesterday?"

"I'm working on it." Or he would be when he could get to the surveillance room.

She was frowning. "What about the picture in Frank's house?"

"The two of you were embracing."

"It wasn't me, Jake. You've got to believe that."

"It was you, babe. I know what I saw."

Her stomach twisted. "Could it have been doctored?"

"Yeah, sure. But by who?"

She sighed. What was she missing?

Only the last month.

"How about Warner Park," Jake said. "Think you could have written it down wrong? There's a Water Park in Manassas."

She shook her head. Another blank. "I don't know."

"Well the closest one is Nashville. Chicago and Wisconsin after that. And then the Caribbean."

"If I could see them. Maybe it would jog something."

"There are pictures on the Net. I could get you in on satellite. We might have some close enough views. But we'll need a computer for that. I've got a laptop in the car."

They looked at each other. His car was still parked behind the Foxhall Road house, a place neither one of them wanted to return to.

"Brewster said they checked, and it was empty," she said.

Jake didn't like it, but he had a solid reason for returning to the house: the surveillance-room tape of the four men from yesterday. "Okay. If it looks clear, we'll grab my laptop and head out. Won't take five minutes."

Starting a database search would be easy. The hard part would be getting down to the room without Margo knowing.

He looked over at her. The wind through the shattered back windows made a mockery of her hair, which whipped around her head and flew out behind her. He remembered that hair from the night before. A sudden tightening in his groin brought the heat back, and he wondered if she'd need his services again. Soon. As habits went, he could think of worse.

When they got to Foxhall Road, Jake crawled by, checking the house for surveillance, for anything that looked out of the ordinary. He went around the block and reconnoitered again.

But the place was clean.

His car was, too. Picked clean. Front window shattered, tires slashed, computer gone.

"I've got one inside," Margo said.

He should have been pissed off, but he wasn't. Suddenly, he had a plausible excuse for getting into the house.

"Big trouble if they get hold of your stuff?" Margo asked. He noticed she kept a careful eye on her surroundings.

Glum, he stared at the damaged Expedition, which because of the defunct tires sat low to the ground. "Probably not. It'll take them a while to unscramble the passwords and codes. By then, the information will be useless."

"How come?"

"Viral resistance. Anyone trying to break in releases a virus that kills the information. Turns it into gibberish. More of a headache for me to replace than a security risk."

"So why the long face?"

"I hate changing tires."

Despite the situation, Margo laughed. The smile looked good on her. "You're in luck. We don't have time." She looked toward the house; a nervous flutter ran across her face.

Jake followed her glance, took in the battered-in back door with its smashed window. "Okay. We'll get in and get out. Just grab the computer and go."

She visibly shuddered when she stepped into the kitchen. The mess still sat on the floor, and the image of the creeps who had been there last lingered. Just remembering made his ribs hurt.

He paused in the kitchen, wanting to reassure her but unable to. If he hadn't needed those damn tapes he'd be miles away, too.

"We should close this up." He gestured to the back door with its broken window. "Not a good idea to give anyone else easy access."

"I don't think we should take the time."

"It'll take ten minutes to nail up a piece of wood. And it will slow down anyone wanting to get in. Any plywood hanging around?"

"Maybe. In the basement."

"Hammer and nails there, too?"

"Probably."

"Go get the computer. I'll seal up the house."

She took him to the basement and

pointed out some one-by-threes he could cobble together over the broken window. She left him to gather them up, and the minute she was gone, he headed for the back wall.

His fingers trailed the surface, carefully skimming the edges until he found a small, recessed lever on the right. He pulled it down and with a silent lurch, the wall slid ponderously open.

He took two of the monitors off-line and used them to rewind the surveillance tape back to the section he needed. It didn't take him long to find the four men who'd surrounded him in the alley. He isolated the faces and downloaded them to a file to send to Manhattan TCF. He tried not to look too hard at the images of himself being chain-mauled, but he couldn't exactly avoid them either.

His phone rang while he was waiting for the download to complete.

"Wise," Brewster barked in his ear. "Get your client down here. Now."

"Why? What's up?"

"We found a nine millimeter hidden in her office. The one she said she didn't own."

Jake's chest tightened. "Is it a match?"

"We'll know soon enough. But I want her where I can see her."

"You going to arrest her?"

"Whether we do or don't, be better if she comes in on her own."

That fist inside his chest squeezed hard. "I'll see what I can do."

"You do better than that," Brewster snapped. "You get her lying ass down here, or I'll drag her down in handcuffs myself. And I won't mind if she gets a little mussed in the process." He disconnected, and Jake stared blindly at the uplink icon transferring the files to New York.

He'd let down his guard last night. Felt sorry for the woman. Had he been wrong? And yesterday. He'd taken a beating for her. He still felt like a fucking punching bag.

Christ.

Was she a cold-blooded murderer who deserved what she had coming?

Or was she as innocent as he wanted her to be?

Choose, a voice in his head hissed. She'd saved his life. Had she taken Frank's? Could she have done both?

He gazed at the monitors that were still live. Margo had the tower and the computer monitor herded together on a desk, the keyboard and cables wrapped up neatly. He felt sick watching her. Knowing what she might have done. What she'd already done. To him. The dark hair, the slim body, the way she'd felt under his hands.

She gathered up a bunch of discs and tossed them in a tote bag.

Without warning two men crashed into the room. The suits from the car chase.

For half a second Jake stared, disbelieving. They grabbed her and knocked her out cold. He leaped, already running for the door, racing faster than he thought possible. Even so, he was too late. By the time he got there, Margo was gone.

37

When Margo came to, she found her hands bound behind her and her eyes taped shut. Terror skyrocketed through her.

"Where am I? What's happening?" She struggled against her bonds.

"Shut up," a male voice responded.

"Who are you?"

"I said, shut up."

She forced herself to swallow the fear. To focus. Think.

An engine buzzed and whined; she was rocking with movement.

A car. She was in some kind of car.

Not a truck or a van, the engine didn't sound heavy enough.

She strained her ears for more telling sounds. No traffic noises came through. Were they out of the city? Or just inside a moving vehicle with the windows shut tight?

"Where are you taking me?"

No one replied.

She twisted, feeling what she could with her bound hands. Was she in the middle of the seat?

"Sit still," the voice growled and gave her shoulder a brutal shove.

The thrust pushed her against something hard. Under pretext of settling down, she wiggled her fingers in a desperate search. The door handle? She retraced the shape. Yes, a handle. She was up against the door.

Hands shaking, she slowly lifted the handle. Nothing budged, it was locked. Then she remembered that sometimes the lock was embedded in the handle grip. She stroked the shape. The lock was there; she could just feel the tip of it.

Her mouth was so dry she could make sand castles in it. Her breath was harsh and reedy. Where were they going? What would happen once they got there?

She didn't want to find out.

Behind her back her fingers ached with stretching. Slowly, slowly, she inched her fingertips onto the lock. Slowly, slowly, pushed it away from her.

A tiny click.

Her heart leaped. Had anyone else heard it?

Nothing. Only the rumble of the car moving over the road.

Pulse racing, she waited to pick her moment. The car slowed, seemed to curve.

Were they on a highway? A side street? No time to find out.

Praying she wouldn't get crushed by a semi, she dived for the door.

A meaty hand latched on to her shirt. "Where the fuck you think you're going?"

He pulled her back, hard enough to make her head bounce against the seat.

"Let me go! *Let me go!*" She whipped her body around, heard a grunt as her shoulder landed on something hard. His face? His head?

"Hold her!" the driver yelled.

The man next to her smashed her across the face, got her by the neck, and pushed her into the seat. She tasted lint and smelled fabric deodorizer.

"Shut up." He pressed her down even farther.

She couldn't breathe. She was choking on dust.

Rough hands yanked at her hair, pulled her upright. She coughed, air returning swiftly to her lungs, and he shoved a gun into her side.

"You're making this harder than it has to be, Margo."

She gasped. "Who are you?"

Silence answered.

"Who the hell are you? What do you

want with me? What did I do? Did I do something? Talk to me, you bastards!"

The car swayed, went around some kind of sharp curve. They slanted down a slope.

"Where are we going?" She tried to stop the panic, but it was there and rising.

The road leveled out, and the car stopped. The driver turned off the engine and threw something into the back. She heard a tearing sound.

Tape. More tape.

"No," Margo said, shaking her head violently. "No! *No!*" The tape muffled the rest of her scream.

The door opened, and someone dragged her out of the car. She landed hard on the ground. It was flat, firm. Cement or pavement. Over her shoulder the whoosh of heavy traffic whined. She breathed in exhaust and dust. They were near a big road. An interstate? She calculated the odds; the area was infested with them.

"Get up." One of them kicked her. She tried to roll into a ball, but fingers dug into her hair and jerked her head back again.

"Easy or hard, Scottie," one of them said in her ear. "Your choice. It's going down either way."

"Hard, you bastards," she said, but the tape turned it into howling gibberish.

Between the two of them, they bullied her to her feet and heaved her forward. When she resisted, she was cuffed, punched, or kicked. Despite her resolve not to, she stumbled forward, tripped over an obstacle — curb? — fell and was wrenched up again, every step taking her closer to an inevitable end.

They stopped suddenly. She inhaled mold and old garbage. Some kind of dirt smell. A landfill?

Suddenly, grim understanding shook her. They could have finished it back by the car, but they didn't want to drag the body. Dumpsters and garbage would be a good place to stash her. If they were lucky, it would be days before anyone found her. Weeks even. Months.

She moaned. Without knowing how, she knew exactly what they were doing.

But not why.

Inside her head questions shrieked uselessly.

Why me? What had she done? At least, for God's sake, tell her what she'd done.

"On your knees." Someone gave her shoulder a brutal shove while the other one kicked the back of her legs out.

She dropped to the ground. Damp and muck seeped through her jeans. She tried scrambling away, and got kicked back for her effort.

"You're only prolonging it. Stay still and it'll be over with one shot. Clean. Quick. Move around, and it's gonna hurt."

Fuck you, she screamed silently.

She was shaking uncontrollably. Sweat trickled between her breasts. Inside her black world, the gun barrel touched the side of her head. Oh, God. This was it. Blinded and tied, the last seconds of her life. Her stomach heaved.

A shot rang out. Another.

She flinched, but felt no pain.

A grunt. A thud. Bodies fell, but neither was hers.

What had happened?

She was shaking so hard she couldn't move. For half a second she waited, chest heaving. Was another bullet coming?

Footsteps. Running. She struggled to her feet, stumbled. Someone caught her. Ripped the tape from her eyes.

Jake.

It was Jake.

Relief ripped through her, so fierce she almost toppled from it. He tore the tape from her mouth, cut through the crap binding her hands, and wrapped her in his arms. She huddled there, shuddering, clinging, half of her not sure she wasn't really dead.

He squeezed her tighter. "You all right?"

She was still breathing fast and hard. She couldn't talk. He grabbed her head, forcing her to look at him. "Okay?"

She nodded. Oh, God, he was so solid and real. The best sight she'd ever seen.

He shook her a little. "Say something."

She swallowed. Tears threatened the back of her throat. "You . . . you took your damn time getting here."

38

"Here" was the back of the Crystal City Lodge. A derelict motel in a cul-de-sac below Interstate 395, the place shared a lot with a graffiti-covered warehouse, also abandoned. The Lodge itself sported two stories of rooms overlooking the freeway. Iron balconies painted bright red looked grotesquely gay and out of place amid the dilapidated ruins.

Behind the motel, where the two goons had dragged Margo, a strip of dank weeds had become a makeshift dumping ground. Crack pipes and car parts littered the grass. Half a bus sat rusting in one corner. The constant buzz of traffic dominated all other sounds. Not a good place to die.

Jake searched the two bodies for ID, then hauled them into their car, where they'd stew until someone found them. Margo hadn't been steady enough to help him, so he'd propped her against the building. Now he squinted over to where she stood, arms crossed, head bent, eyes focused on the ground.

He appraised her coolly, or tried to, Brewster's words echoing in his head. *Get your client down here.* But he couldn't let go of the terror that had tackled him when he saw her on her knees, gun at her head.

He braced himself against the driver's door, paused a moment to catch his breath. God, he was tired. His ribs were throbbing, and worse than that, he had an aching feeling the nine they'd found in Margo's office would match the bullet they took out of Frank.

A false lead or a true one?

Choose, that voice hissed.

He closed the car door and tramped over to her. Light tremors still rippled through her shoulders. He lifted her chin, stared into the midnight blue of her haunted eyes. "Ready?"

She nodded and pushed herself off the trunk, stumbling on wobbly legs. He put a hand on her arm to help, but she waved him away. "I'm okay."

She took another step, then another, each one gaining strength. It was important for her to have a measure of control after nearly losing it all. He kept a watchful eye on her, but didn't try to help her again.

By the time they reached her Taurus, she seemed to have gained a degree of normalcy. Her breathing was less erratic, the shakes gone.

But she still wasn't saying much. She didn't demand to drive, but went around to the passenger side and hunched in, leaning her head against the window. She stayed that way for most of the ride. But the questions were bound to come, and he was bracing himself for the answers.

How'd you find me, Jake?

Choose. The truth or a lie.

Tightening his hold on the steering wheel, he concentrated hard on the road. Ironically enough, they were ten minutes from Arlington Ridge and the Prospect Hill apartment. He wondered if the two men knew about it. But if they had, why not snatch her there and save themselves a trip from Georgetown?

"They knew my name," Margo said, apropos of nothing.

He looked over at her. She was sitting up now, staring straight ahead.

"It was casebook," she continued. "A professional hit."

"How do you know?"

She shot him a pained look. "I just . . . do."

He took that in, just as she was doing.

"Those two guys had no IDs," he said.

"Nothing. No driver's license. No credit cards. You know who walks around without credit cards?"

"Criminals?"

"Me."

She swiveled around in her seat to drill him with a cold stare. "You mean they were Feds?"

"It's one possibility."

"But you carry a badge. Some kind of federal identification."

"Not if I was on a dirty job. And this was plenty dirty. They weren't arresting you. They didn't read you your rights. It was a mob hit."

"Or supposed to look like one."

He glanced at her sharply. "How would you know?"

Her jaw tightened. "I've seen the movies."

Could that be it? Could she be connected somehow? A made woman? But her gear was military, not criminal. Would a professional hit woman have the thigh rigs, the fence climbers?

All she'd need was a big gun and a silencer. Maybe a sniper rifle.

Then again, a pro was a pro. If it was him, he'd be geared up to the eyeballs. You never knew what the situation would call for.

Christ, he didn't like the direction his head was moving.

They rode in silence, then Margo said, "Do you think Suzanne knew something? Saw something?"

"Like what?"

"I don't know. Something about my trip to Spain maybe."

"So now you're convinced you did go?"

"I don't know. But I have those pictures. Maybe it's time I found out." They exchanged a quick glance.

He had to choose. Trust her or turn her in.

"Brewster's not going to like you running out on him."

"Yeah? Well, there's never a perfect time for a vacation."

39

Margo made Jake drive around the ridge in every direction before she agreed to enter the Argyle Towers garage. They spotted no one. No police. No thugs. No hit men. Neither she nor Jake could explain it, but no one seemed to know about Argyle Towers.

She tumbled into the apartment, grateful for the seclusion it provided whatever the reason. Once inside, she leaned against the door, shivering. She was cold, so cold. She'd been cold since the motel, since . . .

But she didn't want to go there.

Jake disappeared into the hallway leading to the bedrooms and came back with a blanket.

She shook her head. "I'm fine." She waved him away and went into the kitchen. She was not going to fall apart. She couldn't. Someone had murdered Frank Temple. Someone had killed Suzanne. Now someone wanted her dead. Seriously dead.

On your knees. The voice in her head. *His* voice.

The bottle of Glenlivet was on the counter. She dumped half a glassful into a coffee cup and took a gulp. Her hand was shaking, and the liquid sloshed over. She wiped her upper lip with the back of her hand.

Jake stood in the doorway, watching. Always watching.

"Stop it."

He eyed her. "Stop what?"

"Stop looking at me." She turned her back, leaned over the counter, took another gulp of scotch.

"Ease up on that." His hand touched her shoulder, and she jumped a mile.

"Don't do that! Don't sneak up on me."

"Look, Margo —"

"Don't touch me!"

"That's enough." He grabbed for the coffee cup, and she jerked it away. The booze spilled, and the cup went flying, crashing on the floor.

Her heart shot into her throat, and she flinched again. "You bastard!" She lunged for the bottle, but he got there first.

"It's not me you're mad at."

Angry tears welled up. "Give that to me."

"I'll make you some coffee."

"I don't want any damn coffee."

"You don't need any damn scotch either."

"Fuck you, Jake Wise." She dived for the bottle again. He yanked it out of reach.

"You'd like that wouldn't you?" He smashed the bottle over the faucet, and the jagged pieces clattered in the sink.

"Damn you!" She let loose with a right hook and caught him by surprise. His head snapped back.

He rubbed his chin, eyed her narrowly, and clipped her a light one in return. While she recovered, he backed out of the kitchen, urging her into the living room. "Come on, Scottie. Take your best shot."

Fists up, she attacked like a kamikaze, legs flying into a leap aimed squarely at the center of his chest.

But he anticipated it.

She went down, and he dived for her, but she rolled away, bounded to her feet, saw he'd done the same.

He closed in to attack, but she elbowed him in the ribs. He yowled, and she gasped, knowing she'd really hurt him.

"I'm sorry. I didn't mean —"

His fist collided with her chin. Not hard, but hard enough to make her stumble backward. While she was still off-balance, he lashed out with his right leg, but before it connected, she caught him by the foot and twisted. He fell with a thud they probably heard on the first floor.

She plunged, landing hard on his chest, straddling his neck between her knees. He was pinned.

They were both breathing hard. He was helpless but gazed at her as though he were in control. "You going to kill *me* now?"

She stared at him, at the cool calculation that hid something deeper in his eyes, at the sensual lips that had uttered the words.

Jake's mouth. His tongue.

"Come on, Scottie. Kill me." His voice was soft, but it drowned out all the other voices in her head. It made her sleepy, woozy. She sat back on her haunches, taking the weight off his body and freeing his arms. His hands found their way to her back. "Do it," he whispered, stroking, caressing. He urged her lower. And lower.

She slid the length of him and sank into his mouth.

"Yeah, I didn't think so," he crooned, kissing her.

Her lips parted, letting him inside. He was so warm.

Forget. Just make her forget.

His hands found her breasts and stroked

the tips. Her nipples hardened, and she groaned, closing her eyes.

"Oh, yeah," he whispered. "That's it. That's it."

She tugged at his shirt, lifting it over his head. The bruises were still raw, and she kissed them. Sorry, she was so sorry.

He cradled the back of her head while she did it, his hand entwined in her hair.

And then it moved over her back and under her shirt. In an instant the clothing was gone, and he was branding her with his palms.

She clung to him, drinking in the taut skin, the power of his arms, the breadth of his shoulder. So substantial. So constant and real. Her hands couldn't stop moving, she was suddenly ravenous for him, licking, biting.

She couldn't get the rest of their clothes off fast enough, she would burst into flames before they were free of them. His hands ripped at her jeans, his mouth sucked the breath out of her.

Hurry, hurry. Don't let her hear the voices.

Jake was already hard and seeking. His hands guided her hips, and she impaled herself on him, sliding home so easily.

The heat and the slick dance wiped it all

away. The growl of a killer's voice, the bite of steel against her head, the rage and fear and humiliation.

Jake was with her. That was real. Arms taut, the muscles in his shoulders flexed and strained. Veins stood out on his neck. The beauty of his tight body moved her deeply. And his face, intense with passion, sent her even higher.

And suddenly it was more than she intended. More than a need she could fill with anyone. It was him. Jake. Inside her body, the way he was moving inside her mind. Jake, who'd stuck by her. Saved her. Proved his belief in her with his bones and his flesh.

She started shaking again. Tiny little tremors of awareness.

She wasn't dead. And she wasn't alone.

"Come here," he said in a hoarse voice, surging upward, so she was in his lap. He pressed her head down and captured her mouth.

Everything escalated a hundredfold. Heat, desire, connection.

"Jake," she moaned softly.

"I'm here, baby. You're alive. It's okay. I'm here."

Sweat slicked his chest, blending with hers. His hips danced sensually, pushing her away and pulling her close. The length of him was deliciously hard. But his mouth, God, his mouth was soft and wet. Pure liquid fire.

His tongue traced her lips, sucked down her jawline to her neck. She shuddered and pulled up his head to taste him again. His tongue plunged inside her, the way his sex had, demanding, urging, faster, harder, wetter.

She gasped, needing air, and leaned away, back arching. Her breasts jutted up, the nipples tightening in the cold. But his hands warmed them, fondled, rubbed. Then his mouth found them and once more he licked her nipples. White-hot desire exploded right up her center.

Yes, she moaned silently. Touch me. Be my past, my present, and my future.

They were both braced backward on their arms, so they formed a perfect V. She looked down at their bodies, her gaze fixed on that one aching place where he joined with her. She watched him enter her and retreat and enter again. Each movement sent an electric spiral rocketing through her.

God, what was he doing to her?

She stared hungrily at the entrance point, that place of intimate connection. It excited her and also overwhelmed, so vital it scared her. In the free fall that was her life, she was finally tethered to someone.

And then he touched her. His fingers found the exact right spot, and she went off like a Roman candle, screaming and shooting flames.

He clasped her tight to his chest while she came, pulsing around him. At the last, he groaned, raised her up and entered her, then bucked with his own orgasm.

And then, out of nowhere, the tears exploded.

"Oh, God." She gasped, battled for air.

He was panting, still throbbing. But he held her tight, so tight she could feel his heart racing against her own.

"Damn." She struggled to breathe, fought to stop the wrenching, angry sobs. Her hands balled into fists. "Dammit!" She pounded on the broad plain of his back while her body shook.

He didn't flinch or shrug her off. He didn't make soothing sounds or try to comfort her. He just held her while she cried.

40

"Why did Frank recruit you to watch me?"

They were draped on the couch, a naked Margo between Jake's legs, her back against his bare chest. He liked the feel of her there, his arms wrapped around her, his hands on her smooth skin. The crying jag was over, and they'd settled into this ridiculous appealing warmth, like old lovers. An illusion, given what nagged at the back of his mind — Brewster and the gun he'd found — but an illusion he was desperate to believe.

He pulled the hair back from her forehead, lifting his chin to do so. "I've known him since I was a kid. He was a friend of my dad's."

"Mmm," she murmured and rubbed her head against his chest. "That's it? Family connections?"

"That and . . ." He stroked her neck, down one shoulder and arm. He loved the taut, silky curve of her. "He called in a favor."

"Must have been some favor."

Jake shrugged, but it was more a way of avoiding her unspoken question than anything else. It had been a long time since he talked about Danika. "I had a friend who died on a mission. Frank helped me get the body out."

"A friend? Like me?"

"She was —"

"She?" Margo twisted in his arms, and he went silent. "More than a friend," she guessed, looking at him.

"Yeah, well . . ." He sighed. "It was a long time ago."

She watched him closely, and he fought to keep his face a mask while he counted back to 1999. Two years after he'd joined the TCF. Serbia had been his last Special Forces post, and Frank had sent him back to Belgrade as part of a team funded by a hodgepodge of government-affiliated agencies to help a group of young people who'd started a grassroots resistance movement. They used stickers and flyers, graffiti and T-shirts to poke fun at the Milosevic regime.

Ostensibly Jake was the resource person, the guy with the money for spray paint and silk screening. His true mission was to scope out the connection between the Serbs and the narco traffickers from Tajikistan who were funding terrorism cells in the Balkans. But he got caught up in the sheer exuberance of what the kids were trying to accomplish.

"Kids?" she asked. "Or one kid?"

He gave her a rueful smile. "One in particular. Danika. My contact." He pictured her, a little blond dynamo with a smile that never quit. He'd liked her instantly. Grew to admire her dedication and commitment to unseating the vicious nationalists who'd stolen her country and plunged it into dictatorship. "She was all of nineteen, part of a group who lived in poverty compared to other Western teenagers, and she helped take down a government by meeting in clubhouses and basements."

Margo settled back against him. "So they killed her?"

"She was fearless. Took too many risks." He sighed. "I used to scream at her, and she'd only laugh and agree, then do what she planned all along."

"And she loved you."

"That's what she said."

"But?"

He squeezed her a little tighter against him, inhaled whatever it was in her hair — shampoo or her own unique fragrance — and recalled the distant pain of those memories. "But does anyone know anything at nineteen? Truth was, she didn't need me. Not really. Except to fuel her battle." He grinned thinly; there was sadness in the smile. "Come peacetime, we'd have made a lousy couple."

He stared over her head at the window of glass, seeing only the blur of sky and the edge of darkness that was Margo's hair.

She needed him.

Weird the difference that made.

Unsettled, Jake found the curve of her hip. "How'd you get this?"

"What?"

"The scar."

"What are you talking about?"

"This." His fingers traced the spot. "Knife wound."

She twisted around to look at it. The fear and bafflement on her face told him she hadn't known it was there.

Her face scrunched into a scowl. "I'm sick of this." She leaped up, grabbed her clothes, and pulled them on. "Sick of not knowing who I am, what I am."

He scrambled to pull on his own clothes, caught her as she was raging down the hall. "Okay." He pulled her into his arms. "So you've got the mark of the devil. So what?"

"Easy for you to say."

And it was. She gazed up at him within

the circle of his arms. Her navy eyes looked black again. Was he looking into the eyes of Frank's killer? Were they the last things Frank saw?

Unease rippled over him. He released her and stepped back. "God, I'm hungry. Are you hungry?" He wasn't, but he needed space; he couldn't think with her staring at him like that. He ambled into the kitchen, and she followed.

"One thing still bothers me," she said.

He opened the fridge. The sandwich she'd brought back for him the day before was the only thing sitting on the wire shelves. He reached for it. "Yeah, what's that?"

"At the motel. How'd you find me?"

His hand faltered, his whole body froze, half-in, half-out of the fridge.

"Jake?"

"Yeah?" He closed the door, stood like an idiot staring at the brand emblazoned on the front: AMANA. The name reverberated inside his head, *Amana, Amana, Amana,* the meaning only sounds. But below the sounds was a frantic hunt for an answer that wouldn't destroy whatever trust she had in him.

Because none of this was real. How many times did he have to remind himself of that? Whatever intimacy they'd shared was a fantasy created by circumstance. It was what he needed to do to hold her together until he could find the truth of what happened to Frank. And yet part of him, the part that kept coming back to her, wanted to grab the warmth and make it last.

"How did you find me?" She stood in the doorway across the room.

He turned, leaned against the fridge, and absorbed the expectant, even trusting, look in her eyes. "Would you believe telepathy?"

She blinked, her expression growing wary. "As much as you believed the alien-abduction theory."

"Yeah, didn't think so."

"So?"

"So . . . what?" He was stalling.

"How did you know where I was?"

He didn't answer.

She stepped closer. "Jake?"

He sighed. Fished in his pocket. Pulled out the GPS locator and handed it to her. Then he walked away. Out the door. Into the living room. Suddenly he wished he hadn't smashed that bottle of scotch.

She trailed behind him. "What's this? Some kind of tracking device?"

"Receiver." He wheeled about, slouched

against the wall, and waited for her to figure it out.

"What does it receive?"

"You."

She came forward, staring at him. Slowly, he raised his hand and touched the back of her neck. The contact sent a shiver through her that he felt in his fingertips. "You've got a signal device implanted here." He touched the underside of her left arm. "Or . . . here."

She blinked. "Implanted?"

He nodded. She looked sick. He didn't feel too good himself.

"By who?"

"I don't know. But Frank gave me the locator." He nodded toward the piece of equipment in her hand.

He opened his mouth to tell her everything, then hesitated. Maybe he could keep the rest under wraps.

But she caught him. "There's more, isn't there?"

Reluctantly, he nodded. "The house. Aunt Frances's house."

"What about it?"

"It's not" — he cleared his throat — "Well . . . it's not your aunt Frances's house."

"What are you talking about?"

276

"It's a TCF safe house. Wired from top to bottom for twenty-four/seven surveillance."

Her face paled. She grabbed the back of the leather armchair. "That's impossible. I remember —"

"Frank's full name is Francis. Francis Augustus Temple."

A small cry escaped. She sank into the chair. "You're telling me that Frank Temple is my aunt Frances?"

"Yes."

"But what about my memories? My sister, my — Oh, God. It's all false? My parents, my —" Her face crumpled, and he wanted to crawl into a hole. Her aunt, whatever blurred recollections she had of her family — and that was precious little — he was carting them away, shoving them into a deep abyss from which she could never redeem them. And he had nothing to give her in return. No knowledge of who she was or what had happened to her.

She shook her head wildly. "No. I don't believe it." Her expression hardened. "I don't believe you. I don't believe any of this."

"Christ, I'm sorry. I wish —"

She leaped up. "Show me."

"What do you mean, sh—"

"You want me to believe that every

memory I have is a lie, you're going to have to prove it to me."

He shook his head emphatically. "It's too dangerous."

"I don't give a damn how dangerous it is." He'd put the car keys on the coffee table, and she swiped them up. "Stay here if you're scared."

She ran out the door.

"Margo!" He jogged after her, grabbed her arm, and spun her around. "They could still be watching the house. You can't go back there!"

She swung her other arm and slammed him in the shoulder, right in the worst of the bruises. He yelped and dropped his hold.

She flew down the hall to the stairs.

"Jesus Christ." He ran after her, but she was already in the car by the time he got to the garage. She would have dodged out without him, but he raced to block her way. She almost ran him down before screeching to a halt.

Silently, he got in.

41

Her face set, her hands white-knuckled on the steering wheel, Margo drove a relentless course down the ridge, into Pentagon City and onto Memorial Parkway. Neither of them spoke until they got to Foxhall Road, and then it was only Jake directing her to the alley.

She parked, practically wrenched the parking brake out of its housing, and challenged him with a lethal stare: go ahead, her face said, prove it.

He led her to the shed, gaze set on nonstop scan, every inch of him waiting for someone else to drop from the trees. But he punched in the code without interruption, and the door slid open soundlessly. She slipped past him, her face a cold, hard mask.

When they got to the surveillance room, she pivoted slowly, taking in the cot with its rumpled blankets, his duffel and clothes lying around, then shifting to the screens and taking in every monitor, every view. Right now they were all frozen on a picture of her with the two goons, one of whom had a hand clamped around her mouth.

"You bastard."

He didn't argue with her.

Quickly, he punched the reset button and the monitor went live. A picture of the now-empty bedroom filled the screen. The computer was still neatly wrapped and tied on the desk.

"How does this work?" Her voice was icily calm.

He showed her what buttons to push and she sank into the chair and pressed one. The data loop rewound. The monitors blurred as images raced by. She pressed the stop button and watched herself tearing apart her bedroom. Her whole body stiffened as she did so, her chin raised, her back rigid.

"Margo —"

She stabbed the rewind button again, stopped it again, and saw herself get undressed, every inch of skin exposed on every monitor.

Quickly, Jake reached over her shoulder to shut down the machines. The monitors went dark.

"Get out," she said quietly, still facing the bank of screens.

"It was to protect you," he said, not knowing if even that was true.

"Like hell it was. Get out. Now."

He spun her around, braced himself on the chair arms, loomed over her. "I saved your life. Be a little grateful." She kicked out at him, but he blocked the move and wrenched her to her feet. "Try that once more, and —"

"We're even." The loathing in her face was palpable, and he hungered to smash through it.

"Actually, I'm one up on you. Brewster found a nine millimeter in your office. You know, the one you said you didn't own?" He examined her face for any sign of the lie, any sign of the truth, but all he found was a pale deadness. He ignored it and pushed on. "Ten to one it matches the bullet they found in Frank. Brewster wants to see you, babe. He's practically got an arrest warrant signed."

"And you're going tell him where I am?"

"Maybe. I haven't decided yet."

From somewhere at her back Margo whipped out a knife — where the hell did she get that? — and before he could defend against it, the blade was at his throat. "Well, make up your mind, *babe.*"

He'd barely seen her move. Her eyes dug into his, hard and ruthless. The knife cut into his throat. He raised his hands and she backed him to a post.

"On the ground. Move!" He sank slowly to the floor. She grabbed a belt from the pile of clothes on the bed and wrapped his hands around the post with it. "Better decide, Jake. Fish" — she cinched the belt tight — "or cut bait."

She came around the front and stared at him. "One more thing." Carefully, she bent to the ground and searched his pockets. She had to get close to him to do it, and her skin, soft over hard bone, caressed his. She smelled of leather — from the knife handle maybe — and shampoo, a wicked combination that pulled him back a few hours to the apartment and the floor and the sex.

"Get too close, I might bite," Jake said softly.

She tensed for a moment, then continued her brisk search. It didn't take her long to find what she was looking for. "No worries. I've got your teeth." She tossed the locator in the air and caught it.

"So we're back to telepathy," he said.

Rising, she dropped the knife and toed it just beyond the reach of his right foot. "I'm either on the side of the angels or I'm not. Let's see how long it takes you to figure it out."

42

At the most, Margo guessed she had an hour, tops, before Jake freed himself. She wasted little time racing to the car, but had trouble getting the key into the door lock, and once she accomplished that, had equal difficulty fitting it into the ignition. She seized the steering wheel, clutching it fiercely to stop the shakes, which refused to let go. She'd been cut off, set adrift on an ice floe, the only human in a dark frozen sea.

Alone, alone. The word echoed in her head.

She swallowed the panic, forced the fear away. Trusting Jake had been foolish. Alone was better, wasn't it? Alone was safe.

She turned the key. But before she zoomed away from that godforsaken house for what she hoped was the last time, she opened the car door and leaned out to toss the locator under the back wheel. She backed over it once, then crunched it a second time. The satisfaction was huge.

Traffic was light, so she arrived at the apartment in half the usual time. The fact that Jake had been there with her only a short while ago, that an hour ago he'd touched her, warmed her, invaded her, body and heart, that hurt she pushed to the back of her mind, where she wouldn't have to think about it.

Instead, she dumped the contents of the *Don Quixote* box onto the coffee table. Three of the passport identity bundles and the cash went into a purse. She found a suitcase in the second bedroom closet, tossed some clothes into it, and was already making flight reservations as she walked out the door. Two stops later she was on her way to the airport. By five she was on a flight to London.

As soon as allowable, she unlocked her seat belt and headed for the nearest bathroom. Closeting herself in, she clipped up her hair with swift efficiency and turned her back to the mirror. She'd bought a handheld mirror at one of her stops and now she held it up, positioning it so she could see the back of her neck.

She traced the area, searching for a bump, a scar, something that would give away the location of Jake's implant. She'd tried this once, before she left the apartment, but her patience had been short, time equally so, and she'd given up, anxious to leave before Jake freed himself and came after her.

She'd already examined her arms and found nothing. Now she conducted a slow, meticulous search, her shoulders aching from holding her arms up. She was sweating by the time she found the infinitesimal lump. It was obscured by the hairline, so she couldn't see it with the mirror, but she felt it. A slimy queasiness stole over her. Someone had cut her open and put a machine inside her body.

She undid the clip and her hair fell, covering the offending spot. She felt hot. Her hands were clammy. She had no knife, nothing sharp enough to do the job, but she wanted desperately to dig the thing out.

Quickly, she wet a paper towel and ran it over her face. There was no Aunt Frances, no sister Barbara, probably no parents, no St. Louis.

No. She paused and latched on to the one solid thing she knew. St. Louis was real. The book, the fairy-tale book, it was from the St. Louis Public Library. That was real.

But a voice snaked into her head, hissing

doubt. The book could be a plant, as false as the house. She could trust nothing, no one.

Panic rushed through her. She closed her eyes, reached back for the thousandth time, aching for some connection, some memory that would link her to a real past. But all she came up with was the thud of a body. Blood. The child screamed in her head again, and her eyes flew open. She gripped the tiny metal sink and nailed the images behind a steel door.

With a hard flip, she shoved the bathroom lock open and marched back to her seat.

If the memories of her family weren't real, why did she have them? And if they weren't real, maybe the others, the ones she didn't want to think about, were false, too.

She glommed on to that the way a drowning man hangs on to a life raft, with fierce and vicious willpower. A glimmer of hope wedged its way into her heart.

Dottie MacKay wasn't usually a light sleeper. Even after she'd found Frank Temple's body sprawled in his office in his own blood, she'd been able to fall asleep and stay asleep.

"The sign of a clear conscience," her late husband used to tell her, and she supposed he was right. She was never one to let the worries of the day intrude on her peace of mind.

Since Frank's death, though, the days didn't hold much of interest. The higher-ups had put her on leave as though she were some kind of invalid, and she still hadn't gotten used to not having some-where to go every day. It made her cranky, and when her daughter had left her son with her, she'd snapped at him. His two-year-old eyes had widened, then filled with tears, and she'd had to ply him with a trip to Baskin-Robbins before the smile was back on his face.

"You relax, now," her daughter had in-sisted — and not for the first time — when she picked him up. "Retire. You've given enough. Time to please yourself."

But Dottie wasn't used to pleasing her-self. She didn't know how.

Yesterday, she'd been allowed back in the office. It was only to pack it up, but that at least was a job to do. She put on the navy suit she'd bought on sale at Hecht's for Easter, the one with the long jacket that made her feel stately and dig-nified, and added the gold brooch Frank had given her for her birthday last year.

"A songbird for a songbird," he had said because he liked to tease her about the way she hummed in the office.

Homeland Security had sent a watchdog, as had CIA and NSA, and the stone-faced men had stood around with arms crossed while she went through Frank's files, separating out the classified information, then boxing it up and labeling everything.

If it had been up to her, she would have savored what she could, reminiscing about the years she and Frank had spent together, but the men had made it clear she had a day to finish and no more. At the end, they'd lugged it away, one to carry and two to stand guard. She watched them disappear down a corridor, conveying the better part of her professional life with them.

But she didn't dwell on it. She might not be ready for this new journey she was about to begin, but there wasn't a whole lot she could do about it.

When the last container carrying the last of Frank's papers had gone, she'd boxed up her own things, the paperweight Frank had given her eons ago, the Christmas photo of her daughter, son-in-law, and grandson. She'd come home, made herself a meat loaf, eaten half, and frozen the rest. And that night she'd gone to sleep like every other night, expecting to wake the next morning, refreshed and worry-free.

So when she opened her eyes, and it was the middle of the night, she gasped in surprise. And then she remembered what had woken her.

A name.

43

Margo flew from London to Switzerland, and, after three days in Zurich, on to Spain. By the time she arrived in Madrid the tiny transmitter that had once lodged in her neck, and was no bigger than the tip of her thumb, was a pile of ash, incinerated with all the other medical waste from the Klinik Hirslanden.

Comforted in the hope that Jake could no longer track her via GPS, she booked a flight to Seville.

It was early evening when she landed. The Maria Luisa, a small hotel on the edge of the Plaza Santa Maria la Blanca in the Barrio Santa Cruz, was shrouded in shadow.

The hotel was a far cry from the massive glass-and-cement Marriotts in Rosslyn and Pentagon City. Done in Moorish style, its walls boasted elaborate tile, blue and gold-flecked, a third of the way up from the floor. An interior walkway, ringed in wrought-iron, overlooked the central patio.

The feel was quaint and pretty, but not as anonymous as she would have preferred. But the hotel was scrawled on a piece of paper in the *Don Quixote* box, so she'd booked a room. Maybe she was a history buff and liked the traditional Spanish decor. Maybe she picked the first place she saw. Or maybe there was a specific reason she'd stayed here before. If so, she didn't know what it was, and thinking about it made her crazy.

After she'd checked in, she took a nap and woke at ten. Outside the small, shuttered window, dark had descended over the cobblestone plaza.

She slipped into slim black slacks, a gray tank, and loose black jacket. She hadn't paid attention to the clothes she'd thrown into the suitcase, but she noticed them now for the first time. Silky against her skin, they gave effortlessly and were easy to maneuver in. Which, she knew instinctively, was why they were in her closet.

She clipped back her hair, covering the small incision at the hairline, which was almost healed, and found the concierge. He had to check a map, but eventually found Calle Gitana, and put her in a cab.

The street was buried deep in the Triana section of Seville, on the opposite side of the Guadalquivir River. The cab took her over the Triana Bridge. She gazed at the stone posts that marked the bridge's entrance, tried to see into the water below. Was this the river that had flashed into her head? Was it this dark water, on a night like this, that she remembered?

The cabdriver started to give his tourist spiel. She couldn't concentrate, barely listened. Something about Triana being the traditional Gypsy ghetto, the artisanal heart of the city, an old fishing center.

Past ten, the quarter was just starting to jump. Clumps of people strolled along the river, and the bars and restaurants swelled with customers. The cab continued into the heart of Triana until the streets were too narrow for a vehicle. She paid off the driver and began walking.

The streets grew more narrow and winding, streetlights less plentiful. Unlike the area around her hotel, which dated back to cobblestones, these roads were paved and lined with dwellings whitewashed or painted, some with tile trim. Iron gates showed dim interior courtyards open to the sky and filled with plants. Here and there balconies hung overhead with the occasional burst of hot pink bougainvillea draping over the railings.

But there was also a hardscrabble aura to the neighborhood. Wooden shutters needed paint. Doors were often nicked or warped. She passed the Hermanos de Cristo, an aged and long-abandoned monastery. Clearly gentrification hadn't reached this section of Triana yet.

The cabdriver had given her vague directions, and though she followed them, she found herself in a small plaza he hadn't mentioned.

She leaned against one corner and closed her eyes. Heard the blood pounding in her ears. Somewhere close by were the answers she needed. The answers she might not like.

A tug on her shirt.

A boy stood there. Ten maybe. Skinny, dark-haired, dirt-streaked.

"Bienvenidos señorita. Que placer de verla nuevamente." Welcome, miss. Good to see you again.

She stared at him, the sounds translating and echoing.

Again.

"You have seen me before?" she asked in Spanish, the words coming easily though she hadn't expected them.

He shrugged with a look of calculated innocence. "It is possible."

She knelt in front of him, gripped his shoulders. "Where have you seen me?"

Oblivious to her intensity, he held out his hand. "Ten euros, and I can forget. I am very good at forgetting."

"No, no, no. I want you to remember."

A look of confusion crossed his face. "You do?"

"*Sí.*" She dug in her backpack, came out with a bill and handed it to him. "Tell me everything."

The money disappeared into a pocket in the boy's baggy pants, but he shook his head. "I do not understand."

"How do you know me?"

"You were here, miss."

"In Calle Gitana?"

"*Sí, sí. Calle Gitana.*"

"Can you take me there?"

"You do not remember how to get there?"

"No." She handed him another bill. "I need a guide."

"I can take you to the river. To all the best places for *pescado.*"

"Just Calle Gitana."

He frowned and shook his head. "Oh, you do not want to go there."

"Why not?"

"It is very bad there now."

"Bad? How?" She held out another bill, but snatched it away when he reached for it.

"Okay," he said in English, then shrugged. *"Vamanos."*

He led her back the way she had come, went left where she had gone right at one point, and she noted her mistake. They passed through a tiny square occupied by an emaciated man sweeping the ground with a stick broom, then headed down a narrow passageway that looked less like a street and more like breathing room between two rows of buildings. On the side, high up on the stone, sat the street sign: CALLE GITANA.

She licked her lips; they had suddenly grown very dry.

"Allí." The boy pointed, and she forced reluctant feet to follow.

He led her through the constricted passage, and the farther they progressed, the tighter her shoulders became. She recognized nothing, yet her whole body buzzed with fearful anticipation.

Finally, he stopped at a corner. Or what had been a corner.

Instead, a huddle of blackened stone circled a pile of charred debris.

"Calle Gitana, 44," the boy said.

Whatever had been there before was now razed to the ground. A charred smell still lingered in the air.

She stared at the ruins, confused and appalled.

44

"Not a pretty sight."

She whirled.

Jake strolled out of a neighboring doorway and sprawled against the stucco wall, hands in his pockets. He eyed her coldly.

Her heart tripped over itself at the sight of him, irritating her immensely. She reminded herself of the day she'd spent in the Zurich hospital getting her neck cut open, and eyed him right back. She'd been an idiot to think she could rid herself of him for good.

For a half second they stared at each other. Then she sprang at him.

But he was prepared this time. He blocked her attack and spun her around. Before she knew it she was facing the wall, her arm wrenched behind her back.

"Don't you ever say hello first?" His voice was a low growl in her ear, his body strong and masculine and pressed deep into hers.

She gritted her teeth. The pain of his betrayal ground through her. "Does this mean you made up your mind?"

One powerful hand in the middle of her spine pushed her into the side of the wall. She inhaled the nauseating smell of smoked wood and brick. The boy watched avidly.

Jake's free hand roamed roughly over her back and waist, her breasts and between her legs. "It means I'm giving you the benefit of the doubt." Having found no weapons, he released her. "You know, it took me days to pick up your trail. I actually had to do some work."

She jumped away, rolling her shoulders and rubbing her back where he'd held her. "A new concept for you."

He gave her a deadpan, that-was-beneath-you look. "I'm getting the idea that you don't think much of my gifts, except when it comes to saving your butt. Or screwing it."

Her fist lashed out, but he stopped it with his open palm before it got anywhere near his face. "I don't think so."

Fine then. She turned her back on Jake and knelt to the boy's level. "How do you call yourself?"

"Name's Amalio," Jake said.

She stabbed Jake with a look. "You speak Spanish now?"

"The high-school version. *Como se llama? Me llamo Juan.*" In rote delivery, he recited what sounded like a conversational drill. "I sent him to find you."

"You what?" She rose.

"Paid him enough to do it, too."

"You paid him?" She shot Amalio a sharp glance. "So did I."

"See, this is why we should work together," Jake said. "Economies of scales."

Amalio tugged at her shirt again, and she gazed down. Once more his hand was out, palm up. "I take. You pay."

She slapped the promised bill in his hand. "You little thief."

He grinned, and once again the money disappeared into the pocket of his oversize pants. *"Y los otros?"* he asked. "They are coming, too?"

Margo narrowed her eyes. "What others?"

"The men. The other two *porteños.*"

"What is he saying?" Jake asked.

"He says there were two *porteños* with me."

"*Porteños* — what's that?"

"Someone from a port city. Usually Buenos Aires."

"And you're carrying an Argentinean passport," Jake said.

She didn't bother asking how he knew.

Amalio gave them both a sly grin. "Some said *Americanos. Como el.*" He nodded to Jake. "But I told them what you said, *porteños.*"

She translated for Jake.

"Ask him about the house," he said.

She turned to Amalio. *"Qué pasó aquí?"*

He raised his hands, the gesture encompassing the entire structure. *"Hubo un incendio. Muy grande."* He shook his head, his dark eyes big and excited. *"La mujer y sus niños. Se salvaron?"*

The night was warm, but a chill ran up her back. "He says" — she breathed deep, trying not to panic — "he says there was a big fire. He wants to know if the lady and her children are okay."

She and Jake exchanged a look. "Tell me about the lady," she asked Amalio, already fearing the answer.

He shrugged, dug a toe into the ground. "I never saw her; she didn't like to come out. Everyone was sad after the fire."

"Amalio!" A woman stood at the end of the street, hands on ample hips.

The boy gave them a last look and ran off toward the woman. She grabbed him by the neck, gave them a scowl over his head, and hauled him away, her espadrilles, worn down at the heel, slapping on pavement.

"Alone at last," Jake said.

Wordless, Margo stared at the ruin. A woman and two children. For half a second she gave the scream in her head free rein. The high, wailing child's cry took flight.

45

Jake put an arm around her shoulder. "Let's go." He pulled her away. "I've got something to tell you."

She twisted out of his grasp. "Not interested."

"How do you know? You haven't heard it yet." He got in front of her, and she stared at him, then walked around.

He dodged her steps. "All I'm asking is a cup of coffee. A beer. Something civilized and friendly. Dilute all this hostility."

"You're kidding, right? *I'm* hostile? Can't get much more hostile than opening up my neck and sticking a beeper in it."

"Yeah, but I didn't do that."

"You didn't tell me about it either."

"Well, if you want to be precise, I did tell you."

"Only when you got caught."

He smiled, all sexy forgive-and-forget. "What does the timing matter? Now you know." He took her by the arm, suddenly sober. "You've got some serious enemies,

Margo, and I can add another potential name to the list. You need help."

"I don't trust you."

"I saved your damn ass."

"How many times are you going to play that card? Besides, I'm sure you had your reasons."

"Yeah, I like the way you shake your booty."

She jerked away, but Jake held her fast and reined her in tight. "Half the cops in Virginia are looking for you," he snarled. "And that doesn't count the troops from the Bureau and the TCF agents. I knew where you went, I know where you are. That's accessory after the fact, obstruction of justice. I'm putting myself on the line here, Scottie, and all I'm asking is a little cooperation."

"Yeah? And why are you being such a hero?"

His eyes could have burned right through her. "Like I said way back when, I want to know who killed Frank Temple."

He released her, and she shook him off. "And what if it was me?"

"Then I'll pull the switch on you myself. In the meantime, we work together."

They were back on the main street now, Betis. Bars and restaurants overlooked the

Guadilquivir. Jake dragged her into the nearest one.

A wide cement cave with a low, humped ceiling, it was dark and cool. It contained no bar with counter and barman. Instead, massive wooden barrels, bigger than a man, crouched in the shadows around the edges. A white-coated server stepped up to one and decanted a glass of deep red wine. *Tinto.* The word appeared in her head. Or *Jerez.* Sherry, from Jerez de la Frontera.

She shivered with the information that was there, unknown, inside her.

Tiny tables crowded the middle, but the place was so packed, she could barely see them. Most people stood, holding crude glasses of wine. The noise ricocheted around the space, doubling and tripling the decibels.

Jake pushed his way through the crowd, pulling her behind him. He squeezed into a corner near the door. A faded poster announced a bullfight in June, the headline blaring GRAN CORRIDA DE TOROS.

"You may not like it, Margo, but I'm all you've got."

"The name's Margarita. Margarita Vargas. And I didn't ask for your help."

"Well, *Margarita.* Doesn't mean you don't need it."

She leaned back against the wall, the cool cement chilling her. The bruises on his face had faded, but she could still see traces of the cut over his eye. Tangible evidence of what he'd done for her. That and taking out the two heavies at the motel . . .

She'd be dead if not for him. God, why couldn't she count them even and move on?

"You swear you don't know who put in the tracking device?"

He held up a hand as if taking an oath. "Swear."

She rolled her eyes. "Like I'm supposed to believe that. You'd say anything to get what you want."

He thought about it. "Yes. I would." He clamped a hand on her throat just below her chin, imprisoning her face. He was close and fierce, and despite herself she felt drawn in. "But I'm not lying." The eyes he turned on her were sober and sincere.

She should be shot for believing him.

46

Despite his grandmother's insistence on keeping Romaní tradition alive, Amalio Baro had only one religion: money. He'd believed in it since he'd been five, when he'd warned a group of *rakli,* non-Gypsy boys, who were meeting to pool the money and credit cards they'd nicked off tourists, that the *pasmas* were almost at their back.

Since then he'd learned to make himself useful to whoever had the coin. His income had brought meat to the table, goat on Easter and sweet, powdered *polvorones* on Christmas. He ran errands for the Turks, and when the pasmas cleaned out the drug dealers, he ran errands for the cops. He wasn't choosy. He'd work for anyone as long as they prayed in the language of euros.

So when Mama Ada dragged him away from the man and woman on Calle Gitana, he was itchy to get out. He let himself be scolded, let himself be sent to his room, then he slipped out the window and

306

shinnied up to the roof, as he'd done a thousand times.

He grinned as he did it, heard Mama Ada in his head say what she'd said ten thousand times before. "He's like a monkey, the way he disappears so fast."

From his roof he scampered to the next and the next. It didn't take him long to return to Calle Gitana. From high above, he spotted the two *extranjeros*, and keeping the man and the woman in sight, followed them until the man pulled the woman into the Bodega Francisco.

His quarry stashed, Amalio raced for the monastery. There, the stone walls were carved with demons and devils that provided many places for hands and feet. He clambered down, touched ground in a flash, and ran to find El Paleta.

Luca Petali had been born and raised in Triana. He could still remember the years before the laws of 1978 when the Romaní, the Gypsy people, were less than citizens, unable to work, spit on, and hated.

A small man, hard-packed and tough, he'd fought his way up from the streets and into the police, though the battle hadn't stopped when he became a brigade member. They still called him El Paleta, the bricklayer, an epithet thrown at him because it was close to his real name and that's what his Gypsy father had been called. But Luca had used it, made it his own. He'd walled up drug dealers and thieves alike, including Osman the Turk, who was now in jail and would stay there a long time.

For six months after Osman's arrest the streets had been quiet. Then a little over a month ago, strange things occurred. Gunshots, like in an American movie. A fire. A family of foreigners wiped out. Two more bodies burned beyond recognition. And no satisfactory explanation.

His superiors were convinced the events were tied to the Turk's drug organization. "The cockroaches always return," his boss had said. But Luca had visited the Turk, and he'd swear the man was telling the truth when he said he didn't know anything about a fire on Calle Gitana.

So Luca forgot to mention the lead he'd stashed away. And he'd put out a quiet word. Cash for information. He trawled the cafes, the beggars' dens, the flamenco bars, and he waited.

When Amalio ran up, breathless and excited, calling, "Paleta, El Paleta!" Luca stilled. But behind the mask that was his face, he hid a small, but triumphant, smile.

47

The blur of voices in the teeming bar washed over Margo like the haze of the past, indistinct yet insistent. Someone backed into her, and she juggled to keep her place near the door. She turned to Jake.

"What about the bookstore and my life, my sister . . . Why do I have these memories and not others?"

"I don't know."

"But you knew the house was a fake."

"The house, not you. Frank told me exactly nothing about you." He squeezed her shoulder briefly. "I'm sorry."

She stiffened. If she felt adrift before, at least she'd had something to tether her to shore — a family name, parents, sisters, an aunt. Now she was attached to nothing.

"So . . ." She gave him a brittle smile. "Let's play Who Am I?"

"Okay," Jake said slowly, and told her about the phone call from Dottie. The phone call about an argument between Frank and Bill Connelly. Frank's door was closed, but Dottie could hear them yelling at each other. Bill yanked open the door and they were still going at it.

"That's when she heard your name," Jack said.

A shiver ran over her. People talking about her. People she didn't remember. "This is Bill Connelly, he's head of the whatsis, the —"

"Deep Cover Ops. Heavy, heavy secret stuff."

"I'm supposed to know Frank. Maybe that's all it was."

"Your name was spoken in Connelly's presence. He must know who you are, too."

Her heart started pounding. Someone might know who she was, what she was.

"So . . . maybe you work for Connelly. Maybe Spain is your base."

The idea set loose that earlier wedge of hope she'd felt on the flight to London. One of the good guys. She could be one of the good guys.

"Then why lie about it?" she asked.

"Protect your identity. DCO doesn't go around outing their agents."

That would be nice. Better than nice. It would be fantastic.

But as quick as the flash of joy raced through her another explanation occurred, one that fit the facts better.

"Or maybe I'm a target." The words edged into her, saying them aloud making the possibility more real. "An enemy. That would explain what almost happened at the motel."

Jake nodded slowly. "And Connelly would lie to protect the case."

The two options warred inside her, voices from opposing sides in a firefight. Where did the house on Calle Gitana fit in? Inside her head she heard screams. Were they the screams of people trapped in a burning building?

God, what had she done?

The crowd pressed in on her, loud and booming. She couldn't concentrate, couldn't think. A burst of laughter hit her like a mortar shot, and she jumped.

Someone bumped into her again.

"Disculpe," the man murmured, dipping his head in apology.

"No es nada," she responded in kind.

"It is very popular here." The man was small and dark and tough-looking.

Out of the corner of her eye she saw Jake observing the interchange. By the look on his face, he had no idea what they were saying and didn't know whether to open his mouth and admit he wasn't native, or keep his lack of Spanish to himself.

But she didn't want to draw attention to herself either. *"Sí, hay muchos turistas."* Too many tourists. She gave the stranger a polite smile.

"Ah, but you are not a tourist?"

The explanation leaped into her head, as natural as the truth. "A businesswoman. I buy books."

She told him about collecting old books and that she was looking for a seventeenth-century *Don Quixote*. He seemed to brighten, though if the truth be told it was more a sharpening of focus, his black eyes glittering harshly. He offered to buy her a drink, but Jake was scowling in the corner, so she declined and signaled him to start pushing past the crowd.

But the man planted his feet, blocking the way. *"Ah. No me di cuenta que estaba compañada."* He didn't realize she was with someone. He turned to Jake and apologized, holding out his hand, which Jake was forced to take.

"Hola," he said with an insincere smile, nearly mangling the greeting.

"You are . . . American?" The man switched to English. As heavily accented as Jake's Spanish had been.

She hesitated. She could easily lie about herself, but Jake spoke no Spanish. "He is."

"Ah," he said. "I thought I placed the accent correctly. And do you also collect the books?"

"Not unless the odds are good," and when the man didn't seem to understand, Jake said, "Never mind. Bad joke. Good to meet you." He pointed over the smaller man's shoulder. "We're on our way out."

"*Ah, sí, sí.* Of course." He made a little bow and stepped aside. "Enjoy your evening."

Jake ushered her out, elbowing his way through the crowd until they finally reached the street. The night was pleasantly warm, and a sudden wave of weariness washed over Margo.

"I suppose you're staying at the Maria Luisa?"

"Where else?"

She sighed.

He patted her back. "Cheer up. I got connecting rooms."

They crossed the bridge into Seville along with dozens of other revelers. Late nights were different here. It wasn't just singles out for a good time. Whole families strolled together, young children included. They traversed the Parque Alcazar, the public park in the shadow of the tenth-century Moorish palace that was home to the Andalusian kings. Strings of lights glowed. Beer gardens dotted the land-scape, along with *freiturias,* where people stood in line for fried fish and homemade potato chips.

They entered the Barrio de Santa Cruz from the southeast, and suddenly, the streets had cobbles and the walls were made of stone. Moonlight grew dim, and they were alone.

Almost immediately, Margo tensed. "What was that?"

Jake put a companionable arm around her shoulder, and leaned in to speak low. "Someone's following us."

Her heart started to pound. "How far back?"

"Not sure."

"Did you see him?"

"Not enough for an ID." They were in a small plaza on the edge of the barrio, and Jake was still holding her. A gallery dis-playing Spanish pottery was squeezed into one corner, and she stopped in front of it. She reached up to wind her arms around his neck, and for a second, their eyes met. She saw in his that he knew exactly what she was doing, both professionally and pri-vately.

"You go around," she whispered, just as

their lips met. His were warm and wet and a current ran through her as they opened.

"Give me a ten count," he whispered against her mouth, and kissed her — unnecessarily — again.

She sank into the second kiss, wanting it, needing to believe in the pretense of it, the sham of belonging. His arms squeezed her tight, his mouth crushed hers. Her legs trembled, and, with a groan, she wrenched away.

His tongue traced his bottom lip as though tasting her. "You'd forget your head if it wasn't glued on," he said out loud.

"I know, but it's my favorite jacket."

He kissed her again, lingering, his eyes saying he was both pretending and not. "Meet me back here."

He went left, walking around the tracker's flank. The plaza was deserted, dark and empty. The slap of Jake's footsteps echoed in the silence, then faded. The impact of the kiss shuddered through her again, and she finished her count.

Without warning, she wheeled about and bolted back the way they'd come. Jake darted in from the opposite direction.

The man tailing them was trapped. Before he could run, Margo tackled him. He landed on the grass at the edge of the Parque Alcazar.

The man from the bar.

Jake dashed up and between the two of them, they jerked him to his feet.

Jake gave him a brutal shake. "Who are you?"

"Release me," the man muttered, cursing. "Let go!" As opposed to the polite stranger in the bar, something about this man now exuded authority. *"Hombres!"* he shouted, and in two seconds, three uniformed and armed men surrounded them. "Cuff them," he ordered.

"Who the hell are you?" Jake demanded.

"I believe we met at the Bodega. Luca Petali. *Inspector* Luca Petali, Policia Nacional."

48

The police station, called a *comisaría*, was an eighteenth-century building that had seen better days.

"Ai, Gitano!" someone called to Petali as he passed with his prisoners. "Arresting the tourists now?" Margo noted the barely concealed contempt.

"At least I am arresting someone," Petali snapped back.

He sent Jake to a holding cell and sat Margo at a chair beside a desk. He cuffed one hand to a steel post embedded in the arm.

Then he sat behind his desk and shuffled papers, letting her wait. Around them, the *comisaría* hummed within its decaying frame. The white walls were yellowed with age, the windows fogged with grime. Centuries of dirt and grime were embedded in the marble floors.

Margo felt herself inspected and turned her attention to Petali. "You came into the bar for us," she said. "Why?"

He'd taken her passport at the park.

Now he leaned back and fingered it. "Your passport is from Argentina. Why haven't you demanded to see the Argentinean Consulate?"

"I want to know why you arrested us first."

"Well, Señorita" — he checked the name on the passport again — "Vargas, you assaulted a member of the National Police. We do not look with favor on such treatment."

"You were following us."

"I am an officer of the law. It is within my job to follow suspicious people. Especially foreigners."

"It was a misunderstanding. Surely you can see that."

He gave her a challenging look. "Who are you?"

She hoped her expression appeared confused. "You have my passport."

He didn't buy it. "Who are you?" The words were slow and distinct. They bounced off her brain like a bad joke, and she skipped to the punch line.

"I don't know."

Petali's face hardened. "Have you ever been inside a Spanish jail, señorita? Assaulting a police officer is not something we take lightly."

She recognized the threat. "Are you trying to scare me?"

"You are not a woman interested in old books, I think. Unless they are burned to a crisp." He drilled her with dark, angry eyes, and she knew immediately that Amalio had sold them out. "We are even less enthusiastic about drug dealers."

That took her aback. "Drugs?"

Swiftly, she ran down the possibilities. Had she been part of a drug deal gone bad? Had someone betrayed them to the police? The man who'd attacked Jake had threatened revenge. Had *she* betrayed them to the police?

Or had she been betrayed? Had there been a firefight on Calle Gitana that got out of hand?

Maybe she'd been part of a chemical team, and the house had exploded while they were trying to manufacture something lethal? Methamphetamine, purified heroin, or cocaine for local distribution? Morocco wasn't far. Didn't she read somewhere that Morocco was Europe's largest supplier of hashish?

But if this was all about drugs, where did the woman and her children come in? Part of some drug dealer's family?

"You were seen at the house on Calle

Gitana," Petali said. "My witness says you were not only there today. You were there several months ago."

"And if I was?" Inside her head she conjured up fragments of images. Heard screams. Smelled smoke.

Her heart started thudding uncontrollably, and she gripped the chair arms to keep from bouncing off the walls. God, what had happened? What was her part in it?

Petali panned the room quickly, leaned in and spoke low. She had the feeling it wasn't solely for her benefit. "You tell me what happened there — the truth, not the *mierda* I've been handed, and I'll see about losing this" — he waved the complaint form in front of her face — *"denuncia."*

She licked her lips. How could she tell him the truth when she didn't know it herself?

"Look, you said something about drugs. Is what happened in the house drug-related?"

"You tell me."

God, she wanted to howl. But she reined in her frustration. The truth was, she wanted to know what happened as much as he did.

No, that was a lie if she'd ever told herself one. She didn't *want* to know; she wanted to go home and forget about Calle Gitana and whatever happened there.

She curled her hands into fists, the nails digging into her palm. Something was inside her head, some terrible memory, and it wouldn't let her forget. Maybe if she and Petali worked together, pooled their knowledge . . .

She took a breath, the decision made.

"Look, I'll tell you everything. Not that you'll believe me, but I'll tell you what I know. But you have to release my friend."

"Give me something first."

She thought about it. What remembered piece of information would set Jake free? "Two days ago, near Washington, DC, four men who looked Middle Eastern came looking for me. They found Jake."

Petali's interest quickened. "Could they be Turks?"

"Release Jake, and I'll tell you the rest."

A quick nod and a rapid order in Spanish. Petali unlocked a drawer in his desk and removed a file. Then he released her from the chair and led her into an interrogation room. A few minutes later, Jake was brought in.

He looked rumpled and tired, but there were no new bruises on his face.

"You all right?" she asked him.

He nodded. "You?"

"Fine."

"Enough!" Petali shoved a chair in Jake's direction. *"Sientate."* He pulled back another for Margo. "So. Who are you?"

She took a breath. "I don't know. And that is the truth." She filled him in on everything that had happened, and he became more still as she went on. When she was done, silence filled the room.

"That is" — Petali seemed to be searching for the words in English — *"asombroso,"* he said at last, as though only Spanish could convey his astonishment.

"I'm not lying."

"I am Rom — *gitano,* Gypsy. My people, we have a saying: there are lies more believable than the truth." His thin lips curved slightly. "I do not think this is one of them.

"Look, I didn't believe it either," Jake said. "At first. But the guys who used a chain on me were real. And so were the two creeps who were about to shoot her in the head."

"The Middle Eastern men. Did you hear them speak?"

"Arabic, I think."

"Not Turkish?"

Jake shook his head, and Petali looked thoughtful. Then, as though he'd made a snap decision, he flipped open the file and slid something across the table toward Margo.

It was a half-burned Argentinean passport in the name of Ricardo Rossini. The cover was charred, the pages black-edged. But enough of the photo was left to see a square-jawed man looking up at her from the picture.

"Do you know this man?"

She shook her head.

"Interesting," he said, sliding the passport back into the file before Jake could see it. "You are fellow compatriots." He hit his forehead in a gesture of forgetfulness. "Ah, but Argentina. It is a big country, no?" He pursed his lips and leaned forward. "Your government, they do not know him either. But you, Señorita Vargas, or whoever you are, do. Because I wager my life he knows you."

Her brows rose in surprise. "Why would he know me?"

"Have you ever seen a burn victim?"

She went cold. "A burn victim?"

He ran the pad of a thumb down the left side of his cheek, thoughtful, calculating. "I wonder what Señor Rossini will say when I tell him the woman who abandoned him to the fire on Calle Gitana has returned."

Her heart was pounding, her hands suddenly filmed with sweat. "Is that what he claims I did?"

"Well, Miss . . . Vargas, burns are complicated wounds, and he has not been well enough to talk. At least, that is what the nuns say. Then again, it has been a while since we spoke. Perhaps he has had a breakthrough."

Petali's words and what they meant — someone knew who she was, what she'd done — exploded inside Margo. She reached across the table and grabbed Petali's wrist. "You must let me see him."

He looked down at her fingers pressing into his flesh. "Do I?" He shot her a chilling look. "Perhaps when I hear the truth."

49

Unsatisfied with what she'd told him, Petali sent Margo and Jake to holding cells in different parts of the building. Since they were holding cells and not jail cells, each was individually locked and unlocked by a single officer, who was dispatched to escort her in and out.

Petali had cuffed her hands, but hadn't shackled her feet. She dutifully entered the cell, but before the guard could close it again, she leaped, chinned-up to a crossbar, and kicked him brutally in the chest. The attack caught him by surprise, and he took it full force, landing across the room. In an eye blink the guard was out cold.

No longer wondering how she could have done what she did, she retrieved the handcuff key and released herself, all the while looking around to make sure no one had heard.

The cell room remained quiet.

She grabbed the guard's gun, tucked it into her jeans, and sneaked away.

Gaze sweeping the walls, she noted

mirrors in the corner but no cameras. The security inside the *comisaría* was a generation behind the times.

She had no idea where Jake was, but suspected the holding cells were all near each other. One eye on the wall mirrors and one eye ahead, she dashed down a corridor. Out of the corner of her eye she saw two men coming. She ducked through a door into an empty office. Footsteps approached and stopped outside her door.

So did her heart.

Two men began speaking. One was Luca Petali. The other . . . she didn't recognize the other voice. Automatically, her mind translated the Spanish.

"You dig your own grave," the stranger said.

"I cleaned out that barrio six months ago," Petali said. "Osman and his Turkish thugs are in prison."

Sweat dripped down her back. Her breathing seemed loud enough to hear through three walls, let alone one door.

"There are always more bad guys," the other voice said. "Whatever you are hiding, wherever you go when you sneak off, whatever you think you'll prove, you'll always be a dirty Gypsy. Do what they tell you and don't screw yourself."

"Tell the boss I had to go out."

"Don't do it, Luca."

"Just tell him."

One set of footsteps marched away. The other man cursed, then he, too, left.

She closed her eyes in relief and waited a moment to get herself under control. So Luca Petali was hiding something. Was he leaving to check on it?

She peeked out. The corridor was empty. She dashed down it, gun at the ready, stopped at the corner, and followed a sign that read *"jaulas"* — cells — to another set of holding cells. The guard desk was empty, so she snuck by it.

The cells here were full, and the minute they saw her, the men inside whistled and shouted. She ignored the ruckus and ran down the cells, checking each one. Jake was in the last.

He took one look at her. "One guard. Heavy smoker. Takes a cigarette break every five minutes. Should be back any time." He nodded to the left. "Jog in the wall."

She saw instantly what he meant. A place to hide.

The rest was easy. When the guard came back, Jake distracted him long enough for her to sneak up and disable him. She found the keys, opened the cell, and tossed them to the guy in the next cell. Shouting and shoving, the prisoners began to let themselves out as she and Jake charged down the hallway.

"Petali. He's hiding something from his superiors." She filled Jake in as they ran.

She'd already scoped out the closest exit. They were out of the building before the general alarm sounded.

Across the street, Petali was getting into a car. There were no taxis conveniently at hand, but Jake found a car unlocked. In ten seconds, he'd hot-wired it. Although it seemed to take them an hour to get going, it actually took only a few minutes. Petali was a block ahead.

They left the city and drove for half an hour, following Petali to a small village nestled against a grove of olive trees. An institution of some kind sat on the outskirts. Brick walls defined its space, and a large brick archway hovered over the entrance to the drive. Petali drove in, and Jake continued, stopping a few feet past the gate.

"Centro de Rehabilitacion de Nuestra Señora de la Sagrada Corazon." Jake read the words over the arch. "Our Lady of the Sacred Heart. What's the first part?"

"Some kind of rehab center." Margo gazed through the arch at the serene-looking grounds. "I think we found what Petali is hiding."

50

Jake parked and Margo left him in the car. The story they'd concocted wouldn't work with a non–Spanish speaker in tow. So she entered the building alone.

Inside it became clear that the place had once been something other than a hospital. A grand estate perhaps. Built over a wide, central staircase, it boasted glossy marble floors and high-arched windows. She looked up. The nurses' desk was on the second floor.

It was past seven, but in Spain, where no one started the evening meal until ten, that was still early. Nevertheless, the hospital was quiet, with few people in the hallways and only one nurse behind the station.

It took a bit of explaining, but Margo finally convinced the staff that her boss at the Policia Nacional, Luca Petali, had left some important papers in a patient's room and she'd been sent to retrieve them.

The ruse got her a room number, but as visiting hours were over and the patient was already tired from Señor Petali's visit, the nurse refused to let her in. She sent someone downstairs to check the room, and when no papers were found, Margo acted the embarrassed underling.

"I am sure he told me to pick them up here."

"He was mistaken," the nurse said firmly, ushering her to the staircase.

Obediently, Margo retreated, but instead of exiting, she ducked into a corridor to scout the layout. Room numbers led in orderly fashion from highest to lowest. Scanning what she could of the floor plan, she figured her quarry's ground-floor room was on the other side of the central stairs. She headed in that direction, but before she could get there, a nurse caught her, and she was forced to leave.

"If he's on the ground floor," Jake said when she returned, "we can locate him from the outside."

They crept out of the car and around the building's exterior.

"Here." Margo pointed to the southeast corner. A window led into the room. She peeked in.

A heavily bandaged form lay on the bed, an IV stand looming over it. From her vantage point Margo couldn't tell if it was a man or a woman, just that it appeared adult.

An eerie sensation filled her. The tightly wrapped body seemed the essence of everything she'd been fighting since she woke up days ago. The truth swathed in so many layers it was impossible to see.

But she knew this: something terrible had happened on Calle Gitana, and whoever lay on the bed knew what it was.

Back in the village, they located a small hardware store four blocks off the plaza. Run by a stoop-shouldered man who shuffled behind the counter, it looked like something out of a Dickens novel, with a weird collection of farm implements, nails, and other tools gathering dust. But they found the suction cup and glass cutter they needed.

Later, they bought food in a tiny place that sold whole chickens roasted on spits over an open flame so the fat from one bird dripped down and basted those below. The man operating the rotisserie cut one down for them, hacked it into pieces, and packaged it up. That and a round loaf of Spanish bread was dinner.

They took the meal to the central plaza and spread it out over a bench. Jake broke into the bread. The hard crust and chewy inside brought back a thousand memories. Some of them must have shown in his face because Margo asked, "What?"

He broke off another piece and stuffed it in his mouth. "What what?"

"Your face went all strange."

She picked at a chicken breast, tearing off a hunk of meat in a brittle, electric slash, then putting it down and tearing off another. The food was shredded, but she hadn't eaten a bite. Ever since the hospital and the glimpse of the mummified body, she'd been on edge. So he stopped her hand from ripping into another piece of meat and told her what he'd been thinking. "You need teeth."

"That's cryptic."

"Not cryptic, Cypriot. Greek, actually. It's something the cook used to say to my mother."

"The cook . . ." She raised one of her black brows. "Did you have a butler, too? Somehow you don't seem the butler type."

He dipped his bread into the drippings at the bottom of the chicken container. "My father was a field officer in the CIA. Beirut was his last posting. Too dangerous to live there, so we lived in Cyprus. My mother was always complaining about the bread. How hard it was to chew. Demetrious, the cook, used to tell her that. You need teeth." He bit into a drumstick.

"Life is rough. You have to be able to attack it with everything you've got. Teeth."

He thought about Margo. She was clearly terrified of finding out whatever had happened in that burned-out ruin of a house. And yet she plunged on anyway, determined to discover what it was. Teeth was something she had in spades.

"And did she?"

"My mother?" He sighed. "No, she was all about making it easy. She wanted to swallow things whole. Soft, easy-to-chew things. White bread. After my father was killed, she took me back to her hometown. A lively little place called Dewey, Indiana."

"A far cry from Cyprus."

"More like a scream. I couldn't get away fast enough."

"So you come by all this" — she waved her hand around to indicate their situation — "honestly."

"It's in the genes."

"And your dad. He was killed?"

He gave her the basics, short and curt. "Embassy bombing — Beirut, 1986."

She absorbed that in silence. "So that's your family connection to Frank."

He nodded.

"You don't like talking about it."

He shrugged, not happy to be so transparent. "Not much to say. We don't know who did it. Not for certain. Not enough to convict and punish."

"And you're all about the punishment, aren't you, Jake?"

He looked at her. "For the guilty."

She tore into the bread. "It must be nice to have memories. Even lousy ones."

Back in the car, they waited for the moon to rise and set, dozing during the long hours. When darkness was at its peak they made their way back to the hospital, parked outside the grounds, and sneaked through the gates and up the long drive.

The place was black and silent, a hulking shape in the night. Clinging to the walls, they crept around to the back, located the appropriate room. In a few minutes, Margo had cut a small hole in the window, reached through, and unlatched the old-fashioned handle lock. She pushed, and the window gave enough for her and Jake to slither through.

Once in they paused, both listening hard for oncoming feet. But the only sound they heard was the steady beep of the machine tolling out electrocardiac life.

Margo stole to the bed, maneuvering carefully between the IV stand and the other medical equipment. The room smelled of ointment and pus and disinfectant. Heavy bandages covered the patient's face, but the eyes and mouth were free. She studied what little she could see, her heart beating so hard she thought it might fly out of her chest. It was a man, definitely, but no one she recognized.

As she leaned over, his eyes opened. They stared at each other for what seemed like an eon. His hand, which was partially encased in bandages, jerked toward hers and she jumped.

He opened his mouth and out came a single word, hoarse and papery. "Scott."

Her heart stopped. She lost the ability to speak.

Jake brushed past her. "Who are you?" The question was low and insistent.

Framed by white bandages, the man's pain-filled eyes moved, gazing from her face to Jake's and back again. The lids came down heavily, shuttering them. For a moment it seemed as if they'd lost him to sleep and morphine, and for just that long she hoped they had.

Then, with what seemed like much effort, he opened his eyes again. Licked dry lips. Spoke. "Richard Carns." The name came out like a hard croak. It meant nothing to her, but it seemed to surprise Jake.

"Dick Carns?" He took a step away, turning to Margo. "I knew a Dick Carns. Worked a case with him."

"Balkans," whispered the man in the bed.

Jake drew in a sharp breath and wheeled back around. He leaned over the patient. "Rumor had it Dick Carns went underground to work for Bill Connelly. DCO."

The man said nothing, only locked eyes with Jake.

Margo, too, remained silent. The murky, dangerous world Jake had alluded to, almost from the beginning, was suddenly there in front of her.

"My God," Jake said. "How long have you been here?"

A small shake of the head, which elicited a groan. "No idea."

"Has anyone made contact?"

"Spanish police."

"No Americans?"

"You're . . . the first." His eyes filled with tears, and he closed them as though ashamed. Margo felt a rush of pity for him, and Jake must have experienced the same.

"It's okay," Jake said quickly. "We'll get you out of here. But we need to know what happened. How do you know Margo?"

He seemed to hesitate, confused, and another wave of compassion and understanding shook Margo. If he thought they were here to rescue him, why wouldn't they know what had happened to him? He looked to Margo for confirmation. Some deep-seated instinct for authority or chain of command took hold. She had no recollection of this man, was dreading what he might say, but she nodded quietly anyway.

"It's all right, Dick. Tell him what you can."

He began to speak, the words faint, the voice as rasping and exhausted as an old man's. But slowly the story came out.

51

They flew into the naval base at Rota near the tip of Spain. There were three of them. Dick Carns, Aldo Rodriguez, and Margo in command. Margo and Dick went to Morocco by tour boat, found the intended targets, and waited for nightfall. Intel had mentioned three guards, but one was missing. That bit of luck made the job easier. Soundlessly, they took out the two remaining guards. Inside the house, they drugged the woman and her two children while they slept.

They brought them across the Straits of Gibraltar by fishing boat in the dead of night, covered in tarps. Aldo, whose Spanish was the most colloquial, waited on the dock at El Puerto de Santa Maria, dressed in the baggy clothes of an Andalusian fisherman. They hauled the cargo into the back of a truck like a load of herring.

Hours later they crossed the Triana Bridge under a moonless sky. The truck continued until the narrow streets no longer made vehicular traffic feasible. Then they transferred the bodies to a wheelbarrow, the woman as small and delicate and motionless as her two sons. By the time the hostages awoke the next day, locked inside the house on Calle Gitana, they were already trapped.

The plan worked perfectly. No witnesses, no delays.

Except for Ruben Cahill, who, despite extreme pressure, was still uncooperative.

Ex–Army Ranger turned mercenary, Cahill was responsible for a wave of bombings, kidnappings, and assassinations from Europe to Iraq and had links to terror organizations across three continents. He'd been a plum capture that so far had yielded little. Taking his Moroccan-born wife and children hostage was supposed to provide the necessary leverage to pry loose his wealth of information. And because DCO handled the mission, everyone could deny it had ever taken place.

Margo and her team set up closed-circuit video and began the battle for Cahill's soul. But two days in, he still refused to speak.

Despite the pleas of his dark-haired wife. Despite the tears of his children.

Desperate for results, the order came

down: eliminate the hostages one at a time, starting with the eldest boy.

The three agents held a tense conference. They didn't make war on children. But orders were orders. They looked to Margo, the agent in charge, and she said she would relieve them of responsibility and do whatever was necessary.

She sent Aldo to bring the boy. They dragged him in front of the camera, and Margo held a gun to his head herself.

The woman was screaming. The nine-year-old was screaming. The twelve-year-old's nose was running, the snot mingling with tears as he shook beneath the muzzle of the gun.

Margo was shouting at the camera, "I'll do it! I swear I'll do it, you bastard!"

The acrid smell of urine filled the air; the boy had wet his pants.

A shot popped. The boy fell.

More shots. Suddenly the room was filled with the sound of gunfire. The third guard had found them and brought men along.

Almost immediately, Aldo took a bullet to the head and keeled over. Cahill's wife ran, but a round jerked her backward. Dick was hit in the leg and the chest. He crawled for cover. Someone fired at him and hit the *bombone,* the propane tank beneath the table in the dining room. Without central heat, many used the tanks to fuel space heaters built into the table frame. This one exploded, shooting flames into the air. The last thing Dick remembered was the nine-year-old, jerking to the rhythm of gunfire as round after round pierced his small body.

In the hospital room, Dick Carns tried to lick his dry lips. He'd woken, horribly burned. He'd only been able to start talking several days ago, but he'd kept quiet to the Spanish police, who came every day to question him.

Now he moaned and fell silent.

Beside the bed, Margo sat as still as stone in a hard-backed chair. Everything was quaking inside her, but she managed to maintain an outward calm by clinging to a tiny bud of hope.

Dick closed his eyes, and she leaned over. "Dick," she whispered, careful not to touch him. "One question."

For a moment she thought she'd lost him again. His breathing was labored, the lungs ruined from smoke and fire. She knew she should leave him alone; talking had exhausted him. But she was desperate to know.

"Dick?"

The eyes inside the bandages drifted open. He groaned.

"The boy. The twelve-year-old. Who fired the first shot?"

There had been many silences during the long retelling of what had happened on Calle Gitana, but this one was the longest. At last, Dick opened his mouth. Sucked in a hoarse breath through his damaged lungs. "You did," he said. "You did."

52

Jake watched Dick Carns's words hit Margo like a slap. She literally shrank, as though all the air inside her had been let out. She said nothing, only stared as Dick drifted into sleep.

A wave of sympathy gripped Jake. What would he have done in her place? Ignored the order? Disobeyed it? Found a way around it? For people like them, catching the bad guy was all that mattered. Getting Cahill to talk could save hundreds of lives. How far would he have gone to make sure that happened?

Footsteps sounded outside the room, and Jake had no more time to think about ethical dilemmas. He bolted to the door and peered out. A nurse with a medication cart was approaching.

He dashed back to where Margo still sat like an empty shell. "We gotta go," he told her.

She didn't move, didn't reply.

"Margo." He shook her. "Let's go." She was limp and unresponsive, so he yanked her to her feet. "Medical staff on the way — we have to boogie! Move!"

He dragged her to the window and shoved her through, tumbling out himself just as the room door swung open. Outside, he flattened against the hospital wall and yanked Margo, who seemed to be in a stupor, beside him. They hadn't had time to close the window. He hoped the nurse wouldn't notice.

Through the open window he heard her humming as she bustled around the room. The medication cart jangled, contents rattling. After a few minutes, the sounds receded. He peeked into the window. She was gone.

"Let's go." He started forward, but Margo didn't move, and he turned back for her. "Come on."

She stared at him, more like through him, then looked away. "I need a few minutes."

The torment in her voice tugged at him, but they didn't have time for anguish. "Take them later."

"I'm taking them now!"

"You may want to get caught, but I'm not crazy about more of Señor Petali's hospitality." He grabbed her arm and she jerked it away. He grabbed it again, pulled her off the wall, and shoved her forward. "Move!"

She rounded on him, fists up, and keeping an eye out for anyone he didn't want to run into, he spoke low and mean. "You want me to hurt you?" He looked directly into her face, the deep blue eyes as black now as the sky. "Yeah, I think you do. A little pain for the child killer? Think that'll make you feel better?"

She drew in a sharp breath, but something loosened in her, and he could tell she wouldn't resist him. He was a shit to twist the knife like that, but it worked. He took her arm, bruising the skin to make sure she couldn't escape, and marched her toward the car. He shoved her in and drove into the night.

Margo sat beside Jake, the scream in her head constant. She knew who it was now. The boy. The boy she'd killed.

All the pieces of her lost life had come together. The water, the men, the heavy cargo.

Human cargo. In a fishing boat in the dark of night.

Oh, the things she'd done.

Suddenly she felt sick. Viciously, violently ill. She told Jake to stop the car, and he took one look at her and swerved to the shoulder without question. She bolted out the door and heaved up every bit of self-loathing onto the grass.

Jake held her hair back. The comforting hand on her neck felt cool against her heated skin, but so undeserved. When she was done, she leaned against the car, wiping the taste and stench off her mouth, but it lingered no matter what she did.

Jake stroked her hair. "Feel better?" he said gently.

She would have laughed if she could. She would never feel better.

"Look, we'll get to the hotel, go up to the room," Jake said, still caressing her head. "I'll order a bottle of scotch. Maybe two. We'll get drunk, okay? Just the two of us. We'll get drunk, we'll have meaningless sex, I promise you'll feel better."

She let him guide her back to the car like an invalid. He was being solicitous, but it irritated her. If she had the energy, she would have told him so. But all her power was concentrated on staring out at the passing darkness. There were few lights in the countryside, and the black looked enviable. She wanted to blend with it. Be invisible. Disappear.

Once they reached the city, Jake ditched

the car; she didn't even know where. He pulled her out, set her on a path. She knew she was walking, knew her feet were moving. She just couldn't feel anything.

Except the scream raging inside her mind.

She stumbled. The street was uneven. Stones. She was walking on stones. It made no sense, but it was true.

A glint of steel caught her eye before her brain registered it. A man in a doorway.

Tall, skinny. Black mustache.

The man who ordered Jake's beating at Aunt Frances' house. But no, it wasn't Aunt Frances' house. She only thought it was. They were watching her. Jake was watching her. All the time, watching her.

The man, he was watching her, too. What was he doing here? Was that a gun in his hand?

Jake yelled, a sound that registered blurred and unfocused. In her head it sounded like the siren blaring inside her. A child. A dead child.

53

In the shadows of the ancient Juderia, Luca Petali slid silently forward, keeping his eyes on the man hidden in a darkened doorway across the cobblestone street from the Maria Luisa Hotel.

Petali liked the Juderia. The ancient Jewish quarter was squeezed under the armpit of the Alcazar, the palace of the Arab kings of Andalus. Here, the streets twisted around worn-down cobbles, and though the wrought-iron balconies created color and interest for the tourists, the place had long been sanitized of its Jews. Their absence reminded him of his own fate, and what could happen to the Spanish Rom if drugs and discrimination had their way. Occasionally he walked here, in secret defiance of the *gaje* who scorned him, living proof that the Romaní would not be wiped out.

But tonight he was not wrestling with the past. Tonight he was protecting the future. He had heard about the chaos at the station and the escape of the prisoners, including the Argentinean woman he'd tied to the events at Calle Gitana and her American friend. The accounts were fuzzy, but he wouldn't be surprised to find the two of them had somehow engineered the whole thing.

They would turn up. He was sure of it. And in the meanwhile, he'd had a report that one of Osman's men had been spotted in the city.

Petali leaned against the hotel's west wall, sharp eyes glued to the man he'd been tailing. He was tall and skinny, cadaverous almost, with a huge black mustache. He was chewing an unlit cigarette, turning it around in his teeth.

Waiting. Waiting for something.

A contact? A meeting? A signal?

Petali waited right along with him.

The man was not familiar. But he had visited Osman in prison. Two days later he'd shown up here. Too much of a coincidence.

Footsteps on the cobbles echoed. Petali tensed. The man with the mustache reached under his shirt and pulled out a weapon. A beat of surprise that didn't prevent Petali from doing the same.

Two people appeared from the side street to the east of the hotel.

The man in the doorway took careful aim.

"Watch out!"

Jake shoved Margo out of the way just as gunshots exploded around them. When he could take stock, he saw the gunman on the ground and Margo still alive.

How had that happened?

Jake spun around in all directions, the gun Margo had taken off the guard in his outstretched hand. "Who the fuck —" He hadn't fired it; he hadn't had time. So who had?

People were piling into the street. Shocked gasps and murmuring. Luca Petali appeared out of the shadows.

"Inside." Petali took Margo's arm, hauled her upright, and threw her forward. "Move. We have to get out of here."

He hustled her and Jake into the hotel and closed the door on the growing crowd outside. Jake was breathless and trying to get that under control. Beside him, Margo stumbled forward, a zombie. Escape from execution twice in less than two weeks. How the hell did she stay upright at all?

Petali commandeered the hotel office, made a quick phone call to the *comisaría.* While he was talking — all of it in incom-

351

prehensible Spanish, of course — Jake pulled out a chair and pushed it in Margo's direction. Small tremors shook her shoulders, but she only gripped the back and held her ground.

Slowly, Jake was getting a handle on what had happened. Mr. Mustache tracked Margo to Spain. Petali took him out. God, if Jake hadn't pushed her out of the way . . .

The Spanish cop slammed down the receiver, then turned to them.

"Thanks for taking out that creep," Jake said.

"I don't want your thanks. And if you want to leave Spain sometime before you're dead, you will tell me who that man was and why he tried to kill Señorita Vargas."

Jake opened his mouth, but Petali forestalled him. "That is the price, señor. The truth. Or I turn you over to the Spanish authorities now." He paused. "Quickly. We do not have much time. A team will be here any minute."

Suddenly Margo seemed to wake up from her long sleep. Maybe the sound of Petali's voice snapped her to attention. Or maybe she enjoyed almost being killed again. In any case, her face lost the misty look, and she spoke. Too bad Jake didn't understand any of it.

"What did you tell him?" Jake asked.

Margo ignored him and continued in Spanish.

"English, Margo. The damn man speaks English."

She and Petali locked eyes. At last the cop turned to Jake. "Get out of here."

"What?"

"You are free to go."

He looked from Petali to Margo. "What about her?"

"She stays."

"Then I'm staying."

"No, you're not," Margo said. "Get out of here, Jake, while you still can."

He didn't like being pushed. And right now he was being shoved right out of the picture. "What kind of deal did you make?"

"Petali will give you an escort to the airport. Take it."

"Fuck you, Scottie."

"It's that or jail. Can't find out if I killed Frank from inside a Spanish prison."

"What are they going to charge me with? Victim of a shooting? Didn't know being shot at was a crime anywhere on the planet."

"Do not worry about that," Petali said. "I will happily think of something to charge you with."

Jake scowled and focused on Margo. "You are not going to do this. What happened — it wasn't your fault."

She laughed, if you could call that twist in her mouth and the sound that came out of it a laugh. "Not my fault? I was in charge."

"It was orders."

"Orders?" Another sardonic snort. "I hear that kid screaming in my head. Do you know what it's like to have a child screaming in your head, Jake?"

"Falling on your sword is not —"

"How do you know I didn't kill Frank, too, on orders?" Her voice was quiet. There was a painful look in her navy blues. He didn't like that either.

"That's ridiculous."

"Is it?"

"Yes."

She smiled sadly, her glorious mouth soft and sweet for the moment. "So, you finally made up your mind."

Had he? The truth hit him like a gale-force wind, like one of those moments in the movies where the camera closes in and everything slows way down. It wasn't that he knew she hadn't killed Frank, though the hope was there like bedrock. It was that he didn't care.

He would support her either way. Fight for her either way.

All his adult life he'd wanted one thing: to make sure the bad guy paid. Now, he wanted desperately for the bad guy — if she was standing in front of him — to get away. As far and as fast as possible.

The ropes securing him to the ground snapped one by one, and he was in free fall. His lungs clogged, and for half a second he couldn't breathe.

Then he anchored himself by focusing on Margo's lithe body, her feet planted, her face vulnerable.

Grabbing her arm, he dragged her into a corner, away from Petali's prying ears. "We can disappear. Go anywhere."

Margo heard desperation in his voice, and in his eyes she saw a hint of shame. Afraid to understand, she spoke carefully. "What are you talking about?"

"You know what I'm talking about."

Her stomach twisted. "Running? You're talking about running?" And worse, she got it. "Oh, my God. You think I did it."

"I didn't say that."

"I was right. You did make up your mind. You think I killed Frank."

"No."

"Liar."

He raised his hands, a futile gesture. "All right! All right." He rubbed his face; suddenly he looked like he hadn't slept in a year. "You want the truth? The truth is, I don't know. I can choose to believe in you. I *do* believe in you. But the evidence is there, and if you go back, you'll go back in chains."

"I thought that's what you wanted."

"Not enough to see you in them."

She looked away, tears stinging the backs of her eyelids. "Well, thanks for that."

He spared a furtive glance at Petali, then came back to her. "So, can we get out of here?"

The sadness inside her chest spread. "You mean, conk our friend on the head and split?"

"Something like that."

"I'm surprised at you."

"Cut the —"

"No, Jake."

"No Jake what? No, you're not going to cut the bullshit, or no you're not going to —"

"No." She picked her words carefully,

trying to be calm, gentle. To explain it to him the right way. "You said yourself you're in trouble for helping me. Go home. No one will know where you've been. I'll turn up, face the music. You'll be out of it."

"I don't want to be out of it."

She sighed. "Now who's throwing himself on his sword?"

"I'm not —"

"You think I don't know what you're offering? What it costs you?" She burst out with the words, voice husky and passionate. "You're the man with the whip, Jake. You're the guy who brings *in* the trash, not tosses it to the wind."

"You're not tr—"

"What you're suggesting goes against everything you believe in. And for what? Me?"

"I just said I believe in you."

Tears welled in her eyes again. She fought them and shook her head. "I'm grateful, Jake. God, more than you can know. But I'm not going to be the load that takes you down."

"No one is —"

"Look, you want it simple? You help me, you implicate yourself. That's not a price I'm willing to pay."

"It's not fucking *about* you."

"You're right," she said miserably. "It's about Frank and those dead kids."

"Christ. Mostly the dead kids. And you know it."

She gazed at the stubborn line of his jaw. He thought she was throwing herself to the lions, but she knew it was the only way to save herself. What she'd done . . . God, she could barely get her head around it. And to walk away, free and clear . . . that was as sick and obscene as the act she'd committed. "Please." She placed a hand on his arm. "Get out of here."

A knock on the door. "Enough of this," Petali said. "We are out of time." He let in a uniformed man from the Guardia Civil, pointed Jake out to him. "This man will take you to the airport." He gave a rapid order in Spanish, and the man clamped one handcuff around Jake's wrist and the other around his own. "The cuffs come off when you get on the plane."

Margo might have wished the cuffs weren't necessary, but she didn't trust Jake not to fly the minute he had the chance. "Sorry," she said.

He gazed at her, his mouth hard, his eyes angry. "You're a regular little martyr, aren't you?"

358

She met his gaze. He looked like he wanted to strangle her. Thank God he would have needed both his hands to do it.

The cop led him away, and Margo breathed easier. No matter what Jake thought, she felt a scrap of peace. A way out. She was taking it. But he wasn't going along for the ride.

54

Three days later, Jake used his TCF badge to get inside Reagan International, and from a window overlooking the tarmac, watched as U.S. Marshals led a cuffed Margo from the plane to a waiting car.

He wanted to feel outrage, to stoke the anger that should be there for Frank's killer. But all he kept thinking about was how long they'd had the cuffs on her. Were her wrists scraped raw?

She'd be processed and booked, arraigned for the murder of Frank Temple. In Brewster's mind the trip out of the country all but sealed her guilt. Not to mention proving her a flight risk — despite the fact that she'd turned herself in — which meant prosecutors would request no bail and get it. All of which could take a day, maybe two, depending on how jammed everyone was.

Jake had hired her a lawyer, a real one, but only on the condition he could be part of her defense team. As such, he could visit her with a little more privacy than the general public.

He did so the next day, in an airless room with a corrections officer stationed outside the door.

Margo shuffled in wearing prison clothes, blue work pants and a shirt with a number stenciled on the back. The color set off her eyes, which looked tired, beaten down. They filled with wary concern as she realized who was seated at the opposite end of the single table in the room.

"What are you doing here, Jake?"

The CO escorting her moved her firmly to a chair. "Sit down first. Then you can talk."

"I shot my mouth off to keep you out of this," she said as she complied. The guard cuffed her to the table, then retreated to a corner. "You shouldn't be here."

Jake took in her haggard face, made even more ashen by the contrast of her dark hair and brows. "You look like crap."

"Thanks," she said dryly.

"Not sleeping?"

She flicked her head impatiently, how she was doing was clearly not something she wanted to talk about. "Why are you here?"

"Right back at you," Jake said.

Her lips compressed into a thin line. "I'm seeing justice done."

"That's a crock."

"What's the matter — don't you believe the evidence?"

"No. Not entirely."

She sighed. "That's because you don't want to, not because it isn't there."

He shrugged. She was right. "Call it a hunch."

"Up until a few days ago, your hunch was running in the other direction."

"A good man admits when he's wrong."

"Yeah, where'd you hear that?"

"The Bible. Or maybe it's Shakespeare. It's always one or the other."

Margo closed her eyes. Her whole body sagged. The struggle to keep herself calm and in control was taking its toll. For days now, she'd roamed her small cell, a single subject occupying her mind. Who would do what she'd done? How had she gotten to the point where it hadn't horrified her? The questions circled, open-ended, unanswered. Jake only brought more of the same.

"Back off, Jake. Please."

But he wasn't listening. "Connelly been here? You work for him, he should get off his bureaucratic ass and do something."

"We talked about this," she said wearily. It was exhausting pushing out the words.

"Talk? Like in conversation? When?"

"In Spain. In the hotel. With Petali."

"I don't think so. You made up your mind and —"

"This is what I need to do."

"Give up?"

His accusation sparked a wisp of anger. "This is not resignation," she snapped. "It's acceptance. Of responsibility. My responsibility."

He pushed back from the table in frustration. "The police looked at that photo in Frank's room. The one of you and him together. It's genuine."

"See? It all works out."

"It only means you had some real connection with him. Maybe he's a relative. An uncle."

"He ever talk about having a niece?"

"No. Doesn't mean he didn't have one, though."

She balked at that. She didn't want relatives. For the first time she was glad she had no connections to anyone. No one to face but herself. Day in and day out.

"Look, Jake, I appreciate the effort, but I don't want —"

"My help. Yeah, I got that."

She looked carefully down at her cuffed hands. She was tired of defending her choice. Tired of talking about it. "We both know someone has to pay. If that's what it takes to stop the screaming in my head, so be it."

Jake rose. "You can hang yourself from the tree outside my window if that'll make you happy," he said stiffly. "But I'm still after whoever killed Frank. I'm betting it's not you."

From the jail, Jake went to see Connelly. He'd tried setting up an appointment to see him, but Connelly was booked solid for the next three days and not even his connection with Melva could get him in on such short notice. So he let himself into headquarters, took the elevator to the twelfth floor, and hung around Connelly's office, hoping to catch the man on his way in or out.

He waited until nearly seven before Connelly appeared, and then it was with briefcase and coat on his way out. Jake pushed off the wall he was leaning against and chased after the man. He was smaller than Jake, rumpled rather than buff, wore a cheap pair of brown-rimmed eyeglasses, and was in a hurry. Jake picked up the pace.

"Sir, can I talk to you?" Jake put on his best subordinate demeanor. Some bosses, like Frank, could command respect without the aid of hierarchical deference. Connelly didn't strike him as cut from the same mold. "Jake Wise, sir. We spoke on the phone a week or so ago about Frank Temple."

Connelly flicked a hard glance at Jake.

"I've got an office, son."

"It's about Margo Scott."

Connelly didn't miss a step. "I'm on my way to a meeting with DOD."

"I'll walk you out."

Another evaluating glance from Connelly. It took less than a heartbeat, but Jake felt like he'd been stripped raw. Connelly checked his watch, looked around. "Five minutes." He gestured for Jake to precede him through a doorway. They stepped into a conference room.

"Go," Connelly said.

"I assume you've been apprised of the situation? She's been arrested."

"I was briefed yesterday."

Yesterday? What the hell had the man been doing? He hadn't contacted Margo, that was for sure. "I'd like to know what your plans are."

"Plans?"

"For getting her out."

He set his briefcase on a chair and his coat over the back. "I didn't know Field

Ops had assigned anyone to the case."

Jake shifted uncomfortably. Connelly had a reputation for going over the line, but who knew how real that was? And how he'd react when the line someone went over was him. "I'm not exactly what you'd call . . . assigned. Not officially."

One eyebrow shot up from behind the glasses, but he didn't order Jake out, which was encouraging.

"Let's say I'm a party of interest."

"Whose interest?"

Jake hesitated, not sure how much he should say, even to the head of DCO. But he didn't have much choice. Not if he was going to get Margo some help. "Frank Temple, sir."

A tiny pause. "Frank is dead."

"Yes, sir. But before he died he asked me to look out for Ms. Scott."

The eyes behind the glasses blinked once. "He did?"

"Yes, sir."

The eyes narrowed. "Look out *for* her? Or watch her."

Here came the tricky part. "I . . . I'm not sure. Frank didn't say. He put me on a round-the-clock. But she's your agent, sir."

"If she's my agent, you shouldn't know about it."

"No, sir. I don't."

He checked his watch. "Are we finished, then?" He moved toward the door, but Jake got in his way.

"She needs help."

"If that's what you're here for, you're wasting your time. And mine. If Ms. Scott did work for me, and I'm not saying she did, she hasn't for six weeks."

Now it was Jake's turn to be surprised. "Sir?"

"We're only human, son. Sometimes we break."

Jake shook his head. "I'm sorry. Still not computing here."

"Have you ever met anyone who went rogue? Broke off contact with their handlers and went out on their own?"

"That's not the case here."

"I understand Ms. Scott's having trouble with her memory."

He gave Jake a deeply direct look. Jake couldn't deny the implication.

"If Frank Temple asked you to watch her, it wasn't because she needed protecting. Believe me, son, she's a danger to herself and others. She's better off where she is. Excuse me." He stepped aside and headed for the door.

Jake heard Connelly through a rising

film of anger that pushed him to raise his voice. "If something happened to her," he called, speaking to Connelly's back, "if, as you said, she broke, it started in Spain. With orders you gave."

Slowly, Connelly turned.

"You can't abandon her," Jake said.

Connelly's small, unassuming face sharpened. "What do you know about Spain?"

"Enough. I spoke with Carns."

"Agent Carns is dead."

"What?" That shook him. He remembered the hospital and his promise to Carns to get him out. But when he attempted to notify the proper authorities, he found that Margo had already done it when she made her deal with Petali. He'd imagined Carns already healing in some high-tech burn center at Walter Reed. "When?"

"He died en route from Europe two days ago."

"Jesus Christ." He ran a hand through his hair.

"When did you speak with him?"

"Last week."

"You were with Ms. Scott in Spain?"

"I told you, she was my assignment."

"Unofficially. And from a dead man."

"Yes, but —"

"Look, I have to go. You don't keep the secretary of defense waiting. But come back in the morning. We'll talk more then." He clapped Jake on the back. "We'll see what we can do for Ms. Scott."

Connelly had handed Jake a seed of hope. Now he only had to figure out how to make it grow.

55

At two in the morning, though, Jake and hope seemed to be on the outs. The Seville shooter was alive, and Jake had put in a call to Luca Petali to see what he knew, but the cop wasn't there. So Jake sprawled against the headboard in his motel room and kept himself conscious with coffee and a Snickers while he waited for Petali to call back.

Which was why he was awake when the two men burst into his room. Instantly he recognized the assailants: Glasses and No Glasses. Come to play another set.

Jake surged to his feet. "How the hell do you guys get around?" he muttered.

Glasses roared, and Jake met him with a quick right to the face. He went flying.

The fight lasted minutes that slow-motioned into hours, but when it was over, Glasses lay slumped on the floor, his head cracked against the door, and No Glasses sprawled in a pool of blood, Jake's Night Raider sticking out from his chest.

Breathing like a son of a bitch, Jake

wiped sweat and blood off his face.

Glasses seemed out for the count, but Jake tied him up anyway. By the time he'd finished, his own breathing approached something near normal. He slipped out the door and into the night.

Scanning the parking lot, he scoped out the place for a third man. None appeared. The lot was quiet; cars sat still as corpses.

Jake slid into his Expedition and headed out of the parking lot. The new tires rode smoothly, but the fight had taken a toll on his healing ribs and the car ride didn't help. Cursing, he parked in the shadows across the street from the motel and took out his cell phone. He didn't like to think what he was thinking, but the cards were stacking up. And the hand he'd been dealt sucked.

A weary voice answered his call. "Brewster."

"I got more bodies for you, Sammy."

"Who is this?"

"Jake Wise. Econo Lodge in Arlington. Room 12A."

Jake waited in his car for Brewster to arrive. He watched the big man go inside the motel room, gave him a couple of minutes to assess the situation, and called him again.

"I've got your back, Brewster. If you want to know all the ins and outs, I'll pick you up."

"Looks like a nice little prizefight in here."

"I do my best to entertain the troops."

"Pretty impressive. Not much call for lawyers in the ring these days."

"Well, I'm not a lawyer."

"Yeah, I'm beginning to get that."

"Look, I'll spill my guts, but only to you."

"You know I can't do that."

"We're talking national security here, Sammy. Trust me, you're not going to want a crowd. Not until you evaluate what I have to say. Check the desk. I left the gun there. The knife's, well, you know where the knife is. I'm not armed, and I need your help."

Samuel Brewster was not a gambling man. He was careful and cautious. He liked to spend his day putting one foot in front of another. No fancy steps. Trusting Jake Wise was a wildly complex move.

But Sam was curious.

Margo Scott was some kind of big-shot federal agent. He still hadn't worked out what kind, and she wasn't doing too much talking. But no one else was either. He'd had his fill of top secret and classified and being shoved around.

They had a nice case against Scott, maybe too nice.

It was two in the morning, his shift started in a few hours, and it was his turn to take Samuel Junior to school. He was working five other cases, and it would be a real pleasure to sink this one. A hook shot into the basket. Clean, finished. Another win for the home team.

He looked around the motel room. The EMTs would be here soon. The tied-up guy stirred, muttered something in a foreign language.

Allah? Did he say something about Allah?

Sam sighed, not at all happy. The last thing he needed was to catch another round of national security shit.

Sirens sounded in the distance.

He waited for them to get there, then slipped away to meet Jake.

Jake picked Brewster up on the northwest corner. He drove off and kept them moving.

Brewster glanced over at him, then back at the windshield. "So I'm here. What's the big news?"

"You know Bill Connelly?"

"There's a Billy Connelly runs a gas station in Brookland. That him?"

"No. This one runs black ops for TCF. He's Margo's boss."

Jake pulled onto 395 and headed toward Baltimore. The road was wide and clear of heavy traffic, the darkness pierced by streetlamps that lit the pavement but didn't penetrate the shoulder. It gave him the kind of privacy he needed.

Brewster said nothing until Jake was on the interstate. Then, as if the highway gave him permission, he spoke. "You telling me that Margo Scott is a deep secret undercover killer for the USA? Not exactly a recommendation."

"I went to see Connelly. He thinks she's gone rogue. You know, off the charts."

"Well, considering what she's accused of, that scans real nicely for me."

Despite Brewster's skepticism, Jake plowed on. "A few hours after my meeting with Connelly, a couple of foreign nationals show up in my room."

"Yeah, I saw how you treat your guests."

"These same foreign nationals showed up at a TCF safe house a couple of weeks ago looking for Margo."

Brewster flashed him an interested look.

"I take it they didn't find her."

"You remember that fender bender I told you about?"

"That was them?"

"That was them."

"I never did buy that story," Brewster mused. "So you're telling me these . . . foreign nationals are Connelly's goons?"

"Feels that way to me."

Brewster shrugged. Once again, he didn't seem to be buying what Jake was selling. "Well, they attacked you before. Maybe they just wanted to finish the job."

"No, you see, here's the thing. They weren't after me that time. They were looking for Margo. Tonight, they were after me."

"And the difference is your meeting with Connelly."

"Pretty big coincidence. I'm not a fan of coincidence. You?"

Brewster shook his head. "Nah, not so much. But why would Connelly set you up? Why would he set Scott up?"

"He sent her on a real dirty job, then denied it. Said she'd acted on her own. But I talked with someone else who was there with her. It was clear they were acting under his orders."

"Who's this someone?"

"Doesn't matter. He's dead."

"Convenient."

"Look, I need a way to pressure Connelly. I can't go through channels. He's too high up. I need some other kind of leverage."

"And what's all this got to do with me?"

"I want you to let me break Margo out of jail."

56

The corrections officer came for Margo just after breakfast and before her daily round of latrine cleanup had begun.

"Looks like they're going to certify you today," the guard said, supervising the cuffing of her hands and the shackles around her legs.

Margo looked at her. Her name, CROSSCOX, was pinned to her massive chest. A big-boned woman, she seemed like someone who should be hauling steel into a semi.

"You are crazy, ain't you?" Crosscox grinned. Her hard eyes had a hint of meanness to them, but Margo was already getting used to that.

"Yeah. Probably." She wished. Crazy was the easy explanation. How could she have killed a child otherwise? Knowing what she now knew about herself, she'd be surprised if she wasn't certifiable.

"Well, they'll stamp your forehead and make it legal."

She led Margo through the cellblock,

going a hair faster than Margo could keep up with her feet chained together. The shuffle and hop she had to maintain sent the links into a clanking frenzy, an audible reminder of the debt she owed and could never repay.

They slowed at a door for some official paperwork dance, then out to a loading dock where a couple of vans and other guards with sidearms and rifles were waiting.

"Scott," Crosscox announced. "Psych evaluation." One of the guards pointed down the way to the last vehicle.

They hustled her up a ramp and into the yawning mouth at the back of the van. Guards bolted her chains to the floor and her hands to rings on the interior wall. The door slammed shut behind her, and a few minutes later the van took off.

She leaned her head back and closed her eyes, swaying with the movement of the transport. She should have been grateful for the break in routine, but like everything else in the past few days, she made herself numb to the feeling. What was the point in feeling anything if all you felt was sick with guilt?

Twenty minutes later, the van stopped. She wondered vaguely what hospital they'd taken her to. Maybe they'd shoot her full of Thorazine. It would be nice to float away on a drug-induced fog.

The van door opened and someone came in. The driver, she presumed, but didn't bother checking. The bolt holding the leg irons to the floor was released.

Not very smart. One kick and she could take the guy out.

But she didn't move. She sat passively, waiting for him to release her hands.

Instead, he spoke. "You ever been psyched out?"

She stilled. That voice. It shattered her carefully controlled indifference.

She groaned. "What are you doing here, Jake?"

"The Brittany-Jennifer maneuver."

She opened her eyes. He was standing over her, keys in hand.

"You know — Brittany and Jennifer want to spend the night with their boyfriends, so they tell their parents they're staying at each other's houses."

She cocked her head, frowned. "Come again?"

He gave her a patient, long-suffering look. "The jail thinks you're being transferred to the hospital for a special top secret psych evaluation. The hospital thinks the jail canceled your appointment." He grinned and shook a scolding finger at her. "Bad behavior." And reached for the handcuffs.

She jerked away. As much as she could jerk, given she was locked in. "Cut it out."

Without missing a beat, he proceeded to unlock the cuffs. "You're not going to be difficult, are you?" He pulled her to her feet.

"I thought we cleared this up. I'm doing what I need to do. I'm not running."

"You *are* going to be difficult. Shit."

The last thing she saw was his fist flying at her chin.

Margo had no idea how long she'd been out, but she woke in her bed at Aunt Frances's house.

No, not her bed.

And not Aunt Frances's house.

The chasm inside her yawned wider, and she closed her eyes, willing it away. She had to get out of there. The place, just being there, made her skin crawl. She tried sitting up, but something clanked and pulled her back.

Her ankle.

It was cuffed to the foot of the bed.

"Jake!" she howled, fury and frustration making her roar.

Instantly, he appeared in the doorway. "Right here, sleepyhead."

She growled. Her jaw ached from his punch, and he was grinning. "What do you think you're doing?"

"Giving you what you want. Justice."

Uh-huh. "Unlock this." She shook her leg and the cuff scraped her skin.

He shook his head. "I don't think so."

"Dammit! Let me go!"

"No can do."

"Why not?"

"Because Brewster's put his ass on the line for you. Not to mention me and my ass, which are already hung out to dry."

God, could the man never answer a question straight up? "What are you talking about?"

He told her about his meeting with Connelly, the subsequent attack at his motel, and his deal with Brewster.

"You know, you're the one who needs a psych evaluation. Why would Connelly kill Frank?"

"I don't know yet. I'm hoping he'll tell us."

She looked at him like he was crazy. No, he *was* crazy. "You're kidding, right?"

Jake shook his head and raised a finger in a gesture for her to hold her argument.

He took out his phone, punched in a number. "This is Jake Wise." He gave his ID code in a fast, agitated voice. "I have to speak to Deputy Director Connelly. It's urgent. Tell him it's about our previous meeting. He'll understand."

In the pause while he waited for Connelly to pick up, Margo said, "What are you d—"

But Jake held up that finger again and spoke into the phone. "Yes, sir. About that person we discussed. She's out, sir. Of jail. Escaped. No, I don't know the particulars. Police are looking for her, but yes, sir, I agree. Be better for us to find her. Especially after our last conversation about how she could be, well" — he looked over at her, his eyes amused — "a danger. I've got a few ideas, places she might hide out. No. No one else. And sir —" He lowered his voice. "Been having a little trouble myself. Last night at the motel. Don't know if it's connected, but I'm keeping a low profile. I'd appreciate your keeping this close to the vest for a few days. Just you and me. Yes, sir, I got it. Private line — 555–7600. As soon as I know something."

He disconnected and gave a little tight-lipped whoop. "I knew that bastard was dirty."

"Private line?"

"He would never have agreed to keep it secret if he was for real."

"He'd go through channels."

"That's right. Even the DCO has channels. And Connelly's only deputy director."

She let out a huge breath. "Okay. So now what? We just . . . sit around and wait?"

He grinned. "Well, I have to catch you first. Might take a few hours."

57

Jake waited until dark to contact Connelly, figuring the night might be more conducive to confession. Plus he needed time to make sure all the equipment was in place and working. So he arranged to hand Margo over to Connelly at the Foxhall Road house at midnight.

Ten minutes prior, the motion detector Jake had rigged to go off if anyone breached the surveillance room beeped.

Jake listened to the sound over the wireless earpiece he wore. "He's here," he whispered into the hidden microphone. As arranged, he began pacing back and forth in the front entry, giving Connelly — who would soon be able to check everyone's position on the monitors — what Jake hoped was a picture of anxious waiting.

"You called that right." From her post upstairs in the bedroom, Margo's voice sounded grim in his ear.

He'd told her about the black hole in the surveillance tape on the night of Frank's murder, the hole that had given her a potential opportunity to sneak out and kill him. Jake had always wondered it if had been tampered with.

"At least now we've confirmed that Connelly is familiar with the house and the surveillance setup."

Brewster broke in, his voice inside Jake's head tinny over the transmission from the van parked across the street.

"Lights out at the front door, and" — he paused — "at the bedroom."

A small beat of satisfaction: as hoped, Connelly had taken the cameras off-line. It was the signal to go dark. The signal to begin.

Jake removed the earpiece and stuffed it in his pocket. He checked the setup once more. The dim lights gave the illusion of stealth, and as promised, the door was unlocked. A quick glance in the corners told him the tiny webcams secreted there, the ones broadcasting to Brewster out in the van, were on. He pictured Margo removing the cuff around her ankle and getting into position behind the door.

Christ, she'd better stick to the plan. He thought about the last woman who hadn't followed the rules. He'd personally checked the route Danika was supposed to take and assured her of its safety. She'd kissed his cheek and told him not to worry. Then she took the road she'd wanted to take all along, the alternate route that allowed her to check on a comrade she'd been worried about. She never arrived. She was dead before word even came down that her car had been ambushed. It took him six months and Frank's help to track down the bastards who'd done it. Fat lot of good it had done Dani.

He'd be damned if he'd be left with nothing but a body again.

Mouth dry and heart pumping, he positioned himself at the foot of the stairs. The door cracked open, and Connelly entered. He wore a tan raincoat over a rumpled suit, one that had seen better days.

The only greeting he gave Jake was a terse nod. "Where is she?" His tone was furtive. Behind the brown rims of his glasses, sharp eyes scanned the interior.

Jake had to admire the man's gall. Having just come from the surveillance room, Connelly knew full well where Margo was. But he was playing the game as though he'd just arrived. Jake did the same, thumbing over his shoulder and pitching his voice equally low. "Upstairs."

"Secured?"

"Got her cuffed to the bed. Had to

knock her out, sir. You were right. She's something wild."

Tight-lipped, Connelly pushed past Jake and began to climb. He didn't rush, but trudged the stairs with slow deliberation. If Jake didn't know better he would have sworn the man was about to be browbeaten. He looked small and weak on the stairs. Defeated.

And man, did he use it. How many times had an enemy lost because he'd underestimated him? It gave Connelly a great tactical advantage. Jake reminded himself that Connelly had just come from disabling every scrap of audio and video in the place. Whatever he looked like, he was hardly beaten. Yet.

With that cautious thought, he made to follow, but Connelly forestalled him.

"I appreciate the excellent work, Agent. I can take it from here."

"But sir —"

Connelly gave him that hard stare again, and despite appearances to the contrary, waited with authority for Jake to obey. He took his foot off the steps and backed away.

"Thank you," Connelly said with a grim nod. Then he pulled a gun from his raincoat pocket and fired at Jake. Point-blank. In the chest.

The impact threw Jake against the door. Shock and pain ricocheted through him. For a blurred minute, his eyes met Connelly's. The man looked . . . satisfied.

Then the world went black, and Jake saw nothing more.

From her position behind the bedroom door, Margo jumped at the sound of the shot. Icy fear washed over her and she gripped the weapon she held even tighter. Oh, God, had everything backfired? She should never have agreed to Jake's asinine plan. Never.

A beat of pure, agonizing silence ensued.

Then the stairs creaked again with the weight of footsteps. Ignoring the sweat pooling beneath her arms, she closed her eyes and strained to listen.

The footsteps came closer. Halted.

Slowly, the door swung open.

From the doorway, an arm shot out, a gun gripped in the hand. Shots ripped into the form lying on the bed, making it jump and dance.

Margo's stomach heaved and she bit down on her lip to keep from crying out. That was supposed to be her exploding on the mattress, not a pile of blankets and sheets.

The firing stopped.

Bill Connelly stepped into the room, walked to the bed and into Margo's line of sight. Jake had described him, but she still wasn't prepared for how unassuming he appeared. If he hadn't just shot the living hell out of what should have been her body, she might not have believed him capable of it. Appearances aside, she wasted little time disbelieving her own eyes.

She shoved her gun in his back. "Put down the gun, Mr. Connelly." He stopped short. "No, don't turn around. Just stay where you are." She relieved him of his weapon.

"Nice to see you again, Margo," he said.

"Not alive, I'll bet."

58

Margo took out Jake's handcuffs and shackled Connelly to the bedstead, his arms wrenched painfully behind him.

"We could . . . talk about this," Connelly proposed as calmly as if he were negotiating a bar bill.

"I'm sure we'll be doing a lot of talking before the night is over."

They'd set up Margo's computer and now she typed in a few commands. Connelly watched with an expressionless face as the scene played out on the monitor: himself shooting a federal agent for no cause at point-blank range.

The broadcast stopped. Silence held the room.

"What do you want?" Connelly asked at last.

"I've downloaded everything to disc. You tell me about Frank Temple, and I'll make sure no one ever sees it."

"What exactly do you think I know?"

"Who killed him."

His mouth curled into a small,

knowing smile. "I thought you did."

"Then why can't I remember?"

"You're having a nervous breakdown."

A small flag of fear unfurled inside her. What if he was right?

She opened the drawer on the desk and retrieved the cell phone she'd placed there earlier. "I've got Detective Brewster on speed dial. Have you met Detective Brewster? He's working on Frank Temple's murder. I'm sure he'd love to throw you and your little killing spree into the mix." She punched in a key.

"Wait."

She glanced at him. He gave her a tiny nod of acquiescence. She put down the phone.

"So . . ." She crossed her arms and drilled him with an uncompromising look. "Do you know who killed Frank?"

"Yes."

She waited. The moment stretched interminably, the end of her agony in sight. But when he spoke, he merely said, "Do you know how long you've worked for me?"

"What does that have to do with —"

"Six years," Connelly said. "Though you were Frank's before that."

She thought of the picture. Her arms

around Frank Temple's neck. She straightened. "What do you mean, I was Frank's?"

"His little protégé." A light emphasis of scorn coated the last word. "His little rescue mission."

"Rescue from what?"

"A life without purpose."

She stared at him, uncomprehending.

"It was his standard recruitment tool," Connelly continued blandly. "He looked for young men and women at a crossroads. People with skills but no goals. Restless people. Rootless. Maybe with a bit of idealism left. People, for example, whose hitch in the military was almost up."

"People like . . . me."

"He plucked you out of nowhere, made you feel special, trained you, and set you on a path of his choosing."

"I have no military record."

"A small adjustment we made when you came to work for us. You were scrubbed — your records eliminated — so there's no trace of your previous life."

She watched him closely, but he didn't flinch, and the explanation made sense. "If Frank and I were so close, why was I working for you?"

He shrugged. "We had a job that required an edged-weapons specialist. You were one of the best I'd ever seen with a knife. And you always went for the kill. Frank agreed to lend you out."

Edged-weapons specialist.
Went for the kill.

She felt hollow, the words echoing deep, confirming what she already knew, but dreaded, about herself. "And I never went back?"

"Some people like wearing the mask. Gives them a reason to keep their distance."

Inside, the dread deepened. "Drifters you mean. Loners."

Rootless. The word ricocheted inside her head.

"Whatever. I'm not a psychiatrist. You stayed. That's all I know."

She scowled at him. "Why should I believe you?"

"I don't care whether you do or you don't."

He spoke with utter calm and certainty. The lack of emotion behind the glasses, neither regret nor triumph, was unsettling.

She hardened her tone. "What does this have to do with Frank Temple's murder?"

"He died because he was protecting you."

"Protecting me from what?"

"Your own stupidity."

The baldness of that statement silenced them both for a moment. Then Connelly continued, "I wasn't lying when I said you were having a breakdown. The Spanish fiasco was . . . difficult. Two agents lost, hostages killed. When you turned up, you were shaken to the core. You threatened to go public." He shifted his position, winced at the pain of the cuffs. "I couldn't let you do that."

"Go public?"

"*Larry King, Meet the Press,* the *Washington Post.* We live and die by our secrets, and you wanted to tell all. It would have been a feeding frenzy."

Something clicked inside her head, and she saw herself tearing through a mound of newspapers. My God, was that why she'd been so obsessed? Not because she was hunting for a story, but because she had one to tell?

She rounded on him, her voice tight and hard. "You didn't want me to tell the world that you ordered the execution of an innocent twelve-year-old."

"There are no innocents in war."

"That's a load of crap. You gave an illegal order, and you know it."

"Yes, I've had this argument before. With you, with Frank. He swore he could convince you to keep quiet, but I believe in facts, not promises. The scandal would have been fatal for the department and the agency. For the country."

"For you."

"Oh, yes, for me as well. Quite, quite fatal. Whatever hopes I had of promotion, of running the agency or a political appointment would be shattered. If the story had broken it would have been worse than Abu Ghraib. Those were adult prisoners. This was —"

"— a child."

"Indeed. I felt it my duty to make sure you didn't talk to the media."

"By killing Frank?"

"By killing you, my dear."

His words floated in the air between them. Once more the picture of her and Frank rose in her head. The happiness on her face as she hugged Frank Temple. Not her lover or her uncle. Her friend. A wave of sadness washed over her.

Angrily she asked, "Then why didn't you leave Frank out of it?"

"He had a . . . a fondness for you. Emotion can be crippling in our business. Frank could not bring himself to do the hard thing. He had a long career and a lot of personal power. He could have stopped me, and I couldn't allow that."

Unthinking, she slammed his face with the back of her hand. "You bastard."

"Yes." He'd barely flinched.

They stared at each other. Margo was breathing hard. Connelly didn't seem to be breathing at all.

"What about Suzanne?"

His expression barely changed. "Suzanne?"

"You don't even know who I'm talking about, do you?"

"Enlighten me."

"Suzanne. The woman they found dead in my office. You do that, too?"

"The deal was information on Frank in exchange for the destruction of the disc. I've given you what you want."

She slugged him again, and his head snapped back.

"Tell me about Suzanne."

The eyes behind the glasses grew cold, reptilian.

Her hands twitched. She wanted to wrap them around his throat and . . .

She changed the subject. "What happened to my memory?"

He continued mute. She aimed his gun at him and growled. "My memory, you piece of shit."

The eyes remained chilled and hard. He said nothing.

She shot him in the shoulder. A nice piece of fleshy meat that would hurt like hell and not do too much damage.

He screamed in pain, his composure lost for the first time. Glaring at her, he spit. "Shoot me again; I'm sure you'll enjoy it. You've spent your professional life hurting, maiming, killing. Little girl is just coming home."

The words were meant to dig deep and she knew it. But it didn't stop them from sinking their sharp teeth into her.

She stepped back, ashamed. Lowered the gun.

Through the pain, he gave her another tight smile. "So . . . we are done here. You've had your little bout of physical aggression. You have what you want. Destroy the disc."

"Oh, I'll do that." Jake waltzed into the room, cutting Connelly a razor-edged look. "Be happy to." She handed him the disc, which he sliced in two with a pair of heavy-duty shears. "There you go." He tossed the pieces at Connelly. "Sir."

Connelly sat stoically as the edges of the disc hit him in the face and dropped to the floor.

Jake wiggled a finger through the hole in his shirt. "You know, that hurt," he said reproachfully.

"I'm just sorry it didn't hurt more," Connelly said. He didn't like being tricked. Who did?

Jake wagged a finger at him. "You are not a nice man."

He stripped off the shirt to reveal the vest beneath, then stripped that off as well. He went to the mirror over the dresser and fingered the red, raw place on his chest where the bullet had had the most impact. "Christ almighty," he said to Margo, "since I met you I've had more aches and pains . . ."

She snorted. "You're just damn lucky he didn't shoot you in the head."

59

Jake slipped Margo back into jail the next morning, the Brittany-Jennifer maneuver working like a charm.

As for Connelly, they'd planned to let him stew while Margo was returned to jail, but the bullet in his shoulder botched that. Brewster picked him up immediately.

It took a couple of days to get Margo released, and though she wanted to be grateful, she was too busy feeling at sea. The words Connelly had said about her echoed over and over again.

Loner. Rootless. A life without purpose until Frank Temple taught her how to kill.

Little girl is just coming home.

She remembered the neighbors who didn't know her. Remembered the bartender saying she never came in with anyone. Remembered the unsettled feeling when Jake got too close.

She'd had a life filled with masks. With hiding. Covering up what she did and who she was. No one knew her. Not even herself.

It made her skin crawl.

And it didn't stop the nightmares. Or the child screaming in her head.

The boy. The boy she'd executed. On orders.

The self-loathing was so vicious, she had to scour herself of all emotion just to function. And even so, it was hard getting up in the morning. Every day she had to break through the black net holding her down. She'd crawl up out of sleep, punching at the darkness with weak fists, craving to stay buried in the shadows.

So when Jake told her he'd set up a visit with Connelly, she was reluctant to go.

"He's holding something back."

"I don't care." They were supposed to be having breakfast. Jake had barged in with a dozen eggs, dragged her out of bed, and made coffee. She didn't have the energy to tell him she wasn't hungry, only pushed the eggs around on her plate.

"You don't want your memory back?"

"What am I going to learn except more about the heartless bitch I am?"

"Margo —" Jake reached out for her, and she jumped up.

"Don't."

He leaned back in the chair, eyes narrowed, and stared at her. "Don't what? Touch you? Comfort you?"

"All of the above."

"I saved —"

"My ass. I know. You never stop reminding me."

He gave her a penetrating glance, which she did her best to avoid. "TCF wants me back in Manhattan," he said at last.

"So go."

His eyes refused to quit. She went into the kitchen and pretended to pour a cup of coffee, but her hands were shaking so much she had to set the cup down.

Jake came up behind her, gently gripped her shoulders. "I don't want to go."

She jerked out from under his touch. God, he was everywhere. "Leave me alone. I don't need you to hold my hand."

"Maybe I want to hold your hand."

And that was the problem, wasn't it? He was the only living creature she had any attachment to, and she wanted to cling to him like Krazy Glue.

But how could she trust that any of the feelings were real? And if they were, how could she figure out who she was, who she wanted to be, if he was always there to cushion her fall?

And more than that, much, much more than that, was the deep-seated feeling that she didn't deserve him. Not now. Not ever.

So she whipped around, gave him a little push, and strode past him. "You don't get it, do you? I've tried being polite, tried not rubbing your nose in it, but here's the thing, Jake" — she wheeled around, gave him her deadliest look — "I don't need you. I don't want you. We're over."

For half a second he looked stunned. Then the sly look was back in his face. "Over?" He pointed between the two of them. "You and me?"

"Read my lips."

"I'm trying to, but I keep wanting to do something else with them."

God, was the man never serious about anything? She inhaled a shaky breath; this was going to be harder than she thought. But she strengthened her resolve and spit it out. "I look at you, and all I think about is how screwed up everything is. You remind me of the worst part of myself. The worst. It makes me sick looking at you."

"I make you sick," he said mildly.

"That's right."

He nodded thoughtfully. "I don't think so, Scottie. I think it's you making yourself sick."

"You see? That's it. That pitiful psychobabble. That's exactly why you need to leave. Now." She marched to the front door and yanked it open.

He followed more slowly and slammed it shut. Then he slouched against it in that lazy, sexy way, crossed his feet and examined the floor, not her. "You know, I read Cahill's file." He looked at her from under his brows. As if what he said wasn't all that important. As if *she* wasn't all that important. "Can't get much worse than him. He's a murderer and a traitor."

She struggled with her patience. She wanted this over with. Now. "Cahill. Not his wife. Or his kids."

"Sometimes it's not what's right or wrong, it's what's more right, less wrong."

"That's a pretty fine wire you're balanced on."

"You did what you had to."

"Now you sound like Connelly."

He threw up his hands. "Hey, I'm just trying to help you come to terms with it."

"I don't want your help!" she shouted.

The noise seemed to penetrate. He straightened, gave her another of those eerie, piercing glances — as though he saw right through her to the lie on her soul — and said, "Well then, no point hanging around. I mean, if you're going to heave all over the place. Been there. Done that."

He walked out. Closed the door behind him and left.

That night he called, and she let it ring. He called again in the morning, and again she let it ring. To keep herself strong, she deleted all his messages without listening to them.

A week later he called one final time, and it was all she could do not to answer it. She tried deleting the message, but her fingers wouldn't punch in the buttons. Weak and stupid, she let herself hear his voice one last time. He'd been assigned a case, the message said, and would be out of the country for a while.

He didn't say where he was going; if she could, she wouldn't have asked. But deep inside, she felt bereft. The last cable tying her to earth had snapped.

Two weeks later, she surfed up from a drug-induced sleep to the sound of the phone ringing. Her body felt heavy, slug-gish, the Ambien still floating in her system. Ambien. A guilty conscience's best friend.

Fumbling for the handset, she noticed it was almost two in the afternoon. She scrubbed her face to try to get some life into it and answered the call. It was Brewster. She hadn't heard from him in weeks, hadn't expected to, and if she could find the energy she would have been surprised.

"Something wrong?"

"Don't think so," Brewster said. "How about your end? That lawyer friend of yours still treating you right?"

She stiffened, made sure the pang of loss stayed deep below the surface. "Jake's gone."

"Gone? That boy left you?"

With rigid determination, she clutched the handset, keeping thought and feeling under strict control. "He went back to work."

"I always knew he was a son of a bitch."

Despite her resolve to stay detached, she couldn't let Sam get away with that. "Not fair, Sam."

"Why? You give him a nice big push?"

"I didn't stand in his way, if that's what you mean."

"Hmm."

She yawned brutally. The day was half over, and she didn't want to think about what she would do with the rest of it except pop another Ambien and go back to sleep. "Is there a purpose to this call, or did you just get the urge to play big daddy?"

"Well, I suppose you could say I had an ulterior motive."

"Get on with it, then."

He paused, and she wondered if he was searching for the best way to say whatever he needed to say. "Sam, I'm dying here."

That got him off the pot. "Connelly cut a deal," he said.

"Big surprise."

"He agreed to cooperate fully in exchange for taking the death penalty off the table. He's been talking up a storm."

"I'm not interested in anything that s.o.b. has to say."

As if he didn't believe her, Brewster plowed on. "He planted that nine we found in your office. The one we matched to the slug we took out of Temple. Your friend, Ms. DeForrest, caught him snooping there. That's why he took her out."

Pain ripped through Margo. Unexpected and unfettered, it broke through the fog. Suzanne. Dead. Her fault. Suzanne never would have believed the world would hurt her. All it took was being her friend. She fisted her free hand around a glob of blankets and squeezed until she could breathe again.

"You okay?"

She swallowed hard. "Uh-huh."

"And there's something else," Brewster said. "You remember Warner Park?"

Her mind fought to change course. Clicked. "The place on the back of the business card?"

"It's not a place."

"It's not a . . . what do you mean?"

"It's a person."

"What?"

"Some cold-war buddy of Temple's, turns out. Specialized in psychological warfare, chemical mind-fucking, stuff like that."

Her skin went cold.

"You still there?" Brewster asked.

"Uh-huh." Though she could barely get the response out. Why was the news always bad?

"Look, I spoke with the man. He won't confirm or deny his involvement, but I got the feeling he's the one responsible for whatever happened to your memory."

Silence stretched like a black hole, sucking in everything in its wake.

"I take it you're not jumping for joy," Brewster said. "I'm sorry, I thought you'd be —"

"Got an address?" She cut the sympathy short, unable to deal with kindness. Not now.

She agreed to meet Warner Park a week later at what used to be a pharmaceutical lab. The lab was pushed into a forgotten section of the tech corridor around Dulles, a hurriedly built, low-slung complex of buildings that was only half filled.

Margo pulled into the compound and stopped at the top of the drive, staring at the buildings. Had she been there before? What had she thought? Felt? Did she know what they were going to do to her?

She tried to picture the place. Test tubes and microscopes? Gurneys with IV stands? Mobile surgical units? Had they cut up her head? They'd have to cut something to implant the transmitter. Instinctively, she reached around and felt the place where the device had been. But it didn't help her remember how it got there. She wracked her brain and came up with nothing. Absolutely nothing but sweat and the shakes.

From a distance a siren sounded. Seconds later a fire engine charged toward her, clanging and wailing. Flashes of memory erupted. The blur of bodies, the smell of smoke. The child's scream reverberated, high and terrified, mingling with the air horn. Get out of the way! Get out of the way! With a wrench on the steering wheel, she turned and fled.

It took her another week to gather her courage again. This time, she made it down to the parking lot. Heart pounding, she gripped the steering wheel and gazed at the building entrance as though it were the doorway to hell.

Did she really want to remember? What if every memory was drenched in blood and the shrieks of suffering people?

She was so focused on ramping up for the trip inside she didn't see the man come around the back of the car to the passenger side.

The door opened and she jumped a mile.

Jake slid in.

Breathless with fear, she stared at him, disbelieving her eyes.

He waved at her. "Hey."

When she finally managed to find her voice, she stumbled over the words. "How . . . what are you —"

"Doing here?" He shrugged. "Heard you needed company."

Her vision blurred, but she steeled the emotion away. She swallowed. "How did you . . ."

"Find you?" He cocked his head, the

corners of his mouth twitching up. "Would you believe telepathy?"

She shook her head, but that loosened the tears she was trying so hard to repress. One leaked down her cheek.

Jake reached over and caught it. "Park called Brewster when you didn't show last time. Brewster called me."

"I thought . . . I thought you were out of the country."

"I was." He cupped her cheek with his hand, his touch soft and inviting. "I'm back."

"But I said . . ."

"Yeah, I know what you said. You didn't think I bought all that crap, did you?"

And then, somehow, she was in his arms.

"I'm so scared." She burrowed into his neck. His arms felt so good. Strong and steady.

"I know." He held her tight. "I know."

60

Warner Park proved to be a bent, grizzled man with fuzzy white hair in a dark blue suit that hung on his thin body. Despite the white shirt and tie, he hadn't shaved in days; white bristles sprouted over his chin and cheeks. There was something scattered about him, as though he'd left part of himself elsewhere and was constantly trying to catch up. But he smiled with almost childlike glee when he saw her.

"Ah, you are here at last." He rubbed his hands together in delight. He had a slight European accent and that plus the hair and the suit gave him the air of a distracted Einstein-turned-grandfather.

"Mr. Park?" Jake kept a protective arm around her, which she sank into when she saw the man who would soon be playing with her mind.

"You do not remember?" he asked Margo.

She shook her head. Her mouth was dry, her tongue and lips glued together.

"Excellent. Excellent!" His smile grew

wider. "You know, my work . . . it has been highly experimental. And, well, all right, I admit it, a teensy bit controversial." He giggled. Was he insane? No, she was the insane one, to let him get anywhere near her head.

But if he sensed her misgivings, he ignored them and chattered on. "To tell the truth, I wasn't sure this would work as well as it has, and I told Frank that. But he can be very persuasive, Frank Temple. And he said it would be only short-term. Of course" — the smile faded and his face sobered — "that did not prove to be the case." A moment of sadness passed between them. Then he clapped his hands together and smiled. "Come, children, we have work to do."

Park led them to a couch with an IV stand beside it and a table with syringes and vials.

Margo blanched, but the sight propelled her into words at last. "What . . . what will you do exactly?"

He explained the procedure, a combination of hypnosis — what he called Neural Linguistic Programming — and thiopental, a truth serum and hypnotic drug. Together they would loosen the synaptic connections that controlled memory and allow him to remove the hypnotic block. He'd work in stages, gradually increasing the chemical load and layering the NLP process.

"I must warn you that the block has been operative for far longer than intended. I can't guarantee everything will return. It will be a gradual process. But we will try, eh?"

He told her to lie down, and gingerly she sat. She was trembling, and Jake squeezed her shoulder. "I'll be right here," he said softly.

She nodded, but couldn't make herself move. What's the worst that could happen? She'd wake up this side of an eggplant, right? She shuddered. No, the worst that could happen was that she'd wake up at all.

And remember.

She took a breath, closed her eyes, and laid back. Terror, icy cold and relentless, rippled through her chest and belly. Jake slipped his hand in hers, and she held on tight as Park rolled up her right sleeve.

This time, the experience stayed with her. The harsh smell of chemicals that lingered in the disused lab. The IV needle sliding under her skin. The cold sensation as the drugs flooded her system. The groggy, dreamlike state they produced. The rhythmic, relentless thrumming of

Park's grandfatherly voice, urging her to remember.

Remember.

The rest was a blur. She knew Jake brought her back to Argyle Towers; she had a vague memory of him carrying her into the apartment, a distant feeling of warmth and safety.

Later, she'd woken with a raging headache, just as she had the first time. Only this time, no one had implanted a posthypnotic suggestion compelling her to go for a run, or do anything else, so she just had to work through the pain. But she wasn't alone. This time, she had Jake. And slowly, agonizingly slowly, her memories.

Some days they came in a rush, flying at her all at once. Her stint in the army, her TCF training, those memories came back like that. Other days, nothing new occurred. Then two days later, she'd smell coffee brewing, and she'd remember something else.

Frank setting the trap for the memory wipe happened like that.

He'd dragged her down to his office. It was late, nine, ten o'clock, and she remembered wondering what he was still doing there.

He'd shoved a cup of coffee in her hand,

and sat her down at his famous round table. "You need to go away for a while," he told her, his big bony hands wrapped around his own coffee cup. "A week," he promised. "Two at the most. Just long enough to keep you out of the picture while I get everything straight with Connelly."

"You don't understand," she'd said, feeling hot and fierce. "I don't want to get anything straight. I want that man's ass burned. Command will never act, and you know it. The only way is to speak out."

And then the wooziness. What had Frank put in her coffee? At least now she knew how he'd gotten her to Warner Park in the first place.

One day, the bulb popped as she turned on a light, and brought back the flash over a camera. And she finally remembered when the picture in Frank's house had been taken. The day she'd finished her training. Frank had run into her in the hallway and asked what she was doing to celebrate. It hadn't occurred to her.

She'd shrugged. "Nothing, I guess."

He'd slung a fatherly arm around her shoulder. "Can't have that, can we?"

He'd taken her to dinner. A real fancy place, too, with a professional photographer who roamed the restaurant and snapped their photo. She hadn't known what had gotten into her, hugging him like that. Like he was a beloved uncle or grandfather.

"You liked him," Jake said when she told him.

Silent understanding passed between them. Frank had been the closest thing to a father either one of them had had. She wasn't sure how she felt about that. He'd been kind to her, and she felt a pull of warmth when she thought of him.

But Frank had also taught her to kill, had helped her become what she was. And that made her want to shrink away.

"I never knew what happened to that picture," she mused. "I'd forgotten all about it. Strange to think of it sitting on Frank's dresser all these years."

Jake squeezed her hand. "Well," he said with that cocky smile, "he was your aunt Frances."

She recalled her sense of her aunt, the vague, hazy pictures she'd thought were memories: tall, bony, beak-nosed. Frank in a dress.

A week after Warner Park worked his little chemical miracle, she returned to the bookstore and made herself stand in the office where Suzanne had died. Her blood

416

still stained the floor. Scattered over the surface, in the corners where they'd rolled, under the chair, at the foot of the file cabinet, sat a series of round beads. Margo picked up a couple of the happy-colored balls. Plastic. With a stem that allowed one to attach to the other. Margo put them together and pulled them apart. What had Suzanne called them?

Poppit beads.

A rust-colored blemish marred the surface of the second bead. She pictured them ripped from Suzanne's neck, bouncing on the floor, stained with her blood. Margo's stomach cramped, but she stood there anyway, making sure the sight would always be etched in her mind.

Later, she roamed the shelves, fingers tracing ancient copies of *Mila 18* and *Rabbit, Run.* The stacks were filled with other dusty books people traded or gave away. Frank had bought the building, store and stock included — when, she didn't know. Only that it was ready years ago when she needed to step inside.

It was still strange to acknowledge that sham. Legacy Books *had* belonged to her aunt. To Frank. It was an agency cover. Her cover.

Buying rare books gave her an excuse to

travel all over the world. And the name was apt. The store was her legacy. A fake business for a fake persona.

Even the books inside the glass case were a sort of counterfeit — real enough, but not for sale. They were carefully collected, illustrated books, mostly for children. And they were hers. Her own personal collection. Why only children's books, she still didn't know, but she got the same comforting feeling holding them that she did with the fairy-tale book in the apartment.

The rest? Bogus.

But the bookstore was just part of what was phony about her. The rest was, too, although she was from St. Louis. When developing a cover it's always good to stick to as much of the truth as possible, Frank always said.

And the truth was, she had no family to speak of. Her father had died a few months before she'd been born, one of the last soldiers killed in Vietnam, so she only had a hazy memory of a stranger in uniform staring out from a photograph with the same dark blue eyes as hers. She didn't know what had happened to that picture. If she'd ever known, the knowledge had disappeared into the still-present fog of forgetfulness.

But she remembered its existence one day out of the blue when she was sitting at Eastlake's, nursing a scotch and waiting for Jake to come back from TCF headquarters.

Days ago, she'd slipped the picture of the woman from the fairy-tale book into her wallet. She found herself taking it out, as she'd done before, staring at it, studying it. She was young and pretty, someone important, someone Margo should know. Sister? Cousin? She shuddered. Victim?

She was fingering the face, rubbing her thumb obsessively over the image. Like a balloon drifting free, her identity suddenly floated up from somewhere deep inside, as if she'd always known it.

Mother. *Mother.*

Then, like an avalanche, the memories crashed down on her. Librarian. Her mother had been a children's librarian. They'd read together at night. To her. With her. Big books with strange, exciting pictures.

She forgot Jake, forgot everything, and raced back to Argyle Towers. She skidded into the bedroom, rammed open the Arthur Rackham book, ripped through the pages. Fairy Lake. God, yes, she remembered that. Those tiny winged creatures fluttering above that dark, mysterious lake.

And Sleeping Beauty. There she was, all somber and asleep, a black throw draped dramatically around her seemingly dead body.

No happy creatures here. All odd fantasy. Dark and weirdly detailed. An entire strange world on a page. They'd talked for hours, she and her mother, about those pictures.

Tears filled Margo's eyes. Her mother had come back to her. God, she remembered. They'd gone for walks in a park, hadn't they? Wasn't there something about monkeys in the zoo? And the art museum. She remembered her footsteps echoing in the art museum. Her mother, Laura. But not Scott. Vaughn. Laura Vaughn.

The name slipped out on a cry, and suddenly Margo remembered everything, including the day her mother died.

Margo had been ten. They'd been in the kitchen, her mother making popcorn, because sometimes they liked to make popcorn for dinner and watch *The Brady Bunch* together. Only this night, her mother turned from the microwave with the bag of popcorn and got a funny, cross-eyed look on her face. She put a hand to her head and the bag dropped from her fingers. It bounced once, twice, popcorn scattering like yellow puffs of air. Her mother staggered and fell like a stone. Margo screamed, but couldn't wake her. No one could wake her.

She closed her eyes. No wonder she couldn't stand the smell of popcorn.

In her head, she heard that scream again, and it was so familiar and so sad. She hugged the fairy-tale book to her. It hadn't been the boy from Spain. That terrified, howling child had never been him.

It was her. That screaming child had been her all along.

She shivered, tears leaking over her face, tears for herself and her lost childhood, tears for the boy whose childhood she'd taken away.

How could she bear it? How could she endure the pain of knowing what she'd done?

And that's how Jake found her, moaning and sobbing.

"Jesus Christ," he said, wrapping her in his arms. "Didn't you hear the phone? I was out of my mind. I thought something had —"

She shuddered with great, wracking sobs. "I remembered, Jake."

"What? That you have a fat husband and two kids somewhere in Delaware? Tell me that's it, and I'll cry, too." He held her tight, stroked the back of her head, and it felt so good to have shelter.

"My mother. I remembered my mother."

He pulled away, cupped her tear-streaked face with his hands and looked at her with great kindness. "Oh, baby, that's good. That's real good."

Under Jake's gentle hands, she managed to calm down, to ease the tears of joy and guilt. She swiped at her eyes. Her whole face felt swollen, the skin tight and dry from crying.

The rest of the story spilled out in stuttered details. After her mother died, her father's sister in Des Moines had taken her in.

"She liked frilly things," Margo said. "Dresses and little white socks with ruffles."

She finished out fourth grade in Iowa then went to her mother's cousin in Florida, who dressed everyone in jeans.

"She had a pool. Other kids. We ate at McDonald's a lot."

"That means you have cousins somewhere, right?"

Cousins. A bright spot opened inside her, but she shut it down. The thought of meeting anyone, telling anyone who she was, what she'd done, made her nervous and queasy.

"How long did you stay there?"

She shook her head. "I don't know. The summer, part of the school year. Then I think there was another cousin. New Jersey. That didn't last very long and after that . . . foster homes."

She learned to be whatever they wanted, whoever they wanted. It was easier that way. And she'd learned not to get too close because she never stayed. She took the fairy-tale book with her everywhere, the one constant in her unstable life. Books were always more reliable than people anyway. Stories never let her down. No matter where she went there was a bookstore or a library. New worlds, better worlds. Her favorites were in easy reach. Suddenly she understood her anonymous donations to the Roland Carroll Children's House.

At eighteen she found the army, maybe following in her father's footsteps, maybe just looking for something, anything, to belong to. Then Frank Temple found her, and suddenly she had a new family.

And now, like her parents, it was gone.

"Only if you want it to be," Jake said. They were side by side on the bed, leaning against the headboard. Jake was holding her hand. He'd held it throughout the entire afternoon while she vomited up the fits and starts of her forgotten life.

She felt the solid strength of his fingers, and not for the first time wondered if she relied on him too much. "I still feel like I belong in jail."

Jake put an arm around her shoulder and pulled her close. "Someone has to do what we do, Margo. You know that. And that means following orders."

She shook her head. "I can't . . . I just can't accept that. I can't even imagine a time when I could."

But clearly there had been a time when she did what she had to, no questions asked. And it had been only a few months ago.

"You still haven't remembered anything about Spain?"

She shook her head. The truth was, she didn't want to remember. She hoped those memories never came back.

"But I did figure out what the last key on my key ring opens."

She'd dropped her purse at the door when she ran in, and now she slipped off the bed, rummaged inside it, and pulled out the keys. Together they unlocked nearly everything about her life: the store, the apartment, the *Don Quixote* box. But there was still one more door that needed opening.

She held them up. "Feel like going for a ride?"

61

Margo took Jake to Old Town, where she parked in front of a row house on Saint Asaph Street that was in bad need of a coat of paint. Four mailboxes hung to the side by the front door, which was a washed-out turquoise.

"And we are . . . ?" Jake asked, looking around. "Looks like a halfway house for college students."

She set the parking brake and turned to gaze over Jake's shoulder at the house. "Didn't you ever wonder why no one found me at Argyle Towers?"

"No," he said with a smug smile. "They weren't as good at dodging and weaving as we were."

"You wish. Connelly knew about the safe house, and he had people watching it. So why not Argyle Towers?"

Jake gave her a thoughtful look. "Because he" — his eyes narrowed — "didn't know about it," he said slowly.

"Give that man a cigar." Margo got out and Jake followed. The step up to the door was a little rickety, the door itself a little sad. After the sleek, clean lines of Argyle Towers, Margo felt disoriented to be staring at it again. As if it represented another life. Another her.

"How'd you remember this place?"

"I was looking through the pictures in the fairy-tale book," Margo said, "and there's one — well, it's a lake, a kind of secret lake where fairies hang out."

Jake quirked a skeptical brow. "Fairies?"

Her face heated. "Don't yank my chain, just listen. The point is the lake was secret. A hidden place. A place only a few creatures knew about. And suddenly, I remembered my own secret place."

Jake looked around. "Here?"

"No, this is where I lived. The secret was Argyle Towers. It's where I went before and after every assignment. To" — she took one of those breaths, as if she needed the extra air to face the past — "to gear up, to prepare myself going in. And to shake it all off coming out."

"A safe house."

She nodded. "It's still a little hazy, but I know I never told anyone about it."

"Not even Frank?"

She shook her head. "There was never any official record of my residence at Argyle Towers."

"Which is why Connelly never found you there."

"That's right."

"So what about this?" Jake indicated the door they were coming to.

She opened it, went left, and stopped at a door labeled B. "This is the apartment everyone knew about." She took out her keys, made to fit one into the lock, but the door swung open without it.

"Damn," Jake said softly.

The place had been ransacked, cushions split, drawers upended, glass smashed.

She smiled bleakly and picked her way in. "Once I remembered this place I suspected they would have been here."

She replaced a cushion on the couch and sat down, studying the mess.

Jake retrieved a framed photograph from the floor and handed it to her. "Who's this?"

The glass was cracked but she could still see the picture clearly. A man in uniform smiled up at her with the same dark blue eyes as hers. "My father." She rubbed her forehead. "I wondered what had happened to this picture."

She examined the photo, feeling nothing but a vague yearning nostalgia, as though she were looking at a museum piece. Depressing, but oddly impersonal. At first, she thought that was just another memory trick, but then she realized it was her true feelings. He'd died before she was born. She'd never known him.

Carefully, she set the picture on one of the empty bookcase shelves. He'd been a soldier at war. Had he done things he was ashamed of? Would he have understood what she'd become? Find a way to explain it to her mother? Margo was glad she'd never know. Hard enough facing her own disappointment, let alone theirs.

Then again, she'd served her country, as her father had. There was honor in that. Why wasn't it enough?

As they cleaned up, other photographs surfaced from the clutter. Her parents together. Her mother with a young Margo. Outside a small house, by a park bench, a birthday party. Silly pictures, mostly, but dear and precious because they were so innocent. And because they gave texture to the life she'd lost.

They spent the rest of the day there, but when the place approached livable again, she realized with sudden, painful insight that she didn't want to stay.

Jake must have seen it on her face. He dumped the last of the debris into one of the garbage bags they'd found under the sink, and straightened. "What's wrong?"

"This." She waved a hand to indicate the apartment.

"Okay, so it could use a damp mop, but —"

"It's the lie, Jake. This place. It's so . . ."

"Normal?"

She nodded. "Like I was normal. A seller of books. Someone who got up in the morning and went to work, came home, went to bed." She looked down at her hands. They were streaked with dirt. A trace of spiderweb had stuck to her thumb. She could remember when they were marked by more gruesome muck. And not for the first time she wished the memories had stayed locked and she was swimming in the dark tunnel again. "But you and I know that never happened. The guns and gear at Argyle Towers, that was the truth. This is just as fake as Legacy Books."

Abruptly, she rose. How many more secrets would come barreling out of her head, ready to knock her down? And when every memory was drained out of her, would she know who she was even then?

"Come on, let's get out of here." She gathered the photos and a handful of books, and ran outside.

"Wait a second," Jake said, hurrying after her. "Where are you going?"

"I don't know." She opened the car door, dumped the books and souvenirs in the backseat. "Mars would be nice. I could start all over on Mars."

She got into the car and gripped the steering wheel. She couldn't wait to get out of there.

Jake had other ideas. He stood outside in the V of the door, leaning against the roof.

"Get in," she called.

"I could take you there," he said. He had an odd, thoughtful expression on his face. "To Mars. My grandfather Wise farmed outside of Dewey. Soybeans. Pigs. The land's rented out, but I still own the house. It's quiet. As close to Mars as you can get without a spaceship."

She searched his face, saw the promise there. A refuge. Far away from the TCF and DCO, the XYZs of her remembered life. A chance to decide what to do next. What life she wanted to lead.

So she packed up the apartment in Argyle Towers. Closed the door on the guns, the gear, and the knives. Jake asked for a short leave to take her to Indiana, found someone in town who would get the

431

farmhouse ready, and by the end of the week, she found herself ensconced in the Wise family farm.

62

The field seemed to stretch for miles, but that was only because the horizon was so low. Margo sat on the steps of the farmhouse's back porch and gazed out at the vast emptiness. She knew what it was like to be cut off from the past. Had it been the same for Jake's ancestors, who came out here when there were no phones, no air transport, no connection to whoever or whatever they'd left behind? The stillness of the flatland could be terrifying. Did they see it that way or did they appreciate it as she did? Because the prairie welcomed her. There were no voices in the emptiness. Only blessed silence.

In the distance a storm was brewing. It hadn't rained in the weeks she'd been there, but now thunderheads gathered, dark and heavy with precipitation.

She went inside where the reports Jake had sent her waited on the kitchen table. They were copies of the depositions associated with the investigation into the DCO's activities. She was finally working her courage up to read what they had on the debacle in Spain. She scanned the pages. Suddenly lightning cracked, followed by a hollow thud of thunder. Isolated and exposed on the prairie, the house shook with the sound. She bent her head, trying to concentrate on the words, but again the weather attacked the house. The snap and crash roared through the walls, ripped through the air, and pierced her skin, her bones, and her soul. Something shifted inside her head.

"Don't hurt him!" she heard a woman scream.

Another lightning flash, and another face swam up into Margo's consciousness. A crying, sniveling, pleading face.

A boy's face.

"Don't hurt him!" Rana Cahill screamed in heavily accented English and grabbed Margo's arm.

She shook the woman off, pivoted away from the video camera. Jerked the boy with her, the gun still ready in her hand, and rounded on the mother.

"You tell him to drop," she commanded, as cold and deadly as a hangman, but with a prayer playing silently inside her. *Listen to me, woman. Don't make me do this.*

"You tell him to drop when I fire or so help me I will kill him."

In the background, Ruben Cahill, the husband and father, the man on the other end of the camera, was also yelling. She knew who he was, knew the blood and bodies he was responsible for, knew he had to be stopped. Knew it was up to her, here, now, to stop him.

And she hated him for it. It was ripe that hatred, a feral, ugly, hot anger. It boiled inside her gut and chest not only for what he'd done, but for what she was about to do because of it. She was breathing hard, the sickness of disgust nearly overpowering. Her agents reflected it back to her. They were mumbling, on edge, uneasy. The two boys moaned and wept, calling out to their mother. But the woman was blubbering so hard, Margo had to shake her.

"Listen!" She slapped Rana across the face, as much for the benefit of her husband as she was desperate to get her attention. They were running out of time. If the woman didn't concentrate, pay attention . . . Margo didn't want to think about that "if." Didn't want that volcano inside her to explode.

She shook her prisoner again, and thank

God, the woman huffed in a breath, seemed to focus a bit more.

"I'm going to fire," Margo said, low and intense, for her ears only. "Do you understand? I'm going to shoot him." The woman started crying again, and Margo wrenched the arm she was holding. "I won't hurt him. But I have to make it look like I did." Rana's face grew confused. Her eyes darted left and right. Margo could hear her thoughts as though they'd been spoken out loud. Could she trust this American whore?

"If he doesn't make this look real, I'll have to do it for real. Do you understand?" The confusion lessened, distrust replaced by a shred of hope. Margo was counting on that hope. "You speak only to the boy. You tell him what to do. No one will get hurt." The mother began to nod in compliance. "No!" Margo yanked her brutally. "Do nothing. Show nothing. Just tell the boy. Now." She dragged mother and son together. The boy's legs were rubber, and Margo propped him up. There was a quick exchange in Arabic. The boy flung himself at his mother, and Margo had to haul them apart.

She stood him in front of the camera and raised her gun to his head.

Behind her, Rana was sobbing. The little brother was screaming. The boy shook beneath the muzzle of the gun.

Margo shouted at the camera, "I'll do it! I swear I'll do it, you bastard!"

The acrid smell of urine filled the air; the boy had wet his pants.

In the farmhouse, lightning cracked the air, a cruel and vicious sound. Her heart stopped.

And when she could breathe again, she stared out at the innocuous lines of the farmhouse, her vision blurred by tears.

Oh, God.

She hadn't pulled the trigger.

She hadn't shot the boy.

The rest came back in slow motion. The child she was holding, the child she was frantically trying to protect, slumped, suddenly deadweight in her hands.

"Down!" she screamed. "Shots! Everyone down!"

She dived for the other kid, but the line of fire was too heavy to get there. Carns got there first, and took two bullets doing it.

They were coming from the second floor, from the roof. Three men with automatic weapons. She recognized one from the intel on the Moroccan home. The third guard. Dammit to hell . . . She'd been careless, should have hunted him down. Should have made sure.

No time to think about that. Move on. Move on. She fired, keeping up a steady covering barrage. Noted the two others. One she couldn't get a good look at and one with a heavy black mustache.

Rodriguez went down, his arms flailing. "Aldo!" she screamed, but got no answer.

In the next half second she saw the mustached shooter take aim, but not at her, at . . .

"No!" Margo dived for the target, but was too late. Rana Cahill's back arched with the impact of the bullet, and she toppled over, plowing into the table in the center of the room.

Margo landed behind the couch, her brain on speed. They shot the mother. What the hell was going on?

The material on the couch popped as weapons fire ripped through it. Christ, she was pinned down. Ten more seconds and the couch would be in shreds and her along with it.

She took a couple of breaths, knowing they might be her last, pumped herself up, and leaped to her feet, firing.

Suddenly, the room exploded into flames, and she was thrown backward, her weapon ripped from her hand. She landed halfway outside the front door. The house was on fire. People scrambled into the street, shouting and screaming. Someone pulled her the rest of the way out, and she must have passed out because when she woke, she was in a strange house, rescued by neighbors.

People jabbered at her, mouths going but no sound coming out. The explosion. Her ears were blocked. Her head . . . dizzy. She touched her forehead and her hand came away bloody. Her sleeve was tattered and blackened; there was blood under her nails.

The first thing she heard when her ears came back was that everyone inside the house was dead. A fissure of grief opened inside her, but she couldn't think about it. Had to run, get away, make agency contact.

She was due to talk to the police, but she managed to slip away unnoticed before they got to her. DCO had a safe house on the other side of town at the end of Sierpes near the Corte Inglés. She slipped outside and made her way there, where she found clothes and money. She contacted DCO and told them what had happened. All dead, she told them, still trying to piece the disaster together. All dead.

Or so she'd thought.

63

"He was there," Margo said into the phone, the words tumbling out of her mouth so fast, she could hardly control them. "At the house on Calle Gitana. He killed Cahill's wife."

"He what?" Jake's voice expressed her own credulity.

"I saw it, Jake."

"The same guy who was at the Foxhall house? The guy Petali shot in Spain?"

"I remember, Jake. I remember it all."

"Yeah, but, who knows if it came back right?"

"Dammit, it's exactly right."

"But Carns —"

"Was across the room. All hell broke loose. He got confused. I'm telling you —"

"All right, all right." A brief pause, as though he was debating how to handle her. "Look, hang tight. There's a flight out tonight. We can talk more when I get there. I've got something to show you."

Margo showered, pulled on the jeans and black tank top that always lit a fire in

Jake's eyes. An ancient wood-trimmed Chevy station wagon was parked in the barn, the lone farm vehicle that still worked. When he dropped her off two weeks ago, Jake had made sure the tank was full, but she hadn't used it, not even when the groceries had mostly given out and she was living on bread and peanut butter. Now, she dug through a kitchen drawer to find the keys.

The drive to town took fifteen minutes. The drive through town took a whole lot less. A couple of blocks in either direction, five minutes tops to find the grocery store.

Dewey's answer to Safeway was tiny, only a little larger than a convenience store would be in Alexandria or Pentagon City. But it had plenty of what she wanted: bologna, lettuce, and mustard, a couple of bags of chips, beer, Coke, eggs and bacon for breakfast. Coffee. Jake liked coffee. She looked at the collection while running over her mental list. Not much of a gourmet selection there.

Well, hire a cook if you want to cook. Or eat out. That's what she did.

Her lips twitched.

She learned something new about herself every day.

She added ham to the bologna, threw in

a can of tuna, and called it a day.

She was getting all domestic — if you could call bologna domestic — but if Jake wanted a real meal he could damn well take her out for one.

She picked him up at the airport and when he came off the tarmac and into the waiting area, she had to admit that two weeks did a lot for a man. He looked good. Better than good. The jeans hung low on his hips, and the sports coat framed his lean build. He hefted a leather garment bag over one shoulder with a casual grace that set her blood humming.

The lines around his eyes crinkled when he saw her. "Well, well, well, Miss Margo. You here for me?"

"Thought it would save time. No car to rent."

"Jeez. And I thought it was my hardy good looks."

She cut a glance his way. "You wish."

He grinned right back at her. "Yes, ma'am, I do." He threw the garment bag over the back of a seat. "Come here." She let him pull her into a corner. "And I have. For too damn long."

His mouth was inviting, and she opened hers, hot and eager to taste him again. God, that man could kiss.

When she could catch her breath, she gazed into his blue eyes and found the warmth there. An answering warmth pulled inside her, and she found herself smiling at him. "Here's your fairy godmother, ready to grant your heart's desire."

He nipped at her mouth. "Then how about some casual sex, no strings attached?"

"I'll see what I can arrange." She took his hand and dragged him away. By the time they hit the door they were practically running.

The airport was an hour away from the homestead, and Jake didn't waste a minute of it. His hand was on her thigh as she hit the airport road, he stroked her neck as she pulled onto the highway, he nibbled her ear as she tried to switch lanes. Twice she almost ran off the road.

When they finally got to the turnoff that led to the farm, she sped down the narrow dirt drive into the farmyard and barely got the parking brake set.

She was out of the car in a heartbeat and raced him into the house. Her skin felt ready to burst, her pulse leaped out of her veins. She was itchy and trembly with the need to have him touch her.

They stopped inside the door, unable to

wait. His mouth was warm, his fingers fumbling as he went for her shirt, then his, then hers again. They managed to get to the bedroom, kissing and tripping all the way, leaving a trail of clothes.

He caught her against the bedroom door. "You ever make love outside?"

"Not that I can remember." She grinned, amazed that she could joke about it, and he framed that grin with his hands.

"Christ, you have the most amazing smile. I think it's because you have the most amazing mouth." He bent and kissed her, sucking the air from her lungs and making her knees wobbly. "Tomorrow, if the ground's warm enough, I'll take you out to the field."

"I don't care where we go." Breathless, she slid her hands up the hard, smooth plane of his chest. It was familiar in a way that nothing in her life was familiar anymore.

His hands stroked her sides, his thumbs moving tantalizingly close to her breasts but not touching them. "You will when you feel the air on your skin," he said, and kissed her again.

They fell on the bed in a heap. "I only want to feel *you* on my skin," she said, pulling him on top of her. "In my skin. In me."

She gasped as he slid inside her. It felt so good to touch him, to feel him there, moaning her name. That intimate connection held her tight, a coil of razor wire joining them together like nothing and no one ever had.

His mouth, his hands, every part of him claimed her. Over and over he brought her to the brink and pulled back, his body branding her, making her his, until she was delirious with wanting more of him. She was lost in a black void of ecstasy, and when at last he set her free, it was his hands that did it, his body, his mouth. Jake. God, Jake.

She exploded on the sound of his name, and as he shuddered his own release, she felt him clamp around her, his arms tight, his heart hammering, his soul in flight with hers, high, high up in the night sky.

She lay on the bed next to him, letting the night air cool the sweat they'd worked up. The room was shadowed, the only light drifting in from the hallway. Crickets twittered outside; she hadn't heard them before, hadn't heard anything but the pulse of her own desire, but now the faint song chirped in the distance. Alive, happy.

A feather from one of the old-fashioned

pillows tickled her arm and she picked it up, brushed it over her lips. They were swollen from his mouth. Her whole body was swollen from him. A good, round feeling.

"So is this what you wanted to show me?"

He drew her into the crook of his arm. "That and . . . other things."

"What other things?" She was sorry she'd asked the minute the words were out of her mouth. "No . . . wait. I take it back."

He sighed and sat up. "We have to talk about it sometime."

"Not yet."

He swung around to the side of the bed. "I'm starving anyway. Man does not live by love alone."

"Really? Well, I hope you like bologna."

64

Margo showered and dressed. A wired kind of happiness beat inside her, a buzz she'd never felt before. As though the way out was a dazzling arrow with Jake's name blazing in neon.

She found him in the kitchen, his brief-case open on the weathered oak table where five photographs were neatly displayed. Police photos, document photos, surveillance pictures, all grimly black-and-white. The sight dulled the glow a bit, but not altogether. Jake was still there, still with her. She could still feel his hands on her, the taste of his mouth, like coming home.

Gripping the back of a chair, she stood over his shoulder and identified the photos. The guy with the mustache, the third guard, and the other three men from the attack on Foxhall Road.

"This one's Nasim Kamal." He pointed to the mustached man they'd last seen in Spain. "He was the team leader and Cahill's contact to the Red Key terror group. The rest are foot soldiers. We think they were sent to rescue the family, and if that didn't seem possible, to eliminate them."

She snapped her gaze to his. "Eliminate them. Why?"

"They couldn't be used as leverage if they were dead."

A chill settled in her heart. "But that would bring Cahill over to us. If his own people killed —"

"*If* that was the story. And if he believed it. But it all looked like a botched DCO job, didn't it? Easy to blame us. Which is why they were after you. Revenge, yes, for taking the family in the first place maybe. But you were the sole survivor. The only one who could tell the truth."

The circle was suddenly complete. "And that dovetailed nicely with Connelly's objective."

"He used them. Gave them locations, times, whatever they needed. If they did his dirty work for him —"

"All the better."

Jake nodded. "Much better. Of course, you kept refusing to go down. So he sent another team after you, too."

"The guys at the motel."

He nodded. "And then, just in case

everything else went south, he framed you for Frank. Like I said, not a nice man."

She tightened her hold on the chair. For half a minute the information bowed her down like a huge boulder crushing her lungs. Such massive manipulation, so many people and machinations. All to get her, kill her, end her life.

And now, it was over.

She let out a whoosh of breath and ran a shaky hand through her hair.

It was over. The chase to hunt her down was over. It seemed impossible, unbelievable, but there it was.

"One more thing." Jake removed another sheaf of papers from his briefcase and slid it in front of her. "Ballistics report from Luca Petali. After I spoke with you I called him. The story you told me was . . . well, let's just say I thought you should have some hard evidence to back it up. And I had a hunch."

She picked up the report and began to scan. The pertinent information leaped out at her. "AKs?"

"And Makarovs."

"In both the mother and the two kids?" She shifted pages, double-checking.

"You and your men use Russian weapons?"

"Of course not."

"You didn't kill them, Margo."

And suddenly the weight was gone, and she almost collapsed with the relief. It felt as though she'd been playing a long game of tug-of-war, and the other side just let go. She could still feel that weight, still feel her hands wrapped around the rope, shouldering the responsibility. But it was like a phantom limb, and it was terrifying.

What would she do now? Where would she go? The freedom was crushing, mind-numbing. She couldn't see, couldn't breathe. She needed air, space.

She fled to the back porch, leaving Jake to stare after her. The moon was out, lighting the field behind the house with a silver glow. The emptiness comforted. It didn't analyze, didn't judge. It just was.

So technically, no, she hadn't killed the mother and her two boys. But if she and her team hadn't kidnapped them in the first place, hadn't used them, they would still be alive.

There are no innocents in war. Connelly's voice slithered into her head.

Only hard choices and tough decisions.

Maybe she could have done it once, but not now.

Not . . . yet.

"So . . ." Jake came up from behind, put

451

hands on her shoulders, gave voice to her thoughts. "What now?"

She shook her head. "I don't know. First I have to get used to being one of the good guys again."

"How about we don't try to do that in one night?" He pulled her against him, encasing her in his arms. He nuzzled her neck. "Give yourself time to adjust. Breathe."

She nodded.

"And eat. Where's that bologna?"

She laughed. God, he always made her laugh. "Still in the car with the rest of the groceries."

"Okay, I'm on it."

She stood for a moment longer. The air was cool but clean. It smelled of earth and rain and, just possibly, new beginnings.

She returned to the kitchen and set the table with napkins and plates, two bottles of Bud. The groceries still hadn't made it inside.

"Jake?"

No answer. What the hell was he doing out there?

The window over the sink had a view of the farmyard. She shoved the curtain aside. The station wagon stood silent in the yard, a darker shape in the dark of the night. She couldn't make out Jake's form.

Had he come in while she stood mooning over the night? If so, where were the groceries?

She traipsed back through the house looking for him. He wasn't in the old-fashioned parlor or the bathroom at the end of the hall. She hammered down the basement steps. "Jake? You there?" Dank and cool, the room was empty.

She trudged back upstairs, went into the kitchen again and looked out the window. The same dark scene with the quiet hulk of the car greeted her.

Her skin prickled. Something was wrong. She stared out at the yard. Everything was quiet. She couldn't see much, because there wasn't any light, but the shape of the car was there, the barn, everything was . . .

The light.

There should be a light.

A cold warning crawled up her spine. She ducked down behind the cabinet under the sink.

It was just paranoia. This was Indiana, for God's sake.

So where was Jake? Where the hell was he?

She was overreacting. The light had

burned out, and Jake was in the barn. She'd heard nothing. No shots, no struggle. She was making herself crazy. That had to be it. He was in the barn.

She inched the few feet over to the silverware drawer and, feeling foolish, grabbed a knife.

Just in case.

Long and thin, the one she pulled out had a five-inch blade. A boning knife. She hefted it abstractly, calculating the weight and balance automatically while she gauged the distance to the back door. She slithered across the few feet, reached up, and flipped off the kitchen light. In the now-dim room she cracked open the door and slid outside.

Crouching low, she waited, scanning the area, listening. Nothing moved. Not even the wind.

Outside, she had a better angle on the car. The back of the station wagon was open.

"Jake!"

Again, no answer.

She scuttled to the vehicle. The groceries still sat inside. Except for one bag on the ground. The carton of eggs spilled out, smashed and oozing.

Her heart began a wild, frantic roller-coaster ride.

Where was he? What had happened?

She peered around. Empty ground all around until the field. The only hiding place, the barn. Could Jake be inside?

It was the next logical location. She inhaled, bracing herself, then dashed out. She ran a zigzag pattern. Hit the barn wall. Flattened her back against it.

She was breathing like she'd never catch up. She closed her eyes. Sweat dripped between her breasts. Slowly, she crept to the barn door. Nothing approached. No one spoke.

She pushed. The door creaked inward. She counted to five, then darted in.

65

Margo stopped short. In front of her was a sickening, gruesome sight: Jake hanging from a central beam, a rope tight around his neck.

She gagged. Didn't dare breathe.

His head lolled. Blood stained his right shoulder. He was muzzled, his hands and feet tied. A rickety chair was the only thing preventing him from strangling to death.

"Jake!"

She ran to free him, but not before the chair beneath him moved. She froze again.

"At last, Agent Scott. We meet."

She spun around. The man who came from his hiding place behind a stall was lean and hard. His hair was matted, his clothes wrinkled and torn. Several days' growth of stubble covered his chin. He looked exhausted, like he'd been through a war zone, but the deep-set eyes in the narrow face glittered with fierce intensity.

She'd seen that face before. The last time behind a closed-circuit television. A view that had started this whole journey.

Ruben Cahill. Ex–Army Ranger turned terrorist-for-hire. The mastermind behind hundreds of bombing deaths and assassinations. Tactical strategist for Red Key and other terror organizations.

Husband to the woman and father to the two children who had died in the house on Calle Gitana.

The Lord of Vengeance had finally hunted her down.

In one hand Cahill held a gun aimed squarely at her chest. His other hand gripped the end of a rope that was tied around the chair holding Jake up. One pull, and he would hang for real.

"The knife." He indicated the blade in her hand. "Toss it here."

Vibrating with tension, she hesitated a fraction, but he pulled the rope, and Jake swayed. The movement woke him. His eyes fluttered open and he saw her. For half a second their eyes locked. She saw pain in his and an assessing coolness that steadied her.

She threw the knife on the ground halfway between herself and Cahill.

"Let him go," she told Cahill. "This is between you and me. You don't need him."

He smiled. In the dim light of the single

bulb that lit the barn, his teeth looked yellow and feral. "Oh, but it's so much more satisfying with him here."

She swallowed, reaching for composure. She had to buy time. Enough to figure something out. "You were incarcerated. How did you get here?"

"I've got friends in low places, Agent Scott. After you murdered my family —"

"I didn't murder them."

He overrode her protest. "After you murdered my wife and children, my lawyer got me a change of venue. A nice, civilian jail. A little traffic dustup during transportation, another little birdie with an ax to grind whispering in my ear, and voilà, here we are. Just the three of us."

If Cahill had escaped, why the hell didn't anyone bother to mention it to her or Jake?

"And you were so busy fucking, I could have brought an army with me, and you wouldn't have noticed."

The knowing look in his eye made her sick. "You . . . watched?"

"Briefly." He shrugged. "What can I say; it's been a long time." His face hardened. "But I had other things to do." He gestured with his head to indicate the setup in the barn.

"You're too late," she said. "What happened to your family — the story is already out."

"The story?" He laughed. "You don't expect me to believe that crap your people put out to the world?"

"We didn't do it, Ruben." Maybe calling him by his first name would start a connection between them.

"Shut up! Don't say my name! Don't ever say my name!" He tugged on the rope, and Jake cried out, wobbling again.

"All right! All right!" She stepped toward Jake, but Cahill focused the gun on her.

"We are not friends, Agent Scott. You got that?"

She stopped short, raised her hands. "I'm sorry. I'm truly sorry. But I'm telling you the truth. We didn't kill them. Your people did."

"Well, we all have our little fantasies." But he eased up on the rope, and Jake was able to right himself.

She licked her lips. If anything happened to him. If he died because of her . . .

God, she couldn't think about that. Couldn't think about Jake at all. She had to let the calm descend, let her training take over. It was there, in her head, in her body. She only had to let it lead.

"I can prove it. I have a ballistics report. It's in the house. I'll get —"

"A report?" He looked at her, incredulous. "My family is dead, and you have a report? Oh, then, by all means, let's go on our merry way. Agent Scott has a report."

"They were shot with Russian-made weapons. We don't use AK-47s and Makarovs."

"I don't give a shit what you used or what your lying reports say!" His hands were trembling with fury. "Even if you didn't pull the trigger, you took them. You put them in harm's way. You're responsible." He accused her with the gun. "You, Agent Scott."

She inhaled a deep, shaky breath. How could she argue with him? He was right. Absolutely right.

So, she'd let him have his revenge. But not on Jake.

"You're right." She took a step toward him, arms raised. "So shoot me, and let Jake go."

"Oh, I will shoot you," Cahill said with utter assurance. "But first I want to see you try to save your boyfriend as he gags and jerks and slowly suffocates to death."

His gaze pinned hers, the look dark, cold, and endlessly pitiless.

"Don't," she said softly. "Please."

"Please?" His tone softened. "Did you say . . . please?"

"Yes."

There were sudden tears in his eyes. "Did my wife beg for our son's life?" His voice cracked.

Oh, God. She swallowed against the emotion in the man's face. "Yes."

"And did you grant her wish?"

"I intended to. I swear it." She looked him straight in the eye, braced at the depth of pain and anguish there, and tried to convey her sincerity with every ounce of her being. "I was going to stage the whole thing. They would all be alive today if your people had let me finish —"

"Is that what you tell yourself in the dead of night when you wake up screaming?" His soft voice had a merciless center, as hard and sharp as an ice pick. "Now, it's your turn." She saw what he was going to do a split second before he did it.

So did Jake. He grunted and kicked out the chair from under him.

Cahill started, surprised. It gave her a few precious seconds.

And instead of doing what a normal person would have done. Instead of running to help Jake, she moved away. Right toward Ruben Cahill.

She rolled, reached out. Cahill's gun exploded over her head, but her hand was already clutching the knife. In an eye blink she flicked her wrist, and with a powerful arm thrust the blade flew across the barn and landed with a silent thump in the center of Cahill's chest.

He wobbled. Fired a round that missed. She leaped, kicked the gun out of his hand, then ran to Jake. He was twitching, turning blue. She righted the chair, got his feet under it.

Cahill had fallen to his knees. She darted over to him, yanked the knife out of his body. He screamed and toppled over. She raced to Jake and cut him down. He fell with a groan and a thud.

She scooped him up, his head on her lap. "God, Jake. Are you all right?"

He coughed. Shuddered. "Oh, Christ," he moaned. "Never a dull moment."

66

Hours later, Cahill's body was gone, the police and nearest TCF section had been informed and statements given, and Jake had been examined, his shoulder wound treated. Only then, when no one was traipsing through the farmhouse or asking questions or answering cell phones, when the tick of the clock over the kitchen doorway and the crickets outside were the only sounds, when it was all finally over, only then could Margo relax.

Too bad the headache hit, like a fist slamming her head.

"Adrenaline reaction," she said, standing at the kitchen sink and downing aspirin like it was candy. "It'll pass."

Jake gave her a rueful smile. "It's all coming back, isn't it?"

She nodded, remembering other near misses and other headaches. Tension seemed to have been a way of life. Would she ever get used to it again?

"I spoke to the branch in New York," Jake said. "The van Cahill and four other prisoners were being transported in crashed and burned. They misidentified Cahill as one of the dead."

"For the want of a nail . . ."

"There's more."

"Not sure I want to hear it."

"Connelly got his hands on a smuggled cell phone. He received a call from a phone a few miles from the crash site. They think that's how Cahill tracked you down. They're going to use it to put the death penalty back on the table. They've been wanting to do it anyway. They think he had something to do with Carns's death, though they couldn't prove it. Now Connelly's been isolated. No calls, no contact."

She looked at Jake, at the solid strength of his body, and tried to bury the image of him nearly being hanged.

The shakes began again, and she gripped the back of a chair to get them under control.

"Hey" — Jake flung his good arm around her — "it's okay. Connelly is out of the picture for good."

She lashed out at him, pushing him out of the way. "What the hell were you thinking, kicking that chair out from under you?"

"The same thing you were thinking when you dived right into Cahill's line of fire."

"You could have died."

"Oh, and what are you — bulletproof?"

They stared at each other. She knew she was scowling, and she didn't care. Her head felt like a jackhammer had gotten loose inside it, and her chest felt angry and raw.

"Come here." Jake reached out his good hand. "Come on. I'm wounded. Don't make me beg."

Reluctantly, she slid her hand into his, and he led her out to the porch. She breathed in the night air, let the vast stretch of flatland soothe her.

"Now, we're going to move on, okay? We had a great time, it was a nice vacation, a little bumpy, maybe, but it's over. Time to go back to work."

"What are you talking about?"

"You were pretty impressive in there." He spoke carefully as if picking through the words. "I mean, the knife thing, the —" With his good arm he mimicked her throwing hand. "You gotta teach me that."

"I don't think so."

"You're amazing in a fight, Margo. You have skills, training. We need people like you."

"I'm done with all that."

"You sure?" He gave her one of his trademark looks. The thoughtful, penetrating kind. "You're still on the payroll at DCO."

She shook her head. As long as she lived she would never forget the tears in Cahill's eyes when he asked about his wife. "I want to live on the surface, not underground."

"I've got an in at Field Ops. I could —"

"No." She watched a hawk fly across the face of the moon. The bird flew with a cruel beauty, hunting prey. "Thanks, but no."

He slid his arm around her, pulled her back into the shelter of his hard chest. "You could stay home. Have babies."

She stilled, then slowly turned to look at him. "Your babies?"

He had that sly, teasing look on his face. "We've got the drill down. My hair, your eyes. Oh, hell. Your hair, your everything. We could make a real heartbreaker."

An image rose in her mind. Herself pushing a stroller across the quay at Waterfront Park. Jake laughing beside her.

She couldn't sustain it; it was too far from where she was now.

"I don't think I'm the stay-at-home type," she said.

He brushed the aforementioned hair

466

back from her shoulder. "What type are you?"

The question threw her. "I don't know," she said at last. The moon came out from behind a cloud and lit the field with a dim glow. The answer seemed as distant as the horizon. "I need time to find out. Get to know myself again. Get to know you. See if we can make it . . . in peacetime."

He traced a line down her cheek. "Start all over you mean?"

"Like normal people."

He cocked his head. "Never was much for normal. Wouldn't do what I do if I was."

"Yeah, probably true of me, too."

"So let's say we throw out normal and just be our own wacky selves."

She nodded slowly. "Okay."

"But if we're going to start over, we should begin with introductions." He dropped his embrace, stepped away, and held out a hand. "Hi, I'm Jake Wise. Well, Jacob actually, but Jake to those who count."

She slid her hand into his. "Margaret," she said, saying her full name aloud for the first time. "Margaret Ellen Vaughn."

"Pleased to meet you, Margaret." He

smiled. It was warm and sexy and filled with possibility. How could she resist?

She smiled back. "I'm pleased to meet me, too."

About the Author

A native New Yorker, **Annie Solomon** has been dreaming up stories since she was ten. After a twelve-year career in advertising, where she rose to Vice President and Head Writer at a midsize agency, she abandoned the air conditioners, heat pumps, and furnaces of her professional life for her first love — romance. *Blackout* is her fifth novel of romantic suspense. To learn more, visit her Web site at www.anniesolomon.com.

	DATE DUE		